BEAUTIFULLY MENDED

COURTNEY KRISTEL

DEDICATION

Lindsay, my number one reader, thank you for loving Jax and Addie so deeply. Without you, I probably wouldn't have ever finished their story.

Acknowledgments

This book would not be possible without these people.

Lea, THANK YOU for making my vision come to life. The hard work you put into recreating my website and the book cover still blows me away. You are immensely talented and I can't wait to see all of the other book covers you create for me. Also, thank you for putting up with my lack of knowledge of anything technology-related.

Thank you to the world's best editor, Kat Pagan. Kat and her team are everything I was looking for in an editor and more. She has made every step easier and helped make this book even better than I thought possible. THANK YOU for going above and beyond. I can't wait to work with you again!

I also want to thank my family for being there when I needed to talk something out. They've had to suffer through 5+ years of all the different scenarios running through my head with this next installment.

I'd like to give a special shout-out to my sister Monica. Thank you for reading at least four versions of this story. The final is a completely opposite book to what you've read previously. **Spoiler** I did not kill off Jax—you're welcome.

Jenni and Lindsay, thank you so much for being awesome beta readers. Your insight helped me finish this story. Thank you for letting me ruin the rest of the series by allowing me to hash it all out on our lunch dates. Hopefully, you two forget everything by the time the series is complete.

Lastly, I'd like to thank my wonderful husband. Simon, you are everything and more. You are the inspiration behind the love my characters have for each other. THANK YOU for all of your support while I finished this novel. I love you, forever and always.

PROLOGUE

Jax
Nine years ago

Clutching my side, I try to take shallow breaths. Fuck, I think he actually broke a rib this time. He's still awake. I can hear him in the living room, rambling on and on about the wife who left him with his bastard son. If only I were a bastard, it would make this somewhat easier.

Keeping to the shadows, I navigate the path that leads to her house. It's almost one in the morning, but I know I won't get any sleep tonight with him around. I'm aware that he has the next few days off from the hospital, and usually I'm already gone before he gets home. But I fell asleep on the couch, waiting for Logan to get home, and woke up to him hurling my soccer ball at my face.

I make it to her house without being seen. Normally I'd climb the tree and jump to her window. I can't... Tonight was too much. Not wanting to wake her, I go to the playhouse in the backyard. I'll sleep there. Besides, Hadley always leaves blankets out for her imaginary friends.

Before I can get to her larger-than-life dollhouse, I hear the telltale sign of Adalynn swinging her legs back and forth in the water. Yes, it's probably weird that I can immediately tell the difference between her and anyone else. I can't help it though. She's always been louder than anyone else, in the best way.

I should have known I'd find her down here. She's the only fifteen-year-old I know that hangs out by the pool in the dark. Silently, I watch her. She's using her arms as a pillow, while she stares up at the night sky, her feet going in and out of the water. I look up too, trying to see what she sees. But all I see is blackness.

"It's southern California, Ads. There are never stars out," I told her the first time I noticed her doing this.

"Just because you can't see them, doesn't mean they aren't there." She put her hands on her hips, with that serious stance she always takes when she's making a point. "No matter what, the stars are there, whether you can see them or not. That's the magic."

I wish I had her optimism about life. So far, all I've known is pain and disappointment.

Until her. She's the bright star in my darkest night.

"Jax?" she whispers. She's sitting up now, looking into the shadows, her eyes seeking me out.

Even though I didn't move, I must have made a sound. Her ability to sense my presence is not good. This, whatever I've been feeling when I'm around her, is supposed to be one-sided. She can't have a crush on me. Not when she keeps all my secrets. It's not fair to her. Besides, I know she likes Riley from her class. I heard her talking about him to her mom when she didn't know I was there. I shake my head, trying to erase the emotions coursing through me. No, Adalynn Grace Maxwell, the girl who helps me after my dad hurts me, does not like me. She can't. The only thing she can feel is pity.

Stepping out of the shadows, I walk towards her. I don't care how long it takes; one day I'm going to repay her for everything she's done for me.

Over and over again, Adalynn has saved my life. She's helped stitch up my shoulder when my dad sliced me with a knife. She held me while I cried the night my mom left us. She gives me a safe place to just be me. Something my dad stole from me after we were both abandoned.

Like I said, she's the bright star in my darkest night.

I tell myself that I don't care for her like that, that I can't, but the tightness in my chest I only recognize when she's around seems to amplify the closer I get to her. It isn't until I'm right next to her and the pool that I realize I sneaked out without shoes. Pretending as if this is completely normal for both of us to be out here at one in the morning, I sit beside her and submerge my feet in the water. I have to sit on my hands to fight the urge to reach out and clasp hers.

"Hey, Ads," I finally say, my voice cracking a little on her nickname.

I'm pretty sure she just stole a piece of me with that smile she's giving me. I try to swallow this ridiculous need to lean over and kiss her. No, I can't do that. Not like this, not when I'm only here because spending another second in my house may have killed me. No, she deserves better than me.

She turns back to the water. "How bad?"

It only hurts if I breathe. "Nothing happened. Just couldn't sleep." The lie falls easily off my lips. It's not the first I've told her and probably won't be the last. Out of everyone, I hate lying to her but I can't help it. I want to pretend that I'm here just because I couldn't sleep. I want to pretend that my father isn't a monster, one that everyone in this town idolizes.

She tilts her head towards me and opens her mouth, but seems to think better of it and faces the water again. I know she can't see any of the bruises he left. Wyatt is careful to never leave a mark where someone can easily see it. That would ruin his reputation and that's unacceptable. Still, I feel as if she somehow knows. I'm about to ask her but her words stop me.

"Riley asked me out."

Of course that fucking pathetic excuse for a quarterback asked her out. I knew it was coming, wanted it to happen. But, man, I didn't know it would feel like this. I try for nonchalance. "What did you say?" There, that sounded as if I didn't care, even though it feels as if my whole world hangs on this answer.

I keep telling myself that she and I can never be. There's no way she likes me like that, but I really hope she does. I don't think I can watch them be around each other at school. Suddenly the "lesson" my dad taught me tonight is forgotten, and all that matters is Adalynn and her answer.

"Ads?" I prompt, almost afraid to ask again. If she's hesitating, that means...

Her lips are on mine before I realize she's moved. I suck in a painful breath from bracing myself to keep from falling into the pool with the force of the gesture. When she pulls away, I lick my bottom lip, tasting copper. She draws her hands to her face, mortified when she notices what her kiss did. Somehow it's still the best kiss I've ever received, blood and all.

Before I can tell her any of this, though, she runs back towards her house. Fuck, this was not how this was supposed to go. Ignoring the pain at my side, I chase after her. "Ads, wait," I call out.

She stops but doesn't turn around. "I'm sorry. I don't know what I was thinking," she whispers into the night.

Now that she isn't running away from me, I pace myself. By the time I'm standing in front of her, I make sure that she can't see how much effort it took to chase after her. I don't want her thinking of anyone but me. I don't care how selfish that makes me. I'm hoping that after this, there won't be a Riley or anyone else.

I want to be the only guy in her life.

Carefully, as if she'll shatter into a million pieces if I'm not gentle, I cradle her cheeks in my hands and tilt her face up so her lips can meet mine. I pause, my mouth brushing hers as I whisper another lie against them. "I finally found something you're not perfect at."

Before she can reply, I do something incredibly selfish and just for me... I kiss Adalynn Grace Maxwell as if I were born to do nothing but this.

CHAPTER ONE

Kohen

With Jax distracted and time slipping away, I sprint towards the house, hoping they don't come looking for me here. If he's smart, if Adalynn means anything to him, he'll see to her first. I'm so close to my endgame. I can't give up now. Addie isn't the only one counting on me not to mess this up. Sure, this wasn't how I planned tonight going but I'm not one to let an opportunity slip through my fingers.

I rush up the stairs at breakneck speed, taking two at a time, to the open door. Somehow I'm able to catch myself from slipping on the blood soaking the floor. Taking in the state of my once pristine house, my mind runs through a thousand scenarios, trying to come up with a plan that doesn't land my ass in jail. Despite the turmoil coursing through me, I still find myself smirking, remembering the fire inside my Adalynn when she ran away from me. As if I'd let her go that easily...

I can't believe she actually stabbed me. It aches when I move, and without looking, I know I'm going to need stitches. This isn't the first time someone I've loved has tried to hurt me. I was able to teach Em, but something tells me it's going to be a little more challenging to pro-vide Ads with some much-needed manners.

Of-fucking-course, Jaxon Chandler had to come to the rescue. I'm sure that asshole is already filling her head with more lies. If he would have just left us alone, Addie and I would have been safely tucked away from all of them. How the fuck did he find us so quickly? I made sure to disable the tracker on her phone. But that's a question for another day...

The storm outside is no match for the one brewing inside me.

Blood drips from my nose onto the imported tiles from Italy. "Fuck!" That bastard got me good. Wiping my face, I push forward. With each breath, labored by Jax's assault, I vow to destroy his life. That piece of shit should have stayed in the city.

Entering the kitchen, I grab the vials of blood I store in the fridge. Hopefully Addie's injuries will keep Jax distracted long enough that I'm able to set everything up the way it should have been tonight if he didn't show up.

I grab my cell out of my back pocket, my fingers hovering over the name of the only person who can save this shitshow. Sighing, I mutter out a curse. This is going to cost me a fortune but Adalynn is worth it, ten times over. There's nothing I wouldn't do for her.

Me: You're needed.

I quickly share my location with Detective Gary. Because I'm feel-ing generous, I wire an obscene amount of money into his offshore account so he knows how dire the situation is.

Me: Don't fuck up.

I'm tempted to remind him what will happen if he does. I'm going through my pictures, gathering all the evidence I've collected against the pig, but his reply is instant.

Gary: On it. Stay there. Miller will take your statement. ETA twenty-five minutes.

Jax must have just gotten around to calling the police. *Jackass.* Doesn't he know that Ads could be seriously hurt? What has he been doing all this time? Worthless piece of shit! If she dies, it's on him!

Clenching and unclenching my fist, I picture what I want to do to Jax if I had the time. Instead, I rush to the closet and into the timeout area where I've stashed Addie. Pushing the jackets aside, I engage the button that hides the panic room I had installed just for her. I knew that there might be a small chance that she may not see things the way I do, so I took precautions. Like always, Addie doesn't disappoint. Tapping a few keys into my phone, I shut the door to the inner room, making the closet just that—a closet. Without the password, nobody will be able to know that there's a panic room in here.

I survey the scene, scrutinizing my work, ensuring everything is perfect. There're still a few details missing that won't match my story but that's okay. However, just to be safe, I break a few more things, like the vase from the grandmother I never met. I turn our domestic violence into more of a brawl started by the jealous ex-boyfriend. I'm willing to bet that by the time this is all over, Addie will have no choice but to see that everything I do is for her, for us.

A quick glance at my watch shows only ten minutes have passed since I contacted the detective. Which means, if Gary is as good as he claims to be, I really only have about five more before the respected NYPD is at my door.

Ha, *respected,* what a joke! They're clueless, unaware that their superior is in my back pocket, meaning they all are too.

"Where have you been? I've been trying to reach you all night!" Olivia hisses, grabbing my arm and dragging me into the nearest supply closet.

"Thanks for coming."

"You didn't really give me a choice, did you?"

No, I didn't. I needed an alibi and the only person I trust is her. She's just another puppet I control, a means to an end.

"Has she woken up yet?" I couldn't tell from my vantage point if she passed out from sheer shock or from her injuries. I didn't hit her that hard. Addie can handle it. A few slaps across the face are hardly going to do much damage. My girl is much stronger than anyone gives her credit for.

Besides, she deserved it! How dare she try to leave me for Jaxon! She doesn't know everything I've done for us. She thinks she loves him but she's wrong. If she knew the truth, she would never love him, not like she should love me. He lies to her; they all do. Once she knows the depth of my love, she'll forgive me. She has to. She won't have a choice.

Addie is mine. *Not his.*

"They're resetting her ankle. Should only be a six-week recovery time. Grade-two concussion."

"Okay, nothing too serious then." She's strong. I remind myself she's been through worse.

Olivia openly glares at me as if I'm the worst one of us in the room. I am, but everything I've done has been for Ads. Everything I continue to do is for our future. I won't stop until she sees the truth.

"I want no part in this." She turns to leave.

Without a care in the world, I slam Olivia against the wall. Hard, reminding her who exactly is in charge here. "Don't pretend you're innocent! I'd suggest changing your tone when speaking to me. If I'm going down, I'm taking you with me." I sneer as her eyes widen in fear. "This is what we're going to do."

She tries to shove me away. "There's no *we*. The police—"

"Fuck the police! They're not going to touch me after you tell them what really happened." She doesn't know that while Jax was busy saving my girl, I ran back to the house to make sure the evidence matched my story, not theirs. By the end of this, Addie will either come to me willingly or Jax will be in jail. Her choice.

Me or him.

"Kohen—"

I'm already bored with this conversation. Sweet, innocent Olivia White better get with the program before I'm forced to go to extreme measures. "You're involved, whether you want to be or not. You made your choices years ago. No turning back now, Liv." I purposely use Addie's nickname for her, reminding her of all that she's done with that simple three-letter word.

Her eyes cast to the floor in defeat. She's tried to break free of the chains I locked her in five years ago, but there's no going back. We both know it. I would almost feel bad for her but I don't. Each session she has with Addie has been recorded so I can watch it. Sure, it benefits me, but it will break Addie's heart if she finds out about Olivia's betrayal.

"It's time to let her go." That fire is back in her eyes. I'm going to need to be careful with her; she might not be useful for much longer.

Wrapping my arms around her thin neck, I squeeze just enough so she knows how serious I am when I say, "I will never let her go. We belong together."

She gasps in a few choked breaths before uttering, "The cops are searching for you. You've gone too far this time."

She thinks slapping Addie around is the worst thing I've ever done, but she doesn't know about Em. Nobody does. I've made sure of that.

For the first few weeks, I was absolutely gutted. I hated myself for what I did to her, to us, to our unborn family. I still mourn the life we lost that night. I went as far as putting the barrel in my mouth. In the end, I couldn't do it. Something or someone made me put the gun down. To this day, I believe it was my Emily, telling me she forgave me.

It was hard moving on in the beginning, when I thought I lost the only person who understood me, that gave my life meaning, but then came Ads.

Ads is my reason.

No matter what happens, I'll always choose her.

"Kohen, did you hear me? It's time to go. You still have time to make this right."

"For all the degrees you possess, you're really not that smart, Olivia. Do you really think I would just leave this to chance? Not have a backup plan already in motion? You and I are going to walk away from this without a dent in our records."

"What do you mean *you and I*?" Her voice shakes, showing her barely masked fear.

"I've already involved you. The cops think you were there tonight." Gosh, her face is priceless when I share that tidbit of information. "It will even prove that Jax started the fight. I was trying to protect her from him."

"What are you talking about?"

I show her my Trojan horse. "The crime scene investigators are already at the house. Your and Jax's DNA is all over the place." I flip to the next picture on my phone. "This is your blood on the wall from when Addie cut you with a scalpel." I keep flipping, showing her each damning, intentionally placed piece of evidence. "This is where Jax punched me, making me break a priceless family heirloom."

"How?"

I don't even try to hide my eye roll. "The blood drive a few months ago? I may have swiped a sample." I really should be thanking her for how effortless this was. Jax was a little harder, but thankfully it's easier to drug someone when they're not expecting it.

She starts shaking her head and backing away from me. "This isn't what I signed up for."

Perplexed, I study the coward in front of me. "You didn't really think that I would help you get away with Eric, just so you can secretly videotape your session with Adalynn for me, did you?"

"Kohen—" The second she sees what I have on my phone, she stops talking. Finally, blissful silence. Olivia, of course, zooms in to see if that really is her in her office, posed with a baseball bat over her patient's head.

It is.

"H... ho... how?"

Nodding to the phone, I point out the obvious, "There's more. I never really needed you to record Adalynn's sessions. I've been watching you since Logan had you start working with her. I needed to find a crack in your armor. Thankfully for me, a drunk college mistake made it easy."

The slap across my face is well deserved. I'm using the night her daughter was raped against her. Olivia has no idea that when Eric's parents had him start therapy, she would be unmasking the dark family secret. The rich kid from the same private college her daughter went to was more than just the average frat boy with a killer smile. He was the frat boy all the horror stories are made up of. Eric and his buddies never liked taking no for an answer.

It took her longer than me to realize what he'd done and to whom. I think that was more because she didn't want to believe in a world where something so terrible could happen to her daughter. Still, I have to hand it to her... I can't believe she actually had the guts. No, she didn't kill him, even though I would have. She just made sure that what he did to all those girls, including her daughter, would never happen again. Not by him. She got justice for all of them. She's just now realizing the price of my *help* after I made sure he wouldn't die.

Eric has been a proud resident of the traumatic brain injury wing in the hospital for almost five years now.

I nod to the phone. "There's one more."

She flips to the last file, to the video that seals her fate. The sound of her crushing his skull echoes off the walls. Lightning fast, she deletes the video as if that will solve all of her problems. It won't.

If she doesn't do exactly what I say, Olivia will lose everything.

Personally, I'm proud of what she's done, what she still does when she visits him every single week like clockwork. Eric is there, a prisoner of his own body, unable to tell anyone what's happening, all because of her.

"Why?" Her voice grates on my nerves. I may respect what she continues to do to Eric for his victims, but I hate that she has so easily betrayed Adalynn. Though it's not as if I've given her much of a choice...

Scanning the room, I walk over to the next shelf to grab a pair of gloves, which I slowly slide on, my back to Olivia. "Call it my insurance policy."

I can tell she's scared. Good. I need Olivia to be scared. I need her to know that I will stoop to the lowest low to get what I want. Nothing is going to get in my way of finally having Ads, not even her.

"What about Jax? He's already given his statement."

At this, I turn my head to glare at her. She needs to stop saying his name in front of me. Fucking Jaxon. If he keeps interfering, he's going to end up like everyone else. I hate that Addie can't see who he truly is. She's blind to all the pain he's caused her. For years, I've watched them, waited for him or her brother to tell her the truth. They've all lied to her, allowing her to suffer in the gilded cage they've locked her in. But I'm going to set her free.

"It'll be his word against ours." I bet the coward in front of me wants nothing more than to turn me in. If it weren't for her family, the bitch would.

"If you come clean, maybe a judge will cut you a deal. I'm sure you'll have to pay a fine to some charity but this will just be a slap on your wrist. You can still come back from this, Kohen."

Digging into my rear pocket, I grab the tool that's going to help get the police off our backs, and move closer to Olivia. She's so focused on my gloved hand she hasn't noticed the scalpel yet. "This is going to hurt." I slice at her forearm, making sure I cut deep enough that she's going to need stitches. It'll earn us points in court if it goes that far. I toss Liv a towel from my house to wrap around her arm. "Complements of Addie."

While she's occupied with her wound, I text Gary back, letting him know where to find the evidence for Jaxon. Olivia hisses in pain, tears in her eyes.

"Be mindful not to spill any blood on the floor."

"You're a fucking lunatic!"

Wielding the scalpel that Addie so kindly stabbed me with, I hold it to the good therapist's carotid. I press down just enough to get Liv's attention, but not enough to leave a mark, as long as she doesn't breathe. "Listen carefully. I'm only going to explain this once. You were at my place all day, trying to reason with Ads before Jax showed up in a blind rage. He attacked her when we were docking the boat. By the time we came inside, it was too late. Adalynn was already hurt."

She's holding her breath, too afraid to breathe. After a few more seconds, I release Olivia. More so because I don't need her pissing herself. "Nobody is going to believe that."

"Why not?" I think it's a perfectly laid-out plan.

"Jax isn't just going to roll over."

"It will be his word against ours," I remind her, seeing as it doesn't seem to be sinking in.

"You're forgetting about Adalynn."

I roll my eyes. "Let's not pretend as if Adalynn is all there mentally, Liv. No matter how hard you try, she refuses to get better. She doesn't want to get better. She'll believe whatever you say because she trusts you. Besides, it's not like a judge will pay attention to a word out of her mouth. Not with her history." I reiterate all the times Adalynn's attempted suicide in the past six years, holding up nine fingers. "She's tried to kill herself nine times that we know of, Liv! Not to mention, all the other times that didn't warrant a hospital visit. Fuck, she barely remembers half of them. It won't be hard to convince her and every-one else that she went crazy again." Hell, at this point it's almost a normal occurrence in the Maxwell household. Logan should be re-lieved that I'm willing to take her off his hands.

"Jax is just going to be okay with you blaming him for this?" Her tone is skeptical. Fuck the renowned therapist.

"He's just the jealous ex who couldn't let her go." Besides, they should already be finished with planting evidence to show how ob-sessed the bastard is.

"And what about the police?"

There's a knock on the door. I glance at my Rolex. *Perfect timing as always, Gary.* With a shit-eating-grin, I open the door to the two de-tectives. "All cops are dirty if you have deep enough pockets."

CHAPTER TWO

Adalynn

Beep... beep... beep... My leg hurts.

Beep... beep... beep... Everything hurts.

It's hard to tell if I woke up from the pain or the nightmare—though the dreamlike state is fleeting once reality sets in. The crisp linen sheets hold no warmth as I practically choke on the smell of cleaning products, while the persistent noise from one of the monitors I'm attached to can't delude the constant ringing in my ears.

The last time I woke up in a hospital bed, my family was gone. However, unlike that moment six years ago, presently, I don't know what landed me here. My memories are once again stolen from me.

Think, Addie, think. What's the last thing I remember? The fight with Jax, leaving his place... Where was I going...? With Kohen! Okay, I was with Kohen. We were going to his beach house.

Ding... ding... ding...

We went away. We were planning on going on the boat. That's the last thing I remember...

It takes more effort than I'm willing to admit to open my eyes—correction, *eye*. "Ouch," I croak out, my voice too tight, barely above a whisper. I carefully lift the hand not in a sling to my face. A bandage takes up half of my face, effectively blocking my left eye.

I can't even begin to process what that means before I notice the sun streaming through the blinds, telling me all I need to know. The skyscrapers a clear sign that I'm back in the city. Slowly, I take stock of my injuries. We must have crashed the boat. My leg is now in a cast, and with how painful it is to take the smallest of breaths, I'm going to take a wild guess and say I have a few cracked ribs too.

Being broken in a hospital bed is something I'm used to.

Once I'm done taking inventory of myself, I scan the rest of the room, stopping on the sleeping figure in the corner. It's the last person I expected to see. Why is Jax sitting in the chair where Kohen should be? I flick my eyes from corner to corner, desperate to make sure he's okay.

"Hi," I croak, my voice too weak to speak above a whisper.

"Adalynn?" Jax immediately springs to life. "Are you really awake this time?"

"Ko..."

Jax hands me a cup with a straw in it. Bringing it to my lips, I greedily suck it down and my throat instantly feels better.

"Where...is..."

"Shh, you're okay now." He reaches around me to press the red call button.

And I try again. "Ko..."

"Kohen?" Jax asks. All I can do is nod as I attempt to swallow the razorblades in my throat. He opens his mouth to respond just as someone knocks on the door, effectively halting our conversation.

"Adalynn?" A woman with a slight accent I can't place comes into the room, followed by a man in black scrubs. "It's great to finally see those violet eyes your husband hasn't stopped talking about."

Husband?

Jax scratches the back of his neck. "Yeah, about that—"

It takes half a second for my brain to catch on. Jax isn't family. Meaning he wouldn't have been able to get information or possibly see me without lying. It makes sense, but it doesn't explain why his jaw is so rigid. Then it clicks.

"Fo..." A coughing fit wreaks havoc on my already broken body. "For... how... long?"

"You've been in and out of it for a little over a day," the doctor (I'm assuming) answers after I've had another sip of water, my coughing somewhat under control.

I nod as if this is perfectly normal. "Where's Kohen? When can I see him?"

Jax takes a step back. "What?"

Dr. Monroe—I see embroidered on her white coat—ignores Jax's outburst and focuses on me. "Hopefully I can discharge you in a day or two. I'd still like to monitor you."

Jax is looking anywhere but at me, his jaw still set and his shoulders tense. Something is seriously wrong. Why is he acting this way?

"Are you in any pain?"

Only when I breathe. "A little," I lie, hating the effect painkillers have on me. I can't stand the haziness. I point to my eye, too afraid to ask if it's gone.

"We'll be able to take that off in a few weeks," the doctor assures me.

"Is it... still... there?" My voice is somewhat audible.

The nurse—his nametag reads Joshua Greene—raises an eyebrow. "Is what still there?"

"My eye!" I try to scream my frustration but it sounds more like a halfhearted hiss.

At this, Jax comes back to my side. "You still have your eye. You're going to be okay, Adalynn. I promise nobody is ever going to hurt you again."

Dr. Monroe clicks on a tiny flashlight the size of a pen. "Adalynn, I'm going to do a quick exam. Without moving your head, please follow my finger."

Jax sits back in his chair while Dr. Monroe and Nurse Greene conduct their examination. I wince but other than that, I remain quiet. The doctor spends the next ten minutes checking me over and explaining what to expect.

Once they move on to assessing my bandages, I demand, "Where is Kohen? Did he drive me here?"

Parts of that day are starting to come back. I remember getting on the boat. I remember his harsh comments about my attire. I remember wanting to break up with him. But that's it. Everything else is just a blur of images, pieces of something my brain is still trying to put together.

Dr. Monroe explains, "You were flown into the city. The local hospital wasn't equipped to handle the extent of your injuries. We set your shoulder in surgery and placed pins in your ankle." With each word, Jax winces. "You suffered a grade-two concussion but you're expected to make a full recovery." She types away on her iPad. "Can you tell me your name?"

I would roll my eyes if I weren't afraid of the pain. "Adalynn Grace Maxwell. I'm in a hospital. I'm twenty-three years old... what else?" I ask impatiently.

"What's the last thing you remember before waking up here?"

Images from my nightmare, being locked in a dark room, flash through my mind so rapidly that I can't focus on anything other than the feeling of being trapped without a way out. My breathing gets heavy, and I start to shake.

"Adalynn, can you tell me what's the last thing you remember before waking up here?" the doctor asks again, obviously unaware of the fear coursing through me.

"I was on a boat." I turn to Jax. "Was there an accident?"

He shakes his head, his expression harder than stone.

"Is there anything else you remember?"

The more I try to piece the events of that day together, the more panicked I become. The monitors start beeping with the increased strain on my blood pressure.

"I think that's enough, doctor." Jax snaps.

Surprisingly, she appears to agree and drops the interrogation. "I'll be back to check on you later. Nurse Greene will bring you something to eat. You're extremely lucky. It doesn't seem like you're suffering from any residual effects. I'm still going to monitor you closely though." The doctor spends the next ten minutes explaining what to expect in the coming days. The only thing I'm able to retain is that I'll be in pain, recovery will be slow, and I should be able to leave this hell-hole soon.

"Are you sure that's wise?" the traitor beside me asks.

Dr. Monroe doesn't even glance up from her iPad. "Feel free to get that second opinion, Mr. Chandler. You'll be hard-pressed to find a doctor with a more impressive background than mine."

I want to argue that I'm more than ready to go home now, but I don't think the fact I'm presently affixed to a hospital bed is going to sell it, so I keep my mouth shut.

She hands me a remote. "If you experience anything that I mentioned earlier, press this button, and we'll be right in."

I can't even manage a nod. Once again, my world has flipped upside down. How did everything go so wrong?

Hesitantly, I turn to Jax. "What happened?"

"You really don't remember anything after the boat?"

"I was wet. I think I was running for help. Did the boat crash?" I ask again, because that's the only theory my brain's been able to come up with. Did I fall into the water? Is that why I was wet?

"There was no accident, Adalynn."

Adalynn...? Interesting, he only uses my full name when it's serious. I gulp and brace myself to hear the next words out of his mouth. Whatever it is, it's going to have the power to destroy me. I can already feel it. I've lost another person.

"Kohen did this to you. You're here because of him." The anger rolling off Jax comes in waves. I can practically taste the hatred in the air.

I don't believe him. I can't believe him. There's no way Kohen could do this to me.

"You're not making any sense."

He points to my neck. "The reason it hurts so much to speak is because your *boyfriend*," he sneers the word, "had his hands wrapped around your throat when I found you. He was going to kill you."

I'm already shaking my head, refusing to believe that Kohen would do this to me. I glance down at my broken body, again taking stock of my injuries but with a new light. No, Jax has to be wrong. Kohen couldn't do this. He... he...

He's... *passionate*, sure, but I never thought he'd be capable of this.

Didn't you though? That pesky voice in my head taunts me, reminding me of all the times he'd grab me a little too tight, or the names he'd call me when he disagreed with what I was wearing. The chill in the room seems to drop a few degrees as I remember the way I felt at his beach house.

Jax has never made his dislike for Kohen a secret, but he would never lie about something like this. If Kohen really did this to me...

Oh gosh, I feel sick to my stomach. How could I have been so stupid? How could I have let this happen?

I thought we were healing each other. His dark parts called out to my shattered soul. Kohen is the only one who understands me. There are things I've shared with him that I haven't even shared with Jax.

"I was going to leave him." It's not until Jax stills that I realize I've spoken out loud. "I was going to break up with him."

"It's okay Ads. He's never going to hurt you again." Jax wraps his arms around me, stroking my hair and soothing me with his kind words while I sob into his shirt.

As he holds me, he fills in the missing pieces. How he pulled Kohen off me, barely refraining from killing the man in the process. I don't know how much time passes as he continues to hold on to me and I cry into his shirt. It's almost like I'm reliving it with him, but not really. It's just another story that someone is telling me. I can't fully grasp that it was me on the ground while my boyfriend attacked me.

Eventually I run out of tears. "You're going to be okay," Jax vows as he takes the seat beside me.

No, I'm not. It feels like ever since I woke up in the hospital six years ago, nothing has been okay. I keep trying to be whole, but something inside me is broken. As if a part of me is missing.

Everything I do always comes down to that night, to all the mistakes I've made. No matter what I do, I always end up back here, back to knowing everything is my fault. Is life really worth it when it's this hard? How do I keep going when everything in me is telling me to just... stop?

As much as I want to put all the blame on Kohen, I can't. I'm as much at fault as he is.

Maybe if the accident never happened, I wouldn't have thought it was okay to be with a man like Kohen. I've always known what type of person he is. He hasn't changed. He just let his mask down, showing me his true self, and instead of running away, I clung to him. I was sinking and he saved me. He was my life vest. Though I never thought he'd be the one putting holes in it, helping me sink faster than when I was floundering alone. If I'm truly being honest with myself, it's because I thought I deserved him, thought we deserved each other. I'm the girl who survived when everyone else died.

So I did what I do best. I swept everything under the rug. The first time Kohen pinched the underside of my arm while we were at dinner with his coworkers, I reminded myself why I deserved it. I accepted his apology every time because I thought, if either of us were the monster, it was me. It's not like I can even fault Kohen for being jealous. He had every right to be when all I did was compare him to the man beside me. I think on some level he knew he wasn't who I wanted. Jax was... *is*. He's the man I've never been able to truly get over, and somehow Kohen knew.

Even though I denied ever having a relationship with Jaxon, Kohen was able to see straight through my lies. So if he ever pulled my hair a little too tight when he kissed me, I chalked it up to him being passionate. I was using him, pretending that one day I could love him the way I love Jax.

I may have stopped cutting myself but only because I found a new outlet to enact the pain. And Kohen was my blade.

"What can I do?" Jax kisses my knuckles, one by one. "I'm so sorry, Ads. This is all my fault."

"If it weren't for you—"

"If it weren't for me, you wouldn't have been there! If I hadn't been such a coward all these years, this wouldn't have happened. You wouldn't even have met *him*."

"Jax—"

"You should have never been with him."

His words send chills down my spine, and I swallow the sudden lump lodged in my throat. "Don't, Jax. Not again."

He doesn't listen though. "I love you, Adalynn Grace Maxwell. I've loved you before I knew what love was."

The pain I was feeling moments ago is nothing compared to whatever's happening in what's left of my shattered heart. Everything he's saying is... too late... too needed... too EVERYTHING.

He's everything. But he's also wrong. He doesn't love me. Who could?

"Why are you doing this? Why now?"

"Because I can't *not* say it, Ads. I shouldn't have pushed you away, not the other day or any of the times before. I'm tired of pretending you're not the most important person in my life."

I shake my head, refusing to believe his lies. "I deserve more." I wish it didn't take Kohen landing me in another hospital bed for me to know my worth. I deserve more than Kohen... more than what Jax can give me. I'm the girl who survived, and I need to stop punishing myself for it.

"I know." He kisses the inside of my palm, over my bandage.

"Do you have any idea how many times I wished you'd say this to me?" I've lost count of how many times I would sit on the floor and daydream about our lives as if the accident never happened. No matter what he tells me, I know we lost each other because of that night.

Everything was perfect until it wasn't. Now, it's impossible to find our way back to each other, and I don't even remember why. And that's what kills me. That's what keeps me up at night.

"I'm here, Ads. I'm saying I love you. I'm saying I don't care about anything but you."

"You've never made me a priority." My voice breaks as I whisper, "I've always been the one you walk away from. And I'm tired of watching you leave."

"I'm never leaving you again," he vows.

How many times have I heard that line in the past? Why does it feel like we were doomed before we were ever given the chance to begin? Maybe it's because we've never even been in a relationship.

We've always been a dirty secret. Passion-filled, stolen moments.

Even though my heart craves him more than my next breath, I do what is necessary... I pull away from the only man with the power to absolutely destroy me. "Loving you shouldn't be this hard."

"I know I never say or do the right thing. I've done everything wrong by you. I know I don't deserve it but I'm asking anyway." His hands shakes as he asks, "Give me one more chance. I'm done hiding us."

He's done? Why? Because my boyfriend tried to kill me? Would he even be here if he didn't come close to losing me for good? He's too late. His lies are old and used up. I have a long road ahead of me and the last thing I need is to deal with the emotional roller coaster that is Jaxon Chandler.

"There's never really been an *us*, though, right? It doesn't count if it's all behind closed doors, right, Jax?" I ask, throwing his words from the other day back in his face.

"I'm sorry, Ads. I've made every mistake when it comes to you."

I refuse to let him in again. Every time I do, he breaks the best parts of me, leaving me to pick up the shattered pieces. And once I'm mended, he always comes back for more. It's a never-ending cycle. I need to choose myself.

"I almost lost you," he says almost absently.

Ding... ding... ding. That's why he's here, saying all his pretty words.

"Don't you mean you almost lost your best friend's little sister?" My dig hits the mark.

"Ads, I didn't mean any of that. I love—"

I stop him before he's able to say the three words that will break me worse than anything Kohen did to me. "What did you think was going to happen, Jax? I was going to jump into your open arms because my boyfriend beat me up? Does it make you feel better inside, knowing that the person I thought loved me was able to do *this*." I gesture to my broken body.

"Ads—" He makes a move to grab my hand again. I pull away before he can make contact.

I know if I let him touch me the way we both want, I'll never survive it. Survive *him*. I'll fall for his pretty words and I'll let him in. I'll give him the option to destroy me once more. That's the game we play over and over again.

We met when I was eight, and he was my hero... the man I dreamed of marrying one day. But I'm not a little girl with little girl fantasies anymore.

The guy should have come with a warning. Jaxon Chandler has done nothing but pull me apart, breaking me down every time he's walked away and left smaller and smaller pieces behind. Can't he see that I'm a shell? Just an empty, broken body. I have nothing left to give. Not to him or anyone else.

"Don't, Jax. I'm too tired to fight you." *Too tired to tell you why we can never make this work.* I just need to be left alone. I need time to myself. I can't do... whatever this is anymore.

"You don't have to fight. I'm done pretending you're just Logan's sister when you're everything to me."

If I weren't so sure it would hurt, I'd laugh. "Yeah? What's changed? Don't forget that you've used that line on me before. It's getting old and overplayed." I point between us. "Just like us." My lips keep moving, saying words I don't truly mean. "We were never meant to be anything more than friends."

It's not like he'd actually want me. Who would? I'm broken in ways I didn't think possible. My boyfriend tried to kill me. It's slowly starting to come back to me. I can picture fragments of Kohen laughing at me while he had his hands wrapped around my throat. I thought he loved me! I thought I finally found someone that understood and wanted to be with me.

"Do you remember when we were little and we'd sneak onto the roof of your house at night?"

I couldn't forget even if I wanted to. Instead of saying that, though, I remain silent, not trusting myself to speak.

"Every night, when I needed you the most, you'd fix me and help me climb up on the roof. You'd talk until I was finally able to relax." The memories come swiftly, both the pleasant and the most heart-breaking. "You'd always tell me your dreams of the future."

You. Jax was my future. My dreams. I would tell him about all the kids we'd have, how happy we'd be. God, I was pathetic.

"I never told you then, but I'm telling you now." He takes a deep breath. "Under those stars with you cuddled up to my side, I never wanted to leave. That was my wish every single night. I never wanted to leave you then and I don't want to leave you now."

"We're not those kids anymore," I say in a choked whisper.

"No, we're not." I don't stop him when he clutches my hand this time. "But I want to get back to there, back to us, Ads. You're the love of my life. You're my every wish, every dream. I lov—"

My skin is buzzing, and my breathing has picked up. With a simple touch, I'm ready to melt to the floor. This is why I have to put distance between us. I can't trust myself when it comes to him. If I let Jax in, I'm willingly giving him another piece of me that I'll never get back. At this stage, it feels as if it all already belongs to him.

"Don't. Can't you see I can't take anymore, Jax?"

Even though this doesn't feel like a game anymore, I have to protect my heart from him... from losing it to him more than I have. I know this man better than I know myself. I know he means every sweet word out of his mouth. But that doesn't change anything. Instead of bright-ening my soul, it only darkens it more. To be together, we'd have to open up old wounds. No more secrets between us. I say that I'm ready, but I think we both know I'm not. And I don't know if I ever will be. For those secrets to be revealed. For Jax to be mine.

"Ads—"

I can't do this, not here, not now. "I think I need space."

"Ads—"

"Please." Afraid of seeing the disappointment in his eyes, I stare at the blank television. "Maybe you can bring me back something to eat? You know I hate hospital food." Out of the corner of my eye, I see him rock back. In that one move, I know he's going to do what I'm asking. Every cell in my body is begging him not to leave, while my words say the exact opposite.

"I'll call in breakfast and I'll be right outside if you need me." He hands me an iPhone, similar to my old one but distinctively new. "Call me when you're ready."

With each step, I silently plead with him to stay, to fight for me. He pauses at the door, and I turn away from him before he can see me watching him leave. My heart aches for him to close the door and kiss me. It seems like hours go by before he finally exits the room. It isn't until the door clicks shut that I let the tears I was holding fall. I hiccup-sob, clutching my side with the physical pain, which of course makes the tears fall harder. With each gasp, I tell my body I deserve this new wave of agony. I was the stupid one who let myself get in this situation.

I stayed with Kohen, even though I knew what he was capable of. I made Jax leave, even though everything inside me was begging him to stay.

Eventually, I'm able to calm down enough to wipe my face. When the tears finally clear from my eyes, I notice the giant bouquet of peonies with a single Stargazer lily in the center.

Jax. Once again, he's seen me at my worst.

CHAPTER THREE

Adalynn

The soft rapt on the door wakes me. I barely have time to respond before two men enter my room. I sit up straighter in bed, noticing Jax still isn't back yet. "Is there something I can help you with?"

"We're here to take your statement, Ms. Maxwell," the bald one says.

And I immediately know they're not just cops. The lack of uniforms with their badges clipped to their belts gives them away. The bald detective appears to not have smiled in years, or his entire life from the looks of it. The other sports an outdated military-style haircut, a clear bodybuilder with an easy grin. Good cop, bad cop. Check.

The obvious point man introduces himself first. "I'm Detective Miller and this is my partner, Detective Fernandez." Miller's muscles could rival Logan's while Fernandez is tall and lanky. "Is now a good time to talk?" He's already setting a tape recorder on the tray table hovering above my lap.

"Do I need a lawyer?"

"Do you feel it necessary to have a lawyer, Ms. Maxwell? We're just here to take your statement pertaining to the events of this past weekend."

"It's best if we get your statement now while it's still fresh in your mind," Fernandez adds calmly, as if he's rehearsed this a million times before.

"Okay, what do you need from me?" I glance at the clock. Where is Jax? It's been four hours. I reach for my phone and shoot him a text.

Me: Police are here. Can you come back?

"Whenever you're ready, Ms. Maxwell," Miller prompts, and I jump.

I can't seem to focus on anything but the recorder staring back at me from the tray table. I tell myself that this doesn't matter, that Kohen doesn't matter. Nothing does but the truth. Still, I find my hands starting to shake, and I break into a cold sweat as I try to remember everything that took place.

I sigh, already wishing I'd pretended to be asleep. "I remember going away with Kohen. Things feeling... off."

"Off?"

I shrug, not really knowing how to convey the way I felt the moment I stepped out of his car. "He stole my phone charger from my bag so I wouldn't be able to contact anyone, once my phone died."

"At any time, did you ask to use his phone?" Miller asks.

"Yes." The memory of him handing me his phone as a test is vivid in my mind, so is the sensation of being trapped. Even then, I knew something was way off. I hated the terror that came with being alone with him, wanting to go back to the city, but not seeing a way out unless I stuck to the plan.

It's as if I'm finally seeing everything clearly now. The neon lights mocking me, taunting my desperate need to be normal, to be loved by someone. I forced myself to be blind in our relationship, believing we were connected because of our pasts. Evidently, I need more help than my therapist Olivia even realizes.

"What happened after you used his phone? Did you call Jaxon Chandler?" This question again comes from Miller.

I shake my head, realizing how this is going to sound. "No, I never got around to calling anyone."

"Did Dr. Kohen Daniels prevent you from using his phone?"

"Eh, not exactly."

This time, Fernandez takes the lead. "Can you explain further please?"

"It felt like a test. Since he was already on edge, I didn't want to set him off. So I let it go. I knew we'd be heading back to the city soon, so I was just waiting until then."

"Waiting for what?"

"To break up with him."

Miller pinches the bridge of his nose. "Let me get this straight, your boyfriend took you away for the weekend. When you realized your phone was dead and he offered to let you use his, you decided you wanted to break up with him? I think we're missing something, Mrs. Maxwell."

You and me both, Mr. Jackass. "I knew that I couldn't be with him any longer."

"Then why wait until you were back in the city? Why not use his phone to call a car? I think we both know you could have afforded it."

"Excuse me?" Despite having one good eye, I shoot him a glare that I know isn't as intimidating as I hoped.

"What I mean to point out is that you could have used his phone to have someone pick you up. Why stay?"

"I thought it would be best to end things in a public place." Taking a deep breath, I focus on the beautiful floral arrangement from Jax as I admit my deep, dark secret. "This wasn't the first time he hurt me."

"Can you elaborate, Ms. Maxwell?" Fernandez asks as he takes notes.

For the next ten minutes, I'm forced to relive every grotesque detail of how Kohen hurt me in the past. The worst part is that until this moment, as I'm forced to explain myself to these two strangers, I didn't even realize how toxic our relationship was. I pretended as if it never happened and went on with my life. I did what I do best and painted a smile on my face and hid the bruises from everyone.

"Do you have any proof of these alleged assaults?" Every time Miller asks a question, I feel smaller and smaller. This interrogation is pointless. I know they don't believe me.

Still, I answer him. "Nope, just my word against his."

Fernandez writes something in his notepad before peering up at me again. "Did anyone visit the home while you were there, Adalynn? A housekeeper, a friend, a gardener perhaps?"

"We were alone. That's why I knew I needed to wait until we were back in the city."

I don't miss the way the detectives glance at each other. In a nanosecond, they convey something. Something they're keeping from me.

"So, it was just you and Dr. Daniels. In the house. All weekend?"

"Yes."

"You two were alone all day Sunday, correct?" Miller reiterates, his speech slower this time, as if I need help processing his words.

"Yes?" I say it more as a question, since I really can't remember much of Sunday.

"Why did you have Mr. Chandler meet you at your boyfriend's house?"

I glare at Detective Miller. "I didn't. As I previously stated, I had no means of contacting anyone." At least this idiot is asking questions I can answer honestly.

He nods. "So you're saying Jaxon Chandler showed up unannounced and uninvited, correct?"

This gives me pause. It seems like he's fishing for something. Though I'm not sure what. "If it weren't for him, I would be dead right now."

"For the record, can you clarify if you asked Jaxon Chandler to come to Kohen Daniels's property?"

I stare open-mouthed at Miller. This is a trap. I know it is. I have to find a way out of this for Jax. I have to save him. "He knew where I was going. I saw him before I left. When he couldn't get in contact with me, he came searching for us to make sure we made it okay."

"Once again, to clarify, what you're saying is that neither you or Dr. Daniels asked Mr. Chandler to stop by. Am I right?"

"If you know my net worth, you must also know how I got it. Jax was making sure history didn't repeat itself." This gives them pause. *Good.* Hopefully I've led them away from Jax.

"Can you explain how you sustained your injuries?"

Finally, an easy answer. "Kohen Daniels."

Miller raises an eyebrow. "Were any of your injuries from Jaxon Chandler?"

How can one person be this stupid? Is he even listening to a word I've said? "Jaxon Chandler saved me from Kohen Daniels attacking me."

"You remember Dr. Daniels attacking you on the night of September 23rd?"

Not really. "Yes," I lie again.

"What else can you tell us about Sunday?" Fernandez jumps in before I throw something at his partner. *Smart man.*

I shrug. "Not much. We had breakfast on the patio, and in the afternoon, we went on his boat."

"And what happened next?"

I close my eyes and beg my brain to remember. "He attacked me."

"He attacked you on the boat?"

I barely stop myself from shrugging. "Af... after."

"And when did you invite Jaxon Chandler into the home?"

What? "I didn't see Jax until he saved me... on the road," I say, recalling that little detail from what Jax told me.

"So you didn't invite him into the home?" Detective Miller watches my face as he waits for me to respond.

"No, Jax never stepped foot in Kohen's house. He rescued me on the street." At least I think that's what happened. Jax would have mentioned otherwise. Right?

"Just a few more questions, Ms. Maxwell, and then we'll let you get some rest." Miller barely pauses before stunning me with, "Did you assault Dr. Daniels in any way?"

"Excuse me?"

"Your and Dr. Daniels's stories don't match up. He has a witness to collaborate the events of the night in question. We're just trying to figure out what really happened."

"That's not possible." Jax wouldn't lie about something like this. Plus, I'm starting to remember things on my own. Like the closet... I hold up a hand, stopping them from explaining. "Wait... You've found him?"

Holy fuck, this is all over! I don't have to worry about what's going to happen after I leave the hospital. I don't have to live in fear, waiting for him to attack. The next time I see Kohen, he'll be behind bars.

"Found him?" Miller lifts a curious brow. "I wasn't aware he was missing."

Wait... What? "I'm confused."

If I wasn't staring at Miller, I would have missed the way he rolled his eyes. "Who coached you? Who are you protecting, Ms. Maxwell? We can't help you if you continue to protect your abuser."

"Coached? What are you talking about?"

He glanced down at his notepad, flipping a few pages before looking up at me again. "On the evening of September 23rd, Dr. Daniels and Dr. White returned to the residence to find the front door ajar with evidence of tampering. There appeared to be a struggle in the house: upturned furniture, a broken vase, and so on. Dr. White called for help while Dr. Daniels went in search of Ms. Maxwell. When Dr. Daniels entered the far bedroom, he spotted Mr. Chandler with his fist raised above a beaten and bloodied woman, recognized to be the victim in question—that's you, Ms. Maxwell." The detective pauses as if I don't know my own name then continues, "When Dr. Daniels was finally able to restrain Mr. Chandler, Ms. Maxwell ran and Dr. Daniels and Mr. Chandler followed." He flips to another page. "The weather conditions made it difficult for Dr. Daniels to continue the pursuit and when he finally found Ms. Maxwell, she was in the middle of the road." He nods to my neck. "With Mr. Chandler's hands around her throat."

I'm almost afraid to ask, but the words are leaving my mouth before I even realize what I'm doing. "Dr. White, as in Olivia White?" This cannot be happening. Olivia wasn't there. I would remember her being there. I search my spotty memory, trying to figure out what I'm missing.

"Yes, she arrived shortly after you called her from Dr. Daniel's phone." Miller scans his notes. "You talked to her for over two hours. Don't you remember?"

What? Now, I *know* that didn't happen. I have to prove it, but the new phone in my hands is as useless as I am.

"Dr. Olivia White is your psychiatrist, correct?"

I give the detective a tight nod. I'm afraid to speak. Fernandez glances at Miller, then at me.

"Do you not remember her being there?"

No. It's just like before. Missing gaps in my mind.

"Are you okay?"

No. I'm not. None of this makes any sense. I need to talk to Jax. I check my phone again. Nothing from him. That's odd. I fire off another text.

Me: The police are saying Liv was there too...

Me: Please come back.

Me: I need you.

My good hand starts to shake so I tuck it under the blanket, trying to hide the fact that I'm scared. If Liv was there... that means... Did I have an episode in front of Kohen? Oh my gosh, this is bad.

"He's telling you that I'm crazy, right? That I've been seeing a therapist since I was seventeen?"

After everything, he's going to get away with it. I shared too much with him, and he's going to use it against me. Are attempted suicides public knowledge like house deeds? Somehow, I don't break down in front of these incompetent detectives as I recall all the secrets I've shared with *Dr. Daniels*, each one more damning than the last.

"Yes, he did mentioned that, and Dr. White was able to confirm you're her patient." Miller reads from his notepad, recounting Olivia's side of things. It's just like all the times before. I was erratic, holding a weapon, screaming that I wanted it all to stop.

I thought my blackouts were over. I'm lost, struggling to recall what really happened that night. It almost feels as if I'm trapped under water, my memories just above the surface, out of reach. The harder I try to grab on to them, the farther I sink down into the emptiness that is my soul.

Miller continues, unaware that with each word he says, I'm breaking a little more.

"Olivia said that?" Isn't that a breach of doctor-patient confidentiality? I thought there were laws against this type of thing. Does Jax know she was there? "When did she leave? Why didn't she take me with her?" That's usually what happens.

"After Ms. Maxwell locked herself in the closet, Dr. Daniels contacted Dr. White. She was able to coax Ms. Maxwell out but not before the latter attacked the former with the scalpel. Eventually, Dr. White was able to calm Ms. Maxwell down and accompany the couple on a boat ride. The rest of Dr. White's statement is consistent with what we've already shared with you."

I shake my head. Refusing to believe this. "Kohen attacked me," I whisper but I don't think they hear me.

The minutes tick by as I try to see how this is all going to play out. It will be our word against his. I should have known Kohen wouldn't just crawl under a rock and die. No, that would have been too easy. Of course he's going after Jax. He knows that's the only way to really hurt me, because we both know how I really feel about Jaxon.

Kohen isn't going to stop.

"Can you walk us through the rest of the night?" Miller asks.

Why? What's the point? I already know they don't believe a word out of my mouth. Not with Liv claiming I was a threat to myself and others. I've already lost. Kohen is going to get away with this. The worst part is that I can't even remember Olivia being there. This is bad.

However, I find myself giving them a recap of everything I remember as well as the things Jax told me happened. It's evident from their facial expressions that they don't believe a word I'm saying. The more I talk, the more I start to piece together. Just small glimpses of that night. But hopefully it's enough to convince them that Kohen is the monster, not Jax.

"Kohen slapped me across my face for talking back to him." I point to my still-bruised cheek.

"Anything else?"

I start to tell them about the dinner but stop. Liv wasn't there. I would have remembered, right? I can't sort out the details. I just have this feeling that I couldn't go upstairs with Kohen. I *did* have a scalpel. Liv wasn't there though. She wasn't who I stabbed; it was Kohen.

"What time did Olivia arrive?" I dare to ask, afraid that admitting she was there will somehow incriminate Jax.

"Around noon."

I nod, even though it doesn't make any sense. She wouldn't lie. She had to have been there. "Is she okay?" Did Kohen hurt her too?

"She had to get twelve stitches but she'll be okay."

"Stitches? Did Kohen—"

Fernandez shakes his head. "It's from where you stabbed her in the forearm. Dr. Daniels had to get a few in his shoulder."

I don't remember. I can picture the scalpel in my hand. I was sitting at dinner with Kohen. *Liv wasn't there.* I didn't want to go anywhere with him. I wanted to leave. I wouldn't have hurt her.

Where is Jax? I need his help. I'm making things worse.

"Anything else you'd like to tell us, Ms. Maxwell?"

I'm not sure. "I ran out of the house." I pause to collect myself. "He chased me and threw me on the ground."

"Mr. Chandler?"

I shake my head. "No, Kohen chased me."

"He followed you outside... where?"

Again, I'm not sure. "The street." I recite the words Jax said right before I forced him to leave. "He kicked me. Kohen was choking me when Jax threw him off me."

"Anything else?"

I nod. "If Jax didn't stop him, I would be dead."

"So you're claiming your injuries are from Dr. Kohen Daniels and not Jaxon Chandler, correct?"

I glare at Miller. "Correct." Why do I have to keep repeating myself? "And how long have you known Jaxon Chandler?"

I shrug. "Since I was eight. I'm sure you're able to do the math."

"Is there anything you're leaving out? For whatever reason."

I shake my head, and Fernandez reaches into his pocket and hands me his card.

"If you remember anything else, give us a call."

I watch them pack up their things and head towards the door. Everything is a mess and getting messier by the minute. I look at my still-silent phone and quickly ask, "What about Jax? Did you get his statement too?"

Miller is suddenly all smiles. "He's being processed as we speak."

"Processed?" I ask stupidly, because what I'm thinking can't be true. There's no way they'd arrest him. Jax did nothing wrong.

"We apprehended him a few hours ago. We just finished questioning him before coming here for your statement, Ms. Maxwell."

WHAT. THE. FUCK.

Everything that happens after they leave is a blur of my fingers moving rapidly over my phone, sending emails and texts at an impressive pace. I lost count how many times I've called everyone. Logan and Connor's voicemails are full, thanks to me. How the heck is nobody answering right now? Even Harper is MIA. I didn't know it was possible for Logan to go this long without responding to me. There's never been a time where I've reached out to him and he hasn't immediately dropped everything to take my call.

Jax is in jail and I'm helpless in a hospital.

My fingers hover over the name of the one person I know can help but will also mean Jaxon will never forgive me. I'm not even sure if the number still works. I've never once contacted him, but when I saw the crumpled up piece of paper in Jax's dorm room, I saved it, engraved it in my memory. I slowly die inside as I lift my phone to my ear.

Please forgive me, Jax.

Out of all the ways I've replayed this conversation in my head, I never thought I'd utter the words, "Your son needs your help," to the one person who singlehandedly *destroyed* Jax's childhood.

Chapter Four

Adalynn

"Why should I care?" The harsh whip of his voice still makes me cringe even after all these years.

Because he's your son, you heartless piece of shit. "I thought you could—"

"Help? Adalynn, I know you aren't the smart one in the family but I thought you'd have at least picked up on the fact that I haven't spoken to my son in years. I doubt he'd want any help from me."

"Yes, but—"

"After everything I've done for him, this is how he repays me? By dragging our name through the mud? For what? For you?"

Do not yell at him. Do not yell at him. I repeat this so many times in my head it's amazing that I don't say the words out loud. As much as I want to remind him of exactly which one of us would be 'dragging the Chandler name through the mud,' I know it's pointless. He didn't care then and he still doesn't now.

A normal dad would stop whatever they were doing to help their son. But Wyatt Chandler has never been father material. Knowing this, I continue to plead for his help. Being stuck in a hospital bed leaves me limited options.

I don't care that Jax will hate me once he finds out. I refuse to just let him sit in a cell because of me. Once I explain, he'll have to understand that I had no other choice but to contact his father.

"As I mentioned, Dr. Chandler, it's a misunderstanding."

"Tell me why I should stick my neck out to help someone as ungrateful as my son?"

I hear the chime of an elevator in the background. "He needs—"

"I always knew you'd be a stain on our name." The line goes dead.

The hours tick by as I wait for someone to call me back. The food the nurse brought in a while ago remains untouched and is no doubt cold by now. *Yum, cold hospital food.* I'll be eating that any second now, just as soon as any one of them gets back to me.

I've drafted a text, but every time I go to send it to Wyatt, I always end up deleting it. He's right. Jax would rather rot in jail than get any help from his father. Oh gosh, what did I do? If he ever finds out that I contacted that man, Jax will never forgive me.

I'm the only one who knows what he's really capable of, what went on behind closed doors. Yet here I am, asking for his help. *Don't throw up. Don't throw up.* What was I thinking contacting him?

Suddenly the door bursts open. I barely have time to register Logan's furious face before he's closing the distance between us and wrapping me in his arms. I'm so relieved to see him that I don't cry out in pain when he squeezes me a little too tight. My ribs protest but I cling to him as much as he's clinging to me.

"When did you get here? Never mind. That doesn't matter. Jax is in jail."

Logan pulls away. "Don't worry about him. All you need to worry about is getting better. Heard they're going to be discharging you tomorrow."

That's news to me. I've been so preoccupied by everything going on with Jax that I haven't even had the time to think about getting out of here or what that means. I can't go back to my place, not with Kohen living in the same building. Forcing that out of my head, I focus on what really matters. Saving Jax.

"Logan, you need to listen to me. Kohen lied to the police and he's pinning all of *this*..." I wave a hand over my body. "...on Jax. You need to call a lawyer."

"I know." Sighing, Logan takes a seat. "Addie, there's something I need to tell you but I need you to stay calm, okay? I don't want you worrying."

Whatever he's about to tell me is bad. I can tell by the way he avoids eye contact.

"Is Jax still in jail?"

It isn't until he shakes his head that I can finally relax. "He's in the process of being released but that's the least of his worries right now."

Logan goes on to explain everything that has happened since Jax saved me from Kohen's. Connor and Logan rushed back from London the second Jax told them what happened. By the time they made it to the hospital, the police were putting Jax in the back of a cruiser. They followed the car to the station and remained there the entire time, trying to get him released but Logan needed to come back and check on me.

Jax was arrested for assaulting Kohen and breaking and entering. He would have had additional charges brought against him, but since I refused to cooperate with the detectives, they had to dismiss the second assault charge.

The best part is that it's already all over the news. When the most eligible bachelor attacks one of the most respected doctors in New York, the world takes notice. Especially since I'm Adalynn Maxwell, heir to the Maxwell fortune. Sometimes I forget that, because of my parents, I'm from a different world. It's easy to pretend that I'm a no-body when all I'm really able to do is focus on getting through the rest of the day. Still, this shocks me. I thought the rags had long forgotten all about the elusive Adalynn Maxwell.

The longer Logan talks, the more confused I become. How is this even real life right now? "Just take me to the station. I'll clear this up."

He sighs. "It's not that simple, Addie."

"Why not? Jax didn't do anything wrong. Kohen did. That animal should be the one locked up, not Jax!"

"They searched his penthouse, Addie."

"Kohen's?" I don't know why I even asked because I know that's not right... "Jax's? Why?"

"They had evidence suggesting this was planned."

"What was planned?"

"Everything. The police have reason to believe that Jax was going to murder Kohen before kidnapping you."

Logan explains how there's evidence that we're lying to the police. Jax's fingerprints and blood are inside Kohen's house. He tries to make me understand but I can't. Jax would have told me if he were there. He found me in the middle of the road. He almost hit me with his car.

"I never thought he'd be able to do this to you."

What? "Jax would never lay a finger on me! You know this!" I yell at Logan. I don't care that our voices are easily overheard by the hospital staff. There is not a world that exists where Jax would ever hurt me physically. He's not his father.

"The police showed us the evidence, Adalynn. You don't need to protect him."

How could my brother, Jax's best friend, ever believe the police? He's not who they're painting him to be. "That's a lie! Kohen—"

"The police have evidence that Jax has been stalking you for years, Adalynn." Logan barely raises his voice, but with the silence that follows, he might as well have been shouting.

I laugh and instantly regret it. Wheezing through the pain, I grab my side and try with all my might to stop the sound. Logan isn't amused. Judging from the vein popping out on his forehead, I say he's one short fuse away from exploding.

"You can't be serious? On what planet would he even *want* to stalk me?" *Would it be bad if I said 'I wish' right now?* "What do you mean they have evidence?"

Logan seems as frustrated as I feel. "They found stuff on his home computer. There were thousands of photos of you, Addie, spanning the years. There was even a detailed calendar of your and Kohen's daily activities."

"That's bullshit. There's no way Jax would stalk me. Why would anyone want to?" I'm the least interesting person in New York. "Whatever photos they have are fake. Kohen is behind this."

Logan hands me a manila envelope. "I'm sorry," he whispers as my fingers grasp the documents.

My ears ring as the reality of what I'm holding actually hits me. I feel the blood drain from my face as I flip through the stack. I'm in every single picture.

"How did you get these?" I ask, stunned. There are pictures of me in Central Park, on the street, at dinner with Logan, the entrance to the subway. Crap, there's even photos of me coming and going from Liv's office. Every time I stepped outside, someone was there with a camera.

How is this even my life right now?

"I may have given myself access to the police files," he says nonchalantly, as if what he did wasn't 100% illegal. It's times like this I'm glad my brother is a tech genius.

I rub at my temples, trying in vain to fight the headache coming on. "Why didn't I notice?"

"This isn't your fault, Adalynn."

"Someone has been following me for years, Logan! Years, and I never once noticed?" My skin is crawling. "I dated my stalker?" I think I'm going to be sick.

"Addie, this wasn't Kohen."

I pause to look at my brother. "What do you mean this wasn't Kohen? Who else could it be?"

Logan sighs, defeated. "Jax."

"That's not possible! There's no way Jax has been stalking me. Are you even hearing yourself right now?"

He tugs at his hair. "What do you want from me, Addie? I'm even more confused than you are. There's no way my best friend could do this, yet the evidence—"

"Is wrong!" I say with such finality I leave no room for argument.

"Look at what's right in front of your eyes, Adalynn!" He tears the photos from my hand and starts flinging them on the bed so my life is spread out in front of us. "I trusted him!"

"This. Wasn't. Him!"

There's no reality where I could possibly believe Jax could do any of this. It doesn't matter that I can't recall most of my past. I know Jax. He wouldn't do this. The fact that Logan is so quick to punish his best friend is disturbing. He should be on Jax's side. What am I missing?

"We've known Jax since we were kids. There's no way he—"

"There's a lot about Jax you don't know, Addie." Logan takes a deep breath, as if preparing to go to battle. "I saw it on his computer myself."

"Kohen planted it there," I say without missing a beat, like I know anything about computers. I don't. Logan is the mastermind around technology.

My brother pinches the bridge of his nose. "I already checked. Nobody but Jax had access to his computer. Well, besides me. The moment the police turned it on, I entered through the back and went through all his files."

I pretend that all of this makes sense. It doesn't. "If you were able to do it, then so could Kohen."

"There would be a trace if an unauthorized user was on his computer. There isn't." I don't need to take Computer Geek 101 to understand that. Sill, my brother explains it in layman's terms for me. "Until the police confiscated his computer, the only person who had access was Jaxon."

"So what? Jax just had all these photos on his hard drive?" I shake my head, refusing to believe any of it. "Are you really going to sit there and try to convince me that he's actually capable of this?"

Blindly reaching into his bag, Logan pulls out his laptop. "There's more, Adalynn."

"More photos?" I ask, just to be sure. There's already too many as it is.

Without looking up at me, he keys something into his computer. "These are different." He hesitates for only a second before he turns the screen towards me.

Nothing could have prepared me for what's in front of me. I thought knowing that someone has been following me for years was bad. Dating my stalker was even worse. But this...? Fuck, nothing compares to this. I'm vaguely aware of Logan talking but I can't process anything he's saying. My mind is too focused on the images on his computer, of the images taken of me in my apartment. Not from the outside, as if that would somehow be better. No, of me in my fucking apartment. Kohen put fucking cameras in my apartment.

Click... click... click. My finger moves through the files faster than I can keep up. There are thousands of them. "Did you... look... at—"

"Some," Logan admits. "Once I saw the bathroom ones, I stopped."

I nod as if that makes sense because, of course, there's a camera in the bathroom. Why wouldn't there be? There're some of me sleeping, getting dressed, sitting in the living room. The more I flip through them, the more my world crumbles around me. Until I freeze, paralyzed.

That sick bastard took pictures of me cutting myself. There's an entire section just for those moments when life became too hard, too numb, and I was desperate to feel *something*. He watched me at my lowest point and immortalized it. Not being able to take any more of this, I slam the computer shut and curl into myself.

"Did you hear a word I just said?" Logan asks.

I can't get my mouth to work properly. The image of me standing over the sink with blood dripping onto the porcelain is all I see. I remember that day. I cut a little too deep. I knew I needed to call for help, to go to the hospital. Instead, I just watched the blood run down my arm into the basin, transfixed as I watched my life pour out of me. I remember smiling when I felt lightheaded. I thought it was finally the end. The next thing I knew, I was waking up in my bed and my wrist was bandaged. There wasn't any trace of blood in the sink. The razor that I used was gone and so was my hidden stash.

"Oh my god. Oh my god," I whisper over and over.

"Adalynn, what? You're starting to scare me. What is it?"

"Jax. He found me. He knew!"

"What?"

I don't know how to begin. Everything is spinning out of control. My head is a jumbled mess of the impossible. Still, I try to explain, even though I don't quite believe my ears either. There's no way Jax would be capable of something like this but... it's the only thing that makes sense. Kohen wouldn't have been able to gain access to my apartment, only someone with a key...

Jax has a key...

Jax was always there at the right time...

Jax was always saving me from myself...

There are too many incidents where he would just appear. Whenever I needed him the most, he was always there, rescuing me. Especially from myself. Not even my brother knew about that time. Jax was the one who found me; he took care of me when I wasn't able. I let him bathe me and feed me when I couldn't be bothered to lift a fork to my mouth. Thankfully, Logan was away for work at the time. That's the only reason we were able to hide it from him and Connor.

I can't help but replay each instance in my mind. If I was just stuck in my head, staring at a wall, he'd be there to watch a movie. If I skipped a few meals, the next thing I knew, we'd be eating together under the string lights on the balcony.

Every single time I needed him, he was there.

Leaning over the bed, I throw up all over my brother. Logan surprises me by moving my hair out of the way and rubbing my back as I continue to empty my stomach on his expensive shoes, which probably cost more than most people's rent.

"I'm sorry," I finally say when I'm finished.

"What do you need? What can I do, Addie?"

I shake my head. There's nothing anyone can do. My heart is at war with my mind. I can't believe it but... if what Logan is saying is true...

No, it has to be Kohen. It can't be Jax. It just can't. How could he do this to me? To us?

"There's one more thing," Logan says once I'm somewhat composed.

Of course, because why wouldn't there be?

"He had a tracker on your phone."

I freeze. I'm pretty sure time stands still as I let his words sink in, to really grasp what Logan is saying. "Kohen?" I ask hopefully, as if having the ex-boyfriend who put me in a hospital tracking my movements would be the better outcome. Sadly, that's all I want. No, not want, *need*. I need Kohen to be the instigator. I won't accept anything else.

Logan's face falls. "Adalynn—"

I'm already shaking my head. "No. I don't believe you. He wouldn't do this to me." Jax is capable of a lot of things but this...? Breaking my trust like this...? No. I refuse to believe my brother.

"Leave."

"Adalynn—"

"I want you to leave. There's no way Jax would do this to me. There's another explanation. Find it." My voice amplifies with each word. "Jax loves—"

"Loves you?" Logan nods. "I know you don't want to believe this —fuck, neither did I—but you have to ask yourself how he was able to find you? How did he know that you were there?"

"I told him." I think. I must have, or maybe Olivia mentioned it?

"You told him the exact address?" he asks skeptically. When I don't answer, he goes on. "He's been tracking your movements for years."

I'm already shaking my head. "No. Jax wouldn't do that to me."

He eyes my new phone. "I can prove it."

Afraid of what he's going to do, I clutch the device to my chest. Unwilling to let go, unwilling to trust his word alone. Because I don't know if I will ever recover from this level of betrayal. It can't be Jax.

"He's not the man you think he is," Logan states, his voice giving away all the pent-up anger he's holding in.

He would never do this to me. There's no way, not after everything we've been through. He wouldn't...

The door creaks open. "It's true, Ads."

And just like that, my world falls apart. Because the one person I trusted most has betrayed me in ways that I never knew were possible. I thought we'd always find a way back to each other, hoping that one day we could be us again. I was wrong.

CHAPTER FIVE

Jax
Four years ago

"*What do you mean you haven't heard from her all day? I thought you were taking her to breakfast?*" I snap into the phone. I'm already running to the elevator.

I knew I shouldn't have trusted anyone but myself. Connor somehow convinced me that he'd be able to handle her. It didn't help that she wanted to go to breakfast with him. I should have insisted on going with them. I should have never allowed her to leave my sight, not today of all days.

"*She said she'd meet me in an hour... It's been three.*"

I'm not even aware that I've moved until I'm staring at a new hole in the wall right beside the elevator. He's waited this long to call me? Doesn't he know what today is? "*And you're just now calling me? Does Logan know she's missing?*" Flexing my hand, I'm slightly disappointed that it's not broken. At least I'd be able to focus on the pain instead of the dread that's taking residence in my chest.

Fuck, I can barely think straight. My chest gets tighter. I can't lose her.

Connor sighs. "His plane was delayed. He's still in the air."

Of course it was. I don't bother yelling at Connor. It won't solve anything. He's not the one at fault. I am. I knew better. They think I'm being irrational, that I need to move on. They think I'm too stuck on the past and that I need to give her room to breathe. Look at what listening to them has done.

If I lose her, it's all my fault.

This is what I was afraid of. Adalynn is too fragile right now. Everyone thinks that she's healing, but I see the real her. I see the way she's always forcing a smile, how she looks away from anything that resembles what we lost. She's continuing to shut everyone out, even me.

Being with me is too hard. I remind her of him.

I see the effects weighing on her. I see the truth, no matter how hard she tries to hide it from me. She attempts to cover her self-inflicted wounds, but I see those too. I see the way her clothes have changed since that first time. She's smarter now, hurting herself in those places meant for my eyes only. Every time I notice a new mark, I die a little more inside. I might as well be the one with the blade to her delicate skin.

There's no escaping reality: I made her this way.

"Have you checked her apartment?" *I ask, focusing on finding her and not on the argument we had again last night. I keep pushing her, refusing to let her forget.*

"She's gone, man."

"We'll find her." *I always do.*

I'm halfway across the parking lot when Connor's words stop me in my tracks. "No, Jax. She packed a bag. She's gone."

"FUCK! Find her! She couldn't have gotten far without using her cards." *We'll tract those; we'll be able to get to her. I'll be able to save her just like all those times before.*

This is why I wanted to put a tracker in her phone and on Hadley's bracelet that she always wears. Logan and Connor thought that was too extreme. They said we needed to listen to Olivia and give Adalynn space in the new reality she created for herself.

I'm already emailing my private detective to stop what he's doing and to locate her. My heart is pounding so hard I swear I can hear it above everything else. With each second that passes, I'm taken back to the day I almost didn't find her in time. I should have listened to myself and installed the trackers. Trusting that she was getting stronger, that she was finally healing, may just be what finally takes her from me for good. I won't survive losing her too.

"I'm already doing that. There hasn't been any activity since she withdrew cash last night."

"How much?"

"Two grand."

Fuck, she really is determined.

My phone chimes with a new email. A quick glance, and I know I'm too late. She's already back in California. There's no way I'll make it to her in time. She's going back to where it all started, where I ruined us.

Breathing's impossible. It's as if all the air has been sucked out of the world. If I don't get to her... No, I refuse to go down that rabbit hole. This will be just like all the times before. I'll save her. That's the only option. I won't allow anything else.

"Jax? Are you still there?"

"She's in California," *is all I say before I hang up and slide into my car. I break every traffic law to get to the private airstrip where our jet is waiting, praying that I'm not too late. I don't even bother calling our pilot. I know Connor will have everything sorted when I arrive.*

She finally agreed to move in with me and sell her apartment. I thought that meant she was ready for everything I was willing to give her, for what we could be. I couldn't let her move in with me and not show her my secret, what I've kept from her since the accident. Olivia warned me it was too soon but, of course, I didn't fucking listen. I need her to remember as much as I need to breathe. I'm grieving our loss all by myself, trying to piece together everything I broke... everything we lost... all by myself.

Why didn't I lie to her? I never should have told her the truth. Olivia was right. Adalynn's not ready. By pushing her, I've... fuck... no. She can't do this. She can't leave me. I can't lose her too.

I can't be in a world where I've lost them both.

I promise myself if I make it to her in time, if I somehow save her, I'll stop pushing. I'll fall in line. I'll tell her the lies she wants to believe. I'll exist as just her brother's best friend. If I somehow make it to California before she takes herself from me, I promise to never speak of him again.

I need her alive more than I need her to remember. I can live a lie. I can't live without her. And now my selfishness is going to cost me EVERYTHING.

Fuck, please, please let me be wrong.

Chapter Six

Adalynn

"I thought I told you not to come," Logan growls as he moves to shield me from Jax's view.

"I need a chance to explain," Jax pleads.

Time stops. My heart stops. Even though I already know the answer, I have to ask. "So it's true?"

Jax and Logan dance around each other as Logan tries to block Jax's path. "Get the fuck out before I drop you."

"Logan, just hear me out. You're blowing this out of proportion," Jax pleads.

"You've been secretly spying on my baby sister and you expect me to calm down?" He shoves Jax hard, forcing him to stumble back. "Did you fucking touch her?"

Jax's face pales. "Never, you know that."

"Apparently I don't know you at all." If you could kill someone with a glare, Jax would be dead. "I'm not sure what you're capable of."

I can't do this with him here. I need time to think, time to come to terms with what Jax is saying. Did he really think we'd be okay after I found out he put cameras in my place? Why would he do that to me? To us? Didn't he realize he was killing me with each little invasion of privacy?

There's a lot I've forgiven when it comes to us, but *this...*? This is unforgivable. We won't survive this. "Leave. I can't do this with you here."

Logan nods to the door. "You heard her."

"You, Logan. I need *you* to leave." I have to talk to Jax. I have to know why he did this to me. He must realize there's no going back, not after this.

My brother's head whips around so fast I'm surprised he doesn't strain a muscle. "Excuse me?"

"I appreciate everything you're doing, but I need to talk to Jax. Alone."

Jax steps around Logan. Behind the black eye he's sporting are all the secrets he's keeping from me. "Actually, I think it would be best if he were here for this, Ads."

I don't wait for either of them to take a seat. "Are the police right? Have you really been stalking me for years?" His jaw tenses at my choice in words. "Did you really have my phone tracked, Jaxon?"

How stupid could I be? Whenever I broke my phone, which occurred more often than I care to admit, Jax always replaced it. I just assumed it was from my brother and he was the delivery man. I'm such an idiot.

"Okay, this looks bad. I'll admit it but it's not what you think."

"What other way is there to look at it? How long has this been going on?" This question comes from Logan.

"Four years."

My brother is out of his seat so fast I barely see him move. His hands are wrapped around Jax's throat, pinning him to the chair. Jax doesn't make a move to fight back. "Four years. Four fucking years?" Logan screams at him.

If it weren't for Kohen, I would have never known the truth. And that's what *kills* me. "You were never going to tell me, were you? What about all the pretty promises? I thought you said you loved me?"

How are we ever going to get past this?

"Ads, let me—" he chokes out.

I should tell Logan to back off, but the words never come. "Why, Jax?" After everything he's done to us, all the back and forth, why would he even want to do this? "Logan, enough!" I snap when Jax's face becomes shockingly pale from lack of air.

Jax coughs, gasping to get more oxygen into his lungs. Glaring at his best friend, Logan finally reclaims the seat he vacated. Once Jax gets his breathing under control, he looks directly at me. He runs his fingers through his hair, a clear sign that he's nervous. It's his tic. Jax never did have the best poker face when it came to me. Or maybe he had the best poker face of them all, seeing as he's been lying to me since I moved to the city.

He turns to Logan. "Let me just say what I need to say and you can hit me later. I won't even put up a fight, man."

"I'm not making promises. Each word out of your mouth makes me want to murder you. I suggest you speak fast before I lose my patience."

"Do you remember the first time you tried to kill yourself, Addie?" Jax doesn't wait for me to answer him. "I do. I remember every detail. Vividly. To this day, I'm haunted by that memory of your cold, lifeless body."

"What does that have to do with anything?" Logan asks, anger radiating off him in near tangible waves. He doesn't like to relive my darkest moments. And neither do I. It's something we're both aware of but never speak about to each other. We've never actually been able to talk about anything too deep, too emotional.

"We couldn't find you. But you left that note for me. You wanted me to find it."

True. It was in our secret place in my bedroom in California. It's where I kept all the letters we'd write. It was just another way we got away with hiding our feelings for each other from everyone who mattered.

"What letter?" Logan asks, glaring at his best friend.

"That's how I knew how to find you," Jax whispers, ignoring my brother. "I barely got there in time. If I took one minute longer, you would have been gone. There was nothing that I could have done."

I want to crawl under the blanket. I want to hide away from Jax, from the world. I don't want to talk about this. I don't want to remember how I swallowed all those pills, how I looked up into the night sky and imagined I was back in the car with my family.

No, I can't go back there.

"I breathed life back into you." That was the first time Jax saved me from myself. "I wouldn't let you die. I couldn't lose you too."

"You didn't lose anyone! I did! I was the one who lost everything!" I won't let him or anyone else use my tragedy to justify their actions.

Both Logan and Jax turn away from me. I should apologize to Logan but I can't. The words never form. Just like everyone else, he can't fully understand what happened all those years ago. Both of them were tucked safely away while I was helpless to do anything but watch as our family died, one by one.

"Don't you see, Ads? I can't allow you to give up."

"It's your insurance policy," Logan whispers.

Jax points to my phone. "At least I can always find you. So when you need me the most, I'm there. Always." So Logan was right. He's been tracking my movements.

"Why didn't you tell me?"

"Do you really think if I told you, you would have had your phone with you..." *All the other times*. He doesn't need to say it. We all know what he means. Sadly, that night wasn't the first. There were others. And each and every time, Jax was there. How did I not ever notice?

"That doesn't make this okay."

Jax shrugs. "I don't care. Be mad. Scream, hit me if that makes you feel better. I'm not sorry, and I'm going to keep protecting you, Ads."

"Why?" Why can't they just let me go? Don't they see that life shouldn't be this hard? Don't they see that I'd rather be... No, I can't go back down that road.

"Because you saved me when I needed you." Right, his childhood. He's just returning the favor.

"I don't need you looking out for me anymore. I'm fine."

"Like Logan said, it's my insurance policy. And now you know."

"What about all the pictures?" my brother asks.

Jax shakes his head. "I never saw those until tonight when the police showed me."

"And you expect us to believe you?"

Jax looks as if my brother just slapped him across the face. "Logan—"

I probably shouldn't, but I believe him. He has no reason to lie now, not about this.

"No, I might understand the phone thing, but why didn't you tell anyone? Why keep it a secret from me? I could have helped you!"

"I was afraid you'd try to stop me."

"You had nothing to do with the cameras?" Logan asks again.

"No."

"They're on your computer."

"I know. The cops showed me too."

"I didn't find a trace of anyone else in there, Jaxon. I don't see how he could have planted everything. He has a rock-solid alibi."

"I. Know," Jax growls, fist clutching the arms of the chair.

As they go back and forth as to how the photos ended up on Jax's computer, I tune them out. I can't listen to this anymore. How is this my life? How has it all come to this? To me dating my stalker? To the man I love secretly tracking my movements?

It's all too much.

I can't even stomach the thought of what this all means. If what they're saying is true, everything about Kohen has been a lie. It wasn't an accidental meeting in the gym. No, like everything else, it was staged. Kohen wanted me and I gave him exactly that. I told myself we were healing each other, that we were the same, but it was all a lie.

It makes sense now at least. The reason he just happened to know the name of Hadley's stuffed bear, how he knew things about me that I never told him... It's because he's been watching me for years. I gave him everything he wanted—me—and I didn't even stop to see all the red flags. I was blinded by my need to belong somewhere, for someone to actually love me and want to be with me. He used my past to get closer to me. I've never felt so... so... violated.

Did he really even lose his mom to a brain tumor? Was everything he ever told me a lie to build a connection with me? What was his endgame? Why me? I fear that I'm never going to know the answers to all my questions.

I hate that he did this to me. That he turned something I thought was beautiful into this ugly, shattered mess. I thought he really cared about me. I can't believe I thought he was going to be the man to finally help me get over Jax.

Jax... How could he betray me? And, more importantly, why would he go through all this effort to protect me, only to push me away? Time and time again, I thought we would finally be together, only to have him pull the rug from underneath me and leave. For years, we've played this stupid back and forth game. One second, I'm everything he needs, and the next, I'm not good enough for him to stay.

I've lost count of how many chances I've given him. How many times I've hurt myself because of him. How much of myself I've lost to him.

He tells me he loves me, that he's finally ready to give us a real chance. But his promises mean nothing when he constantly breaks them. When will I give up on him?

I know Jax believes he was protecting me. I get that, but why? I've never hid my feelings from him. He's known all along that he's all I've ever wanted. Yet he continues to push me away. So why did he go to such lengths? That's what I can't figure out. I'm missing something.

I finally find my voice again. "Logan, I need to talk to Jax, alone now."

"Addie, I don't think that's a good idea. There are a lot of eyes on us."

"I don't care. I need to talk to him alone," I say again.

My brother must see the seriousness of my expression because he stands, with a huff. "Outside, Jax."

"Logan, I just said—"

"I know, but he and I need to get something clear."

Jax leans over and kisses the inside of my palm, shocking me into silence as he exits the room. "Don't move. Be right back."

The fact that my brother doesn't deck him right there surprises me. Jax has never shown an ounce of affection for me in front of Logan. That's been the unspoken rule we have yet to break. I thought that Jax always pushed me away because of his friendship with my brother. Clearly, I was wrong since Logan acts as if it's completely normal for Jax to touch me as though I belong to him.

CHAPTER SEVEN

Jax

"If you're going to hit me, at least do it where nobody can see," I say as I follow Logan out the door. He doesn't laugh. Crap, I really hope he doesn't hit me. That's the last thing that needs to happen right now. Logan is right. There's too much attention on this already. News crews have been here all morning. I was swarmed by various media outlets when Connor finally got me released.

It says a lot that Connor stuck to my side with everything Kohen is trying to plant on me. I hate that Logan questioned that I hurt her. Even if it was just for a moment, I can't believe he thought I'd ever be capable of hurting her. He knows how much she means to me. I'd never be able to do that to any woman, let alone the other half of my soul.

It's because of *him*. I know Logan. We both know I'm the reason his sister is the way she is. This was just another nail in my coffin. We'll never get back to normal until I honor the promise I made to Adalynn all those years ago at their family's gravesite.

Once she knows the truth, she'll hate me. She already does. She just doesn't remember that I'm the reason she's broken. For us to be together, I'm going to have to tell her everything.

Logan leads me to an empty room across from Addie's. He doesn't wait for the door to click before he dives right into it. "Does she know?"

"Logan—"

"Does she fucking know what we did to Asher?"

Even after all these years, hearing our son's name takes my breath away. Hanging my head, I whisper, "No." Logan studies me, trying to tell if I'm lying or not. "I haven't told her about him. If she's starting to remember though..." I leave the rest unsaid.

"You'll what? Fill in the blanks for her?"

"I'm not going to keep lying to her about him." My head snaps back before I notice that he's moved. Fuck, that stung. Logan's right hook is just as powerful as it was back in his fighting days in college. My mouth fills with blood. I can already feel the left side of my face swelling. Still, I keep my hands at my sides. We both know I'll never fight him, not when I deserve this.

"You will do what you're fucking told, Jaxon! You're the whole reason we were forced into this fucking charade in the first place."

It would have hurt less if he punched me again. "I know..."

"I told you to stay away from her!"

"We love—"

He shoves me against the wall. "Look at what your love has done to her! You made us all lie to her! You can't just decide to stop now, not after everything. It's not fair to her!" It's as if each word spears through me and rips my insides out. He's not telling me anything I don't know. I can't be happy. I don't even know how. I've ruined everything, and Logan isn't shy when it comes to reminding me whose fault this is. "How the fuck do you think this is going to end, Jaxon?

70

Did you honestly think I'd allow you to play house with her and break her all over again?"

"That's not going to happen."

"No?" He shoves me into the wall for a second time. "How do you think she's going to react when she finds out the truth? Did you forget what happened last time?"

I shake my head. "I could never forget." I remember every single time Ads couldn't handle the grief anymore. I remember every single time she tried to take her life. "I'm the one who found her!" I'm the one who always finds her. Maybe that's my punishment, watching the light slowly drain from her eyes, unable to do anything but bring her back to life, back to her misery.

I'm in a permanent state of hell.

"Being with her isn't going to make it okay."

Don't I know it? If loving her were the cure, she would have been fixed years ago. After everything we've been through, I've never stopped loving her. All I've ever done is try to protect her. Protect her from Wyatt... from herself... from... from Asher.

"She's remembering, Logan. You can't stop this from coming out."

"Watch me. I won't lose her again."

"She's stronger than you give her credit for. Look—"

He brings his arm up and presses it into my throat. "How many times does she need to try to kill herself before you realize she's gone too? She's never coming back to us, Jaxon! She might be alive, but she's. Never. Coming. Back. To. Us. A piece of her died that night, a piece that made her who she is. The Adalynn you remember is gone and you need to be okay with that. It's time to move on."

I'm already shaking my head. I refuse to believe that. I can't. She has to be okay. She can't... No, Logan is wrong. She'll remember... she'll remember our child... She has to.

This time is different. It's the first time in years she's started to ask questions. She wants to remember. I shouldn't have pushed her away when she showed up at my place. I wasn't ready. I'm still not. If I'm wrong, it will cost me everything. It'll cost me *her*.

"You can't love her enough to fix her, not after we helped break her!" he reminds me again.

"She's not broken." Adalynn is anything but broken. She's the strongest person I know. Despite everything, she's still here. She's still putting in the work. She wants to get better. Or that's what I tell myself every day and every night.

"And what is this going to do to her when she finds out we've hidden Asher from her? Do you honestly think she's going to forgive us?" He paces the room. "You think she's strong? For years, she's been lying to herself, forcing us to lie to her too!"

"We had no choice!" I remind him this time. The walls are closing in. I need to leave. I need fresh air. I can't keep doing this with him. Over and over, we go again. Whenever Ads and I start to get close to each other, he's always here, repeating all the reasons I can't be with the only person to ever set my soul on fire.

I don't want to hide anymore. I've kept her secrets for six long years.

"I'm done," I say more to myself than to Logan.

"You'll leave her alone."

I brace myself for the hit I know I deserve. "I won't listen to you, not this time."

Instead of hitting me, as he has every right to do, he surprises me by slumping into a chair. "You can't force her to remember to clear your conscience. It won't change anything."

"It could change *everything*. She's ready!"

He peers up into my eyes. "You're willing to bet her life on that, Jaxon? Because that's what knowing the truth will cost her, her life."

"We can't keep doing this, Logan. It's been six years! We have to try something new. Can't you see this is killing her?"

"So you've given up?"

"Logan..." My voice cracks, showing how much pain I'm feeling from that one question. Of course I haven't given up, but it's been six years. There are no more leads. I've exhausted every resource at my disposal. Asher is gone and I don't think he's ever coming back. I owe it to him to make his mother whole again.

"You promised that you wouldn't give up. You swore on their graves, Jaxon!"

"I know."

"So what? Now, after all this time, you're just going to stop?"

"Of course not!" I've dedicated my life to fixing the one mistake I can't take back. Even though it's a lost effort, I won't give up on him. I will continue my search until I take my last breath.

Logan walks to the door. Before he opens it, he asks, "Do you think Adalynn is going to forgive you... forgive us?"

If it didn't hurt so much, I might laugh at his ridiculous question. "No, Logan, she's never going to forgive us. She's going to hate all of us for everything we've stolen from her."

"You can't tell her, Jax. She's not ready." He keeps saying that but we both know it's us. None of us are ready to face the repercussions of what we've done to the most important person in our lives.

I promised her I'd never give up, but four years ago, I did. I stopped believing our love was enough. I stopped trying to let her heal, and I let her believe the lies. I reinforced them with half truths. I've erased the most important part of us because I was too afraid of her hating me, of her blaming me.

I've been a coward, hiding behind her emotional state. Enough is enough. It's time to shine a light on all of our scars.

"No matter what we do or say, it's never going to be okay. We've *destroyed* her, Jaxon. There's no mending what we've broken. The only thing we can do is be here to pick up the pieces."

I'm already shaking my head. "I refuse to believe that. There has to be more in this life." This can't be how our story ends. I won't let it. "The only thing I can do is love her. That has to be enough."

He heads to the door. "Does remembering Asher help you or *her*?"

"What do you mean?"

"Remembering Asher won't fix anything. It will only destroy her. Let her live in her blissful ignorance."

"She doesn't even know she's a mom, Logan."

"Yes, and whose fault is that?" he spits out before leaving me alone.

Mine. He doesn't see what that one question does to me. Crumbling to the floor, I cry for the life we never got a chance to live. And once again, he's right. She's never going to forgive us. How could she?

She's a mom without a child, and I'm the one who helped her forget our son.

Chapter Eight

Adalynn

There's a soft knock on the door before Jax's head pops around. "Can I come in?"

I sit up a little more in bed, somehow managing not to tug on any of the wires currently attached to me. "Yeah."

Since they walked out a few minutes ago, all I've been doing is rehearsing what I was going to say. We need to slow down. There's too much unknown when it comes to him. He keeps too many secrets from me. I don't know how we can get past this... past everything we've done to each other.

I'm starting to think love isn't enough. I don't know how we're ever going to find our way back to each other. Life has gotten too hard. I don't want to keep going down this road with him. It's too painful... too... everything. Too much has happened. I need to tell him to leave me alone, that I don't need him protecting me anymore. At this point, it might be easier for each of us to forget about the other. All we do is break each other's heart.

His mouth opens but nothing comes out. He seems miles away. Jax is standing there, looking absolutely destroyed. Like a light wind could blow him away. I don't know what happened out there with him and his best friend, but somehow I know he needs me. He needs me to be here for him. And with that, everything I practiced evaporates. Everything I've told myself since he left doesn't matter. Nothing matters anymore, just him.

There are a million and one reasons we should stop trying. A million and one reasons we shouldn't be together. He's broken my heart more times than I can count. Yet he's a part of me. Because as many reasons as there are to give up, he's also the reason I keep trying. He's the reason for everything. He's always had a hold of me, and no matter how much I know I should push him away, I can't. I won't give up on him... on us.

I would rather spend a life time with him than without him.

"I don't care about any of it, Jax. All I care about is you," I tell him honestly. I was going to use this as another excuse to distance myself. That's what I do. If he doesn't walk away from me, I walk away from him. I think deep down I know why. I don't think I deserve to be happy, so I do everything in my power to sabotage it. Liv tells me that I need to stop blaming myself, to let myself live in the now and be happy.

Maybe I should start listening to her...

"Adalynn—"

I hate how his voice breaks on my name. "Just hold me. Make me forget."

His steps are slow, almost as if he can't believe what I'm saying. He stops right beside the hospital bed. I scoot over to make room for him. He doesn't come any closer though. With a featherlight touch, he tilts my chin until I'm staring up at him. His lips are inches from mine. Neither of us closes the distance.

"What do you want to forget?" he asks, his breath caressing my mouth with each word.

"Everything that isn't you."

I don't know who moves first, me or him. It doesn't matter. The only thing that does is the way his mouth feels against mine. His tongue traces my bottom lip. I gasp at the contact. Jax doesn't waste any time completely consuming me with his kiss. I feel him *everywhere*. Our tongues fuse together, and his hands cradle my face as if I'm the most precious thing to him. With each passing second, he breathes life into me. His touch brings me back to him.

Jax doesn't disappoint. He makes me forget everything but him. This, right here, feels different.

I can't explain it. I just feel the difference. Something has shifted in us. It's as if we're each finally giving up and trusting the other. It's taken years to feel like this, to have the peace again, and I never want to lose it.

He pulls away first. Breathless, he whispers, "I'm yours," against my lips before diving back in.

I reach up with my somewhat-good hand and tangle my fingers into his soft hair, pulling him closer to me. I need to feel him everywhere. His lips never leave my skin as he kisses a path down my neck. I arch into him, needing more.

"Jax," I moan as he nibbles on my ear.

"What do you need?" he asks, as if reading my thoughts.

"You."

"You have me."

Gripping his shirt, I pull him back to me, needing to feel his mouth on mine. "Jax," I moan again when he presses a featherlight kiss on my pulse point.

He groans into my neck. The sound alone is almost my undoing. His lips find mine again, and this time when he kisses me, it's slower, as if he's savoring the moment, before giving me a quick peck on the lips. He leans his forehead against mine. We're both breathless.

He brushes the hair out of my face. "I'm sorry I wasn't here to protect you, that I didn't get to you fast enough."

I place my hand over his. "If it weren't for you, I would have died," I repeat what I told the detectives, what I believe in my heart to be true. I don't bother mentioning all the times he's saved me from myself. I kiss the inside of his palm. "Thank you for saving me."

"I'll always save you."

"Lie down with me?"

He shakes his head. "I don't want to hurt you."

He starts to move to the chair but I grip his arm before he can get away. "Please, Jax, I need you."

He sighs. "Fine, but if you get me in trouble with the nurse, I'm blaming you."

I can't stop the smile that spreads across my face even if I wanted to. Biting my lip, I keep from making any noise as he crawls into bed with me. As I reposition myself to lay my head onto his chest, I almost hiss from the movement but thankfully no noise escapes. I'm sure if Jax knew how much pain I'm in, he'd be out of this bed before I could blink.

Carefully, so he doesn't hurt me, he wraps his arms around me. It's as if during all the time I was with Kohen, I wasn't really living, wasn't really breathing. Being wrapped in Jax's arms feels right. He makes me feel safe, cherished even, as he presses his lips to my temple. I know we have a lot to talk about, a lot of secrets need to be shared, but not now. Not when we're finally together again. So much has happened, yet here we are. It seems no matter what is thrown at us, we always find our way back to each other.

I smile as my mind continues its train of thought from only moments ago.

There are a million and one reasons we should stop trying. A million and one reasons we shouldn't be together. Yet this feeling of being in his arms, of having his lips pressed against my skin, is the only reason that matters.

"Don't leave me," I whisper.

"Never again, Adalynn. I'm yours."

It's been hours since our kiss. The night nurse checked on me an hour ago. To say she was less than pleased to see Jax in bed with me is an understatement. Logan hasn't returned either. The only thing that interrupts the silence is the constant beeping of the monitors. To anyone else coming in the room, it would look as if we're both asleep. Both basking in each other's warmth, clutching each other's hands, but I know he's not asleep. Just like I know he knows I'm awake.

It's almost as if neither of us wants to break the silence. In the quiet, we can just pretend that this is enough. That we're enough. That no matter what, we can get through anything. In the little bubble we've created, nothing can get to us; the outside world doesn't exist while we cling to each other.

"When did it all change?" My words finally pierce our bubble when I can't take the silence any longer.

His breathing changes, barely noticeable but impossible not to see when all I can focus on is everything that is Jaxon Chandler. I'm already bracing myself for the lies that are going to spill from his mouth. He sighs. "I wish I could tell you."

Carefully, I turn my body as much as I can so I can watch every expression that crosses his face.

Once upon a time, Jax was everything to me. Once upon a time, I was everything to him too. Once upon a time, I thought he would never lie to me...

I'm not that naïve girl anymore. I know better. If someone is keeping my secrets, it's him.

"Tell me something real." Tell me how we went from being each other's forever, to being trapped in this back and forth struggle. "We promised to love each other, in this life and every life after."

He clutches my hand tighter. "Ads—"

"How did we get here?" We were perfect until we weren't.

I feel him take a deep breath. "My feelings for you have never wavered. I've always loved you. I love you more today than I did back then."

I hiccup sob into myself, trying not to let his words affect me.

"Do you remember how I used to paint?"

I nod.

"Every day in that house almost killed me. When he was gone, I was able to paint. Before you, it was the only way I could escape and forget that my life wasn't horrible, that my dad didn't blame me for everything bad that happened in his life. Before you, all I had were those paint brushes. Before you, my life was dark. You gave my life color, gave it meaning. You, Adalynn Grace Maxwell, breathed life back into me." Jax wipes away my tears. "You've always been my forever."

"Then why are we here? How did we get so broken?"

"Do you ever wish we could go back to how it used to be? That we could just be us and our love would be enough?"

Yes. Every second of every day. "What broke us, Jax?"

"Let's just be us, Ads."

I don't even know what *us* is anymore. It's been so long since we weren't hurting each other. It's been years since I've fully trusted him. I was a naïve teenager who believed that nothing could ever come between us. I was foolish, drunk on him.

"How can we ever go back if I don't even remember what broke us in the first place?"

"Olivia says that if we force you to remember before you're ready, you'll end up back in that catatonic state. That if we help fill in the missing gaps, your memory will be distorted and you could lose what really happened... *permanently*."

Turning away from him, I face the window. Even all the way up here, it's impossible to see the stars above the city that never sleeps. Sometimes I wish I was up there, that I was anywhere other than here. Sometimes it becomes too much, and all I want is simple.

Death seems simple. Death is a fantasy for a girl like me. As much as I crave it, I don't think I'll ever reach it, not with Jax still pulling me to him. He's what tethers me to this plane of existence.

"Sometimes it's easy to forget that part of me... to pretend that I was never that weak."

"You're anything but weak, Adalynn. You've gone through more in your life than anyone I know. It's okay to not have it together all the time."

"Give me something, Jax."

"Olivia—"

"I know what she said but she's wrong. How can I heal if I don't even know where to start?"

Seconds turn to minutes. Pretty soon it becomes obvious that he's going to maintain the charade that everyone insists I keep living.

"Promise me something?" he asks, finally breaking his silence.

I don't even hesitate. "Anything."

"When you remember, because one day you will, promise me you'll talk to me before doing anything."

It doesn't take a genius to read between the lines. He means before taking my life... "I'm not that girl anymore." The lie taste bitter on my tongue. "Why wasn't I talking to you before the accident?"

Jax stills. "Ads—"

"Please, Jax, give me something," I repeat. "Give me this."

He kisses the inside of my palm. "Okay, Ads, I'll tell you why we stopped talking all those years ago."

CHAPTER NINE

Jax
Eight months before the accident

I can't believe she's pregnant. We were so careful. I should be panicking. I just got my underage, high school senior girlfriend pregnant. I'm not. Maybe I'm in shock. I know this isn't exactly how we planned things but it doesn't change anything for me. I know Adalynn is the girl I'm going to marry and have a family with. She's the other half of me. Sure, it's going to make our lives a little difficult, but this is right.

She's freaking out, but she has no reason to be. I'm going to take care of her and our child. The only thing I hate is that this is going to change her life more than mine. She's had her entire future mapped out since the first time she got into a pool. I think that's what's upsetting her the most.

Within two minutes, the time it took for the two pink lines to appear, her entire life changed. Everything she's worked for, all the goals she set for herself, have been altered. Still, as hard as this is going to be for the both of us, I wouldn't change it. A small part of me knows it's because she's forever tied to me now. She tells me that I'm all that she wants, that one day she's going to marry me, but I've never really let myself believe that I could be that lucky.

How could I, when the one person who is supposed to love me unconditionally reminds me how much he hates me and wishes that I was never born?

Peering up the driveway, I can't help but smile as I look at my childhood home. This will be the last time I ever step foot in there. After today, I'm done being my father's puppet. I don't give a fuck what anyone thinks. It's over.

The moment Ads told me she was pregnant, I knew that I had to cut all ties with my father. He'll try to tell me that I'm making the biggest mistake of my life. He'll try to ruin it for the both of us. I'm doing this for my child and for my future wife. They will always come first.

I don't need my trust fund. The guys and I are so close to starting our own business, and college is already paid for since I got a full ride. Nobody understood why I wanted a scholarship, why I worked so hard in school. This is why. I didn't want him to be able to hold something over my head anymore.

Today's the day I cut him off completely.

A small part of me hoped he'd change, that maybe if I went away to college, he'd get the help he needs. It never happened; he doesn't care about me and never has. I hate that no matter what he did to me, I always thought that one day, if I was good enough, he'd be the father he once was. The father who didn't star in my nightmares. When he told me to "take care of it," I knew that no matter how much I wanted him to change, he wasn't going to. I need to protect my family from him.

With a deep breath, I finally turn the knob to my childhood home to say goodbye for good...

By the time I come to, blood is clouding my vision and my father is screaming at me. My eyes flick to the side and land on the remnants of the broken vase he used to hit me over the head when I came inside. My balance is off as I try to stand. I don't know how long I was out, but I do know he didn't stop hitting me after I fell. It takes several attempts to get my footing. Of course Father dearest helps by wrapping his hands around my throat and pinning me to the wall.

"You fucking piece of shit! How could I raise someone this stupid?" Wyatt screams into the side of my head. The only plus side is that my ears are still ringing so he sounds muffled as he continues to yell at me. Spit flies in my face as he curses at me. My ribs are throbbing, and I don't need an x-ray to know that he broke them again.

But I find the strength to smile. I'm sure I look demented with my bloodstained teeth. "I hope that felt good. Good luck explaining those bruised knuckles."

Reminding him how he just lost the small amount of control he seems to always be able to maintain whenever he gives me his "lessons" enrages him more. Because of me, he's going to have to come up with an excuse to explain why he won't be operating for the foreseeable future.

Good.

"I thought I told you to take care of it!" The hand around my throat squeezes tighter. Yet, even as the color slowly drains from my face with the sudden lack of air, I keep the smile on my face. No matter what happens tonight, I win.

He no longer has any control over me. We both know it. So, yes, as the blackness starts to welcome me home, a feeling I'm all too familiar with, the fear he used to elicit is gone. I know he won't actually kill me. He'll just make me wish for it. At least when I'm unconscious, I won't be able to feel the repeated kicks.

"Since you can't clean up your messes, I'll take care of everything, just like I always do." His grip on my throat tightens more, making it impossible for me to plead with him. He laughs as he watches me struggle against the inevitable. That initial blow to my head gave him the ad-

vantage. It's been a long time since he's been able to overpower me. But because I was distracted, it's going to cost me everything. He's going to hurt her, all to teach me a lesson.

She always thought I was hiding our relationship because I was too afraid of everyone finding out, that I didn't want to risk losing my friendship with Logan. She couldn't be more wrong if she tried. I've been protecting her from him. I knew if he ever found out how much she really means to me, he'd take her away from me. Just like I took his wife away from him.

I try to fight against him, but it's too late, I've lost too much oxygen. My body sags to the floor at the same time I hear him grab his keys. He's going after her.

Adalynn
Present

"Wyatt was a monster. He should never have been a father," Jax finally says.

"What does Wyatt being a piece of shit have to do with any of this?" I ask, almost too afraid to speak. If this is going where I think it is, Jax will never forgive me when he finds out that I contacted him, that I begged the man to help his only son.

"He's the reason I broke up with you."

I don't even have time to ask for an explanation before Jax starts to ramble, trying to get everything out before I stop him.

"He wasn't happy about us and our plans... He made it clear that I couldn't be with you, no matter what... I couldn't risk him doing anything rash, so I ended it."

"The day at the airport."

Jax nods. "I had every intention of making it right but I had to get out from under his thumb first."

Why didn't he tell me? Would it have made a difference? Would we still be in this exact same spot now, if I knew the truth? My head is full of so many questions but the only one that matters is: "Did he cause the accident?"

I don't even realize I'm holding my breath until Jax says, "No, that wasn't his fault."

"There's more though?"

"When it comes to us, there's always more, Adalynn."

Somehow I find comfort in his words. There're a lot of secrets, but we are so much more than that, always have been. When everything's out in the open, I think we'll find our way back to each other. We have to. There's no way we would go through this much pain just to remain friends.

"So you broke up with me to protect me from him?"

"Yes, and I haven't spoken to him since that night."

And I just brought him back into Jax's life. Crap, I need to tell him. The words get lodged in my throat, and Jax takes my silence for something that it isn't.

"I will never let him get between us again."

"Why didn't you just tell me?"

"I had to make it believable. I had to let him know that you didn't mean anything to me." He grips my hand in his. "Letting you go, letting you believe that I didn't love you, that was one of the hardest decisions I've ever had to make."

"The day of my swim meet, you were trying to talk to me."

He kisses the tips of each finger. "I was trying to tell you how I was going to be able to take care of you, that not a moment went by where I didn't think about you... about our..." He shakes his head. "It doesn't matter. We're here now and we need to move forward."

I know he's keeping something from me, that this isn't the full story, but it's a start. He thinks letting me in is going to scare me away. He doesn't know that no matter what, I'm here. I'm in this. "Before you stopped by tonight, I was planning on telling you that I couldn't do it anymore, that I just wanted a fresh start and for us to be friends. I was going to ask for space," I whisper.

"Please tell me there's a *but*."

I nod. "*But*... I know what it feels like not to have you. I'd rather share my life with you than have to watch yours from the sidelines." He cradles my face with one of his hands, and I turn my head to lay a kiss on the inside of his palm. "I'm done pretending that you're not what I want."

"What exactly does that mean, Ads?"

"If you're done fighting this, and you really want to give us another shot, I'm yours." I barely have time to take in his breathtaking smile before his lips descend on mine. Then it's over before it gets started.

"I'm... never... giving... you... up," he says, breaking each word with a kiss.

"No more tracking my phone though—"

"No." His voice leaves no room for argument.

"No? Jax, you can't seriously think that I'm going to let you track my movements."

"Your safety is all that matters to me. I won't take that lightly. The tracker stays." He kisses the pout right off my lips. "You can track me too if it makes you feel better."

It does, slightly, but I refuse to show it. "Fine, but it's just tracking my location, right? You can't see what I'm doing on my phone or secretly hear my calls?"

He laughs. "I'm not the CIA, Ads."

I squint at him, unsure if I believe him. I know he's not the CIA, but I also know that Trinity has groundbreaking technology that the government wants to get their hands on. It wouldn't surprise me if Jax were able to record every little thing that I did on my phone—well, if not him, my brother. Logan is the tech genius in their company.

"No more secrets, Jax. You need to trust that I'm in this with you. Nothing…" I cradle his face in my hands. "Nothing is going to make me let you go."

He glances away from me as he says, "There're some things that I can't tell you, not yet, but when you're ready, I'll tell you everything."

"But no more lies going forward, right?"

"No more lies."

I let him kiss me. With each sweep of his tongue across mine, I let him wash away the past. I let him erase each and every lie he's ever told me. I let myself get swept up in believing that my life can be different. I don't have to be the broken girl Kohen made me out to be. I can choose to fight with everything left in me. For Jax. For my happiness.

I'm choosing us.

Chapter Ten

Adalynn

It's been four weeks since Kohen attacked me at the beach house. Today is finally the day I get to move into a new place. As much as Jax wanted me to stay with him while I was looking for somewhere to live, I knew it was too soon for us to move in together. So, instead, I've been staying at my brother's place in the room he's always kept for me.

I think it will do wonders for our relationship once we're back to living separately. Whenever Jax and I were cuddling on his couch, my brother would forget what his role was, and I would have to remind him I didn't need a father, that I was an adult, which of course just caused us to fight. To say that Logan doesn't approve of my life choices would be an understatement. Not that I can really blame him. The only reason I'm moving into a brand-new place is because of my stellar decision-making.

The one good thing about living with my brother is whenever I woke up screaming in the middle of the night, he was there. Never once did he try to tell me that I was overreacting. The first night, he thought the worst had happened, that Kohen somehow got into his apartment. After the third night in a row, he decided that we'd both sleep in his movie room. As much as I wish what happened with Kohen didn't affect me, we all know it has. Thankfully, my brother was willing to skip his bed for a few nights in favor of keeping me company. Once Jax found out this was happening, he joined us, much to my brother's dismay.

Jax and I are finally in a good spot. We still have to work on trusting each other, but we're getting there. I think it helps that this is the first time in our entire lives that he isn't hiding us. In fact, he makes it a point to always touch me, no matter who is in the room. The first time he spent the night, even after my brother protested, I fell asleep in his arms.

It was also the first night I didn't wake up screaming. When the screaming stopped altogether whenever Jax stayed over, Logan returned to his room and finally stopped trying to tell Jax that he wasn't welcome anymore.

Tonight is the first night we're going to be alone in a long time...

I keep waiting for Kohen to try to reach out and apologize but I haven't heard anything from him. Maybe it's because Jax changed my number and I haven't had a residence since I bought this modest, at least by New York standards, two-bedroom apartment. It's close to the bakery, walking distance to the park, and right around the corner from Jax's place. It cost a fortune but with the thumbprint elevator and the extra security, I couldn't pass it up.

Even though Logan and Jax try to reassure me that I don't have anything to fear when it comes to Kohen, I know I can't be too safe. I might not remember every little detail, but I remember enough to know that he isn't going to walk away quietly.

"I need to talk to you," Connor whispers as he tries unsuccessfully to keep his attention off Harper.

He's been watching her more. At first, I thought it was charming but then I snapped back to reality and remembered by best friend is a man whore, and that's being nice. I don't want him anywhere near her. The second she's in his bed, things will get awkward. I think she's the only girl in New York immune to his charms.

"You know she's not interested, right?"

He doesn't attempt to look away from her. "Did she ever tell you why she moved to the city?"

Nope. "She moved because of her job," I lie. It's not his business why she moved up here from the south.

"Do you want to know what I found on her background check?"

Looking around, I drag the giant of a man into the next room. "What do you mean her background check?" I hiss at him. He must be joking right? Running a background check on her seems a little extreme.

He huffs. "It was clean."

I could smack him. "Isn't that a good thing?"

"Nobody is that clean. She doesn't even have social media."

Neither do I. "What does that have to do with anything?"

"You don't find it strange that someone like her isn't even on Twitter?"

"I don't know if you meant for that to sound degrading or not, but it did. Knock it off, Connor. She's my only friend."

"Exactly." He tries to step around me, but I grab on to his shirt, halting his movements.

"Leave her alone, Connor. Everyone is entitled to their secrets."

I can tell he wants to disagree with me, but before he can, Logan comes into the room. He looks between us and laughs. "I told you not to tell her."

"You knew?"

He rolls his eyes. "Adalynn, if you think I don't run a background check on everyone in your life, then you're clearly confused and forget who we are. Besides, I'm sure Jax does the same thing."

Connor winks before walking out. Murder. I could murder all of them. "Don't you think that's a little excessive?"

"No," My brother states.

No. That's all he says, as if it's all completely rational. What does he think I'm going to do? Write over my fortune to her or something? The same fortune I have only touched twice: once for college and now for this apartment. I wish I could just give it away. It's blood money. I only have it because they died.

With as much grace as I can manage still sporting the stupid boot on my foot, I stomp—well, in my head, I do anyway—and return to the main room. Everyone has been helping me move in today, but it's almost dinnertime, and I need to finally stop being a coward and talk to Harper.

"Okay, guys, out. Its girls' night," I announce to the room.

The first time Harper visited me in the hospital and saw what Kohen did to me, she immediately started crying and apologizing. She blamed herself, because she knew what he was capable of and still kept my secret. I, of course, wanted nothing to do with any of it, so I did what I always do and swept it under the rug. I excel at avoidance, especially when it comes to her.

Yes, I know I'm a coward. I've been a coward for four weeks. Now that I'm living on my own again, it's time to have the heavy talk that I know she wants to have with me. She tried a few times when I was at Logan's, but I always changed the subject, and thankfully she never pushed me. By the way she keeps checking to see if I need anything, even though I'm almost walking by myself these days, I think we both know what's going to happen once the guys leave.

"I didn't do anything," Jax pipes up while putting together my new bookcase.

I glare at his back. No, he didn't do anything, if you don't count the fact he knew about the background checks and didn't tell me. Since Harper's here and I don't want her to know how crazy the guys are, I settle for asking him, "Do you have a penis?"

He doesn't bother responding.

"Then out." I point to the door. It takes me a little longer to maneuver to the couch because of all the boxes. I may have gone a little overboard with ordering new things. I didn't want a single item in here that Kohen could have breathed on, let alone touched. Okay, so maybe I used my inheritance three times...

"Pizza?" Logan asks Jax. "We're going to go watch the game."

I don't miss the way Connor's eyebrows jump up in surprise—heck, I think everyone's do. Not once since we started dating has Logan treated Jax the same. He pretty much avoids being in the same room as him. Maybe avoidance is a Maxwell trait?

"Don't touch it. I'll finish it when I come back tonight." Jax sets his tools down and points to Harper and then me. "Under no circumstances do you leave this apartment without letting me know where you're going, and don't let anyone up."

Before I can tell Jax what I think of his rules, Logan interrupts. "Bye, Harper. Bye, sis," He waves at us while grabbing his jacket. "I'll be outside, Jaxon."

I tell myself that they're just worried about me and trying to do what they think is best. That's the only reason I let it go and ask them all, "Are we still on for breakfast tomorrow?"

Connor shakes his head. "Leaving first thing in the morning for London." Right, they're working on expanding overseas. Connor is trying to find a location for their new headquarters.

"I'll pick you up on the way to the office," Logan says, at the same time Jax says, "I'll drive us, then have Henry drop me off at work after."

They both stare at each other. They haven't really settled into this new role. Logan has been my protector since we lost our parents. I think he's struggling with leaving the "father" role he took over and becoming my brother again. It's hard for him to see how close Jax and I have become in a few short weeks.

"Great." After breakfast, I have an appointment with Olivia. I haven't told them because I know they think I should find a different therapist with everything going on. I should have enough time for Henry to drop me back off here and make it to her office without any-one knowing. I don't trust Jax's driver to take me without reporting back to him.

It would be easier, I think for both of us, if I got help somewhere else. A part of me wants to continue to see her because she's familiar. Seeing her each week is something I've grown so accustomed to that I often find myself heading towards her office, only to turn around.

Yet she called a few days ago and left a message, informing me that she hasn't filled my spot yet. If I wanted to come back to my normal schedule, it's mine. She also let me know she can recommend me to a colleague if I thought that would be better.

I still have no closure on what the police are saying I've done to her. If it were just Kohen, it would be easy to chalk it up to one of his mil-lions of lies, but I can't find a reason for her to make something like this up. She's been such a huge part of my life and I don't know how to even attempt to apologize. Harper seems to be the only one to fully understand my dilemma. I've finally opened up to Harper and ex-plained who Olivia is, and how long I've been seeing her.

I trust Harper even if Connor is on the fence.

"Want Chinese?" Harper asks, once Connor and Logan close the door. "Usual order?"

My stomach growls in answer. Which of course makes her and Jax laugh. He saunters over to me, because walking would be too simple of a classification for what Jax does. He even kneels in front of me in such a way that causes my stomach to do summersaults.

He cradles my face with his palm. "Are you going to be okay?"

Although I know without asking that he looked into Harper, I can't find it in me to be mad. Not when he's this close and invading all of my senses. "I'll be okay." Besides, he was doing what he thought necessary to protect me. Now that we're back together, I've realized how much he does for me that I wasn't aware of before.

Like how he always makes sure I have ChapStick in the nightstand —even Henry carries a tube for me in the car. If I'm making dinner, he's setting the table, or refilling my wine glass for me. Most days he's waking me up with breakfast in bed. The best part is at night when we're finally back in our bubble cuddling. We stay up for hours just talking, sharing things we've hidden from each other all these years.

I can't believe there was a time when we weren't here. All the games we've played with each other over the years seem unimportant now that we're finally in a good place. Every single day I fall a little more in love with him.

Jax stares into my eyes as if searching for doubt. Since he found me, we haven't really left each other's sides. He's started only going into the office for a few hours every few days. Everything else he needs to do, he does it from wherever I am. Having him leave, if even for a little while, seems a lot harder to do now that he's this close to me.

"I can stay out of the way," he says as if sensing my dwindling resolve.

"Nope, no way, Jaxon I-don't-know-your-middle-name Chandler. You are giving us much-needed girl time."

I laugh. I almost forgot Harper was here while getting lost in his eyes. "Just a few hours."

"Don't fall asleep without me," he whispers right before lowering his mouth to mine. The kiss is short and sweet, just a gentle press of his lips against mine. Still, it leaves me wanting. We've been taking things extremely slow. I think we both have an unspoken timeline: until I'm more healed, until I'm more settled, until I'm not living with my brother.

My eyes dance around my brand-new apartment. Looks like I'm settled, healed, and no more Logan checking on us every few minutes...

Is it too late to change my mind and just jump into bed with him?

Jax's smirk says it all, but it's not until he mumbles, "Lead the way," that I realize I've spoken out loud.

Harper, of course, joins in with, "Yes, it's too late. I already ordered Chinese and I'm starving. Now stop giving her bedroom eyes, Jaxon."

"Bedroom eyes—" I hold up a hand and cut myself off. With her, sometimes not knowing what she means is better. "Never mind." I turn to the man in question. "I'll see you in a few hours."

His sigh leaves nothing to the imagination. He's as frustrated as I am. "Call me if you need anything." Then he addresses Harper. "Don't let anything happen to her."

She salutes him and tosses me the remote. "Find something trashy while I grab us something to drink."

I laugh at Jax's departing huff.

"Okay, now that we're full and working on our second glass, I think it's time we finally have the talk," Harper says after refilling both of our wines.

"As in the sex talk? I think that ship sailed when I was sixteen, Harper."

Setting her glass down, she turns so she's facing me on the couch, tucking her knees underneath her. "The talk about the club we're both members of but never wanted to join."

I'm pretty sure I stop breathing. I think we both know what club she's talking about. There's no way. Not this feisty firecracker. She's the exact opposite of me. There's no way she'd allow this to happen to her. She'd leave at the first sign...

It takes too long for me to find words because she confirms my worst suspicions. "The *I should have left before he put me in the hospital* club."

"Oh, that club." My eyes sting, but somehow I'm able to fight back my tears. "Your ex did this to you too?" I wish it hadn't happened to her, but there's a reason they say misery loves company. To know that I'm not alone, that she gets it... somehow that knowledge gives me a little comfort. Looking at her now, I don't know how long it took for her to be this spitfire of a person, but Harper is who I inspire to be. I need her attitude, her confidence. I need her will to live.

I scoot closer and hold her hand, wanting to give her any comfort I can.

She sighs, long and heavy, as if the world is resting on her shoulders —that kind of sigh. "My husband put me in a hospital... well, he would have if he didn't have an on-call team of nurses and a doctor to tend to me instead. But, yes, Adalynn, I understand." She lifts her glass to mine. "Cheers." It's the saddest toast in the history of toasts. It's also the most broken I've ever heard her voice.

"I hate him. Whoever he is, I hate him."

"I hate that I knew what was going on, and I did nothing to stop him. I'm so sorry, Adalynn." She wipes at her eyes. "I keep thinking if maybe I let you in sooner, this wouldn't have happened. I should have told—"

"There was nothing you could have done to stop me. I don't blame you, Harper."

"Well, you should. I have years of experience when it comes to recognizing the telltale signs. Still, I ignored it." She waves a hand over my body. "I feel so responsible. If I just said something—"

"Do not give him that power. This isn't on anyone but Kohen." I hug her.

"I really wish you weren't in this club, Adalynn," she says into my hair.

I *wish* I was the only member. I hate that she knows my pain. Nobody should ever know what it feels like to have someone they trust, someone they love, do *this* to them. "Me too, Harper, me too."

She leans back against the couch. "I don't think he's going to just go away, especially since the news broke about the incident."

I nod. "Jax and I met with a lawyer the other day, about getting a possible restraining order."

"A piece of paper won't stop him. It never does," she says, as if speaking from experience.

I'm almost too afraid to ask, but my lips have a mind of their own. "How did you get away?"

"The first time he smacked me, I just stood there. I didn't say anything. I just stared in shock, wondering if my husband of all of twenty minutes really just backhanded me. He didn't even apologize. He went to the wedding reception and acted as if nothing happened." Harper fidgets in her seat. She studies the blank walls of my apartment, takes in all the boxes, and just... relives the past.

I can see the pain she's in, the pain she desperately wants to escape, and the wall that she so carefully hides behind finally comes down.

"When my mom found me, she took one look at my face and applied more makeup. She told me to suck it up, that I had guests waiting for me." Her laugh is humorless. "I thought she'd save me, thought she'd at least help me out of my marriage."

Holy fuck.

"It wasn't until I was 30,000 feet in the air, in his private jet, that I finally lashed out. I threw my champagne glass in his face... and woke up two days later."

Two days later... what did he do to her?

"Harper—" My voice cracks.

"I'm glad you were able to get away. Sometimes that's the hardest thing to do. Most can't escape." She grips my hands. "No matter what happens, Adalynn, do not take him back. Men like him, they never get better. No matter how much we want to fix them, we can't. There's something broken inside them. It makes them like that, and that kind of darkness never goes away."

"I could never take him back. It's so much worse than just the beach house."

And because she just shared one of her worst experiences with me, I tell her what's really happening with Kohen. I promised the guys and my lawyer that I would keep everything a secret. They're nervous about all the publicity surrounding the incident, but I know Harper isn't going to sell my story to the rags. I shouldn't have waited until now to tell her. But I was afraid she'd judge me. She saw parts of our relationship that nobody else did. Looking back now, I feel so stupid for being with him. I don't want this to be my story, and saying it out loud makes it real.

After knocking back the rest of my wine, I tell her everything I've kept from her. I tell her everything the police discovered, how they think Jax is actually the one who hurt me, how even our lawyer thinks this won't go our way. I don't know what I'll do if Kohen doesn't drop the charges. I won't let Jax be punished because of him. Because of *me* and my choices. I'm going to do whatever it takes to protect him.

Chapter Eleven

Adalynn

Breakfast was a lot better than I anticipated. It seems that whatever has been bothering Logan and putting stress on his and Jax's friendship is slowly but surely healing. They even cracked a few jokes with each other.

I was somehow able to convince Henry to just drop me off in the lobby. I knew he didn't want to, but thankfully he gave in to me. Once he left, I immediately hailed a taxi.

I hate that it feels like I'm lying to everyone by omitting the fact that I'm seeing Olivia. I'll tell Jax after. That way, I won't have to hear how bad of an idea this is since it will already be done. If I can't continue to be her patient, at least I can explain how sorry I am for hurting her. I just wish I remembered.

Story of my life... wishing to remember.

I was tempted to leave my phone at home, but I knew that would be too much. Besides, with everything going on with Kohen, I can't take that risk. Twirling my cell in my lap, I contemplate what to do.

"Miss?" The cab driver asks, snapping me out of my thoughts.

Looking up, I realize we've arrived at her office. "Right, sorry." I tap my card to the reader and leave a hefty tip for the sheer fact that we've been waiting here for a few minutes while I've done nothing but stare into space. I'm just glad he didn't throw me out. He must not be from New York.

Even though Logan and Jax don't agree with my need to see her, it's something I feel I have to do. She's the only therapist I've seen since the accident who's made me feel more myself since that night.

Without thinking about it anymore, I open the door and head inside the building.

"Thanks for agreeing to see me," I say hesitantly as I take a seat in Liv's office. If I wasn't so hyperaware of everything going on, because of what I did to her, I might have missed the way her hands shake as she places her tea on the coffee table. "I feel horrible for what I did to you. I wish I could—"

She holds up a palm, stopping me. "It's not your fault, Addie. You were in a manic episode. I want to help you, but you have to put in the time."

It takes everything in me not to keep apologizing but something is telling me she doesn't want to hear it. The only way I can prove how sorry I am is to do what she's asking. I need to put in the work and get better so that I don't harm anyone else.

"What do I need to do, Liv?"

Grabbing her ever-present iPad, she clicks to what I'm sure is the very lengthy patient file she has on me. "The last time you were here, we were discussing the return of some of your missing memories. Would you like to start there or..."

I think we both know she's referring to the night at Kohen's beach house, but I don't think it's fair to her to open that up. What if I'm haunting her just as my dead family haunts me?

"Should I even be here?"

"I'm your therapist, Adalynn. I'm here to help you."

"Yes, but at what cost? I attacked you."

She calmly sets the iPad down to replace it with her teacup. "You're in a fragile state, Adalynn. That night, you felt out of control, and you needed to leave. In my line of work, sometimes things escalate. I'm sorry I wasn't able to get there sooner to help you."

"That's just it, Olivia. I don't remember you even being there. I'm starting to remember what happened between Kohen and me... but you... you... I can't picture you there no matter how hard I try."

Her hazel eyes leave mine and focus on the ceiling by her bookcase before settling on me again. "Maybe you need to stop trying so hard and just focus on the now. What can you do now to control your emotions? What can you do now to help yourself heal?"

I grab the stupid bear on the corner of the couch and squeeze it, instead of digging my nails into my palms. That would be so much easier. I'd be able to ground myself more but it isn't healthy. Liv is right. I need to focus on the now.

"Logan has found another therapist for me. I'm supposed to meet with him on Friday."

"How do you feel about that?"

I shrug. "It might be easier to start fresh."

"For whom?"

It feels like minutes pass before I finally answer her. "I think it would be easier for the both of us. You wouldn't have to sit there wondering when I'm going to attack you again."

She types something into the iPad. "I think you should go to the other appointment. If it's easier for you to talk to someone else, then I think that's what you should do. My only concern is for you, Adalynn. I want to help heal you, and if that means you speak with someone you're more comfortable with, then go. I don't want you to be here if it hinders your healing process."

She's giving me the out I desperately need, but don't want. I know Logan and Jax don't understand why I *need* to keep seeing her but I do. I've lost count of how many therapists I've seen over the years; she's the *only* one who has made me stop cutting. She's the *only* one who has made me want to start living my life again.

"But if you want to continue to see me, I think we should get started. The choice is always yours, Adalynn."

"If it's still okay with you, I think I'll stay."

With a smile that doesn't fully reach her eyes, Olivia waits for me to begin our session. I tell her about my migraines.

"When did these start?"

I pause. I don't believe they're related to the incident with Kohen. I'm sure if she thinks the two are related, she will contact my doctor. The neurologist will order an unnecessary MRI just to prove that I'm right and they have no correlation.

Instead of saying all of this, I just shrug my shoulders. "A while." I try to downplay it so Olivia doesn't overreact. That's the last thing I need right now.

"Tell me more about these migraines," she types something into her notes.

I sigh, long and slow. "It's almost as if I'm finally remembering... something. All I see are pieces though. Nothing that clues me in to this big secret everyone in my life seems to know... everyone but me that is."

"I want to try something. Lie back and close your eyes."

Doing as she says, I squeeze the teddy bear to my chest as I get comfortable.

"Okay, slow, deep breaths for me. Count to five, hold, and slowly release it." I follow her instructions and start to relax more. "Two more times, Adalynn." With each controlled breath, the tension in my body dissipates. "Perfect, tell me what you see before you get the migraines."

"A box... more like a present. I know it was for me, but it wasn't my birthday. I keep seeing it in the trash, unopened."

"Good, what else?"

"Hadley." My voice breaks when I whisper my dead sister's name. "I remember her giving me her bear, but it wasn't for me."

"If it wasn't for you, then who was it for?"

The memory is right there. I can almost grasp it. Yet, the closer I get to wrapping my fingers around it, the faster it slips through my hands, disappearing as quickly as it came. "I remember a lot of fighting."

"With whom?" Liv asks.

"My parents, it seems all we did was fight." We were fighting the night of the accident. That's why my dad wasn't paying attention to the road. He was trying to get my attention in the rearview mirror. Maybe if we weren't fighting, he would have been paying attention and they'd all still be here.

"What were you fighting about?"

I shake my head. "I can't remember," I whisper, the lie tasting bitter on my tongue. I may not fully remember but I have a feeling we were fighting about my relationship with Jax.

That doesn't feel right though, because nobody knew about us back then... right?

Sitting up, I turn so that I'm looking out the windows instead of at her. "Maybe Logan and Jax are right," I find myself saying at the end of our session.

"Right about what?"

For some reason, I still can't look at her while I admit, "I think I need to see someone else, Liv."

There's a long pause so I'm forced to face my fears and look at her. Her smile seems strained as she sets her tablet down. "I just want to help you, Adalynn."

How can she help me if we can't even talk about anything related to Kohen? It feels as if we've come to some unspoken agreement not to bring anything up that relates to him. I don't believe either one of us is ready to dissect that yet. What if I say something that triggers what I did to her?

"What are you afraid of?"

"I don't want to say anything that might hurt you," I confess quietly. "I'm so sorry, Olivia."

Getting up from her desk, she walks around it until she's sitting on the coffee table directly in front of me. "Adalynn, you didn't mean to. Your best interests are all that matters to me."

"What about that night? Won't it..." I'm at a loss for words.

"When you're ready to talk about that night, about your relationship with Kohen, I'm here." She grabs my hands and gives them a gentle squeeze. "You don't have to be afraid for me, Adalynn. I'm here to help you."

I find myself nodding.

"What I said at the beginning of our session is still true. If you want to see someone else to determine if they're a better fit, please do. As I mentioned on the phone, I haven't filled your sessions."

"Okay."

She stands, and I follow suit. "Let my assistant know when you make a decision."

I'm not even surprised when I find Henry, Jax's driver, waiting for me outside Olivia's office. I just shake my head in amusement. I guess I won't be able to keep the fact that I came here a secret. I don't really think I was ever going to. If I really wanted to maintain my privacy, I would have left my phone home. I knew he'd be tracking my movements. I think that's why I felt safe to even leave my place. I knew he'd be watching, looking after me.

Henry opens the back door when he notices me approaching, "Miss Maxwell," he greets me.

I barely suppress the urge to roll my eyes, just barely though. "Henry, how many times do I need to remind you to call me Addie?"

"Just once more, Miss Maxwell," he says, just like he says every single time.

"Thanks for picking me up," I say as I slide into the back. "Would you mind taking me home?"

He tips his head. "Of course." Then shuts the door and slips into the driver's seat.

I'm grateful that he's listening to opera and is focused on the music instead of talking to me. I've always found it hard to hold up a conversation after visiting Olivia. Just like all the times before, I'm wrapped up in my head, trying to force my memories back into place. Liv thinks I've made great progress and that my memories are returning, I just need to be patient. Patience has never been my strong suit though. That's why even though I know I should be relaxing, I'm trying to force them back.

She thinks I need to see a doctor about my migraines. She's worried about my well-being and thinks I need to take painkillers. I know it doesn't make sense but what if painkillers fog my mind and the memories stop coming?

Besides, being in pain isn't the worst thing in the world. It reminds me I'm still here.

I'm so focused on what Olivia and I talked about that I don't hear the first alert on my phone go off. The second alert brings me back to the present. Looking out the window, I see that we're only a few blocks from my place. I key in the passcode and pull up the live footage to see Jax disengaging the alarm and making himself at home.

Even though I know Jax invaded my privacy by checking my location, I can't find it in me to care. Besides, he sent his driver to collect me. "Thanks, Henry," I say as he holds the door open for me.

"Of course. Have a good day, Miss Maxwell."

I don't bother correcting him. I doubt there's anything I can do to get him to stop formally addressing me.

"How was your session with Olivia?" Jax says as he greets me at the front door.

"Enlightening." Moving around him, I place my purse on the hook and reengage the alarm system. Not wanting to have this discussion in the entryway, I head to the living room, but stop dead in my tracks. I use the wall to support me as I'm hit with another headache.

I'm back at my parents' house in California. There, on the coffee table, is a small present waiting for me. The same present I keep picturing every time I close my eyes. My mom tells me Jax stopped by and dropped it off. I don't bother opening it. I throw it away and go upstairs to do my homework.

"Ads, are you okay?" Jax asks, transporting me from the lingering memory to the present.

"What was in the small box you gave my mom?" I use my hands to show him the size of it. "Grey wrapping with white birds on it." Before, I could only picture the box in the trash. Now I remember more. My mom dug it out and brought it back upstairs. I remember arguing with her, but in the end, she won and left it on my dresser unopened.

Where is it now? I don't think I ever got around to opening it. I want to tell him that I'm remembering more. I want to ask him why I hated him. It's on the tip of my tongue, but no matter how hard I try, the words never escape.

I'm a coward. I'm afraid of what will happen between us once everything is out in the open. If I'm destined to lose him, I want to enjoy every last moment until I can't anymore. So, instead of telling him what's really on my mind, I ask him about the present again.

He swallows loudly.

"It wasn't my birthday."

Without saying anything, Jax leads me to the couch so we can sit. "No, Ads, it wasn't your birthday."

I wait for him to offer more but he doesn't. I wish I could say that I'm surprised but I'm not. This isn't the first time since I came back from the hospital that I've shared something with him and he clams up. I wish I could say this will be the last, but I both think we know better at this stage.

"Jax," I press.

"I know that I'm being selfish by keeping you in the dark, but I don't know how to open up to you, Ads. Everything was stolen from us six years ago. I want more than our past. I want our future."

"I want that too. I need to know what happened for us to move forward, Jax."

"I'm trying to protect you."

It's the same argument, just a different day.

"Why are you here?"

"I wanted to see how today went."

Maybe if I give him this little piece of myself, he'll give me a little more too. Ever since I left the hospital, we've been trying to work our way back to each other. It definitely hasn't been easy but it's worth it.

He's worth it.

He grabs my hand and kisses my palm. I'd be lying if I said that simple move didn't make me melt into him.

"Liv is familiar. I know you and Logan don't understand, but if she's willing to keep seeing me, I think it's what I need."

"Okay."

"Okay? Just like that?" I nudge him. "I thought you'd put up more of a fight."

"I hate fighting with you, Ads." He hands me a bag on the floor that I didn't notice until now. "I got you something."

Inside is a sketchpad. I trace the cover with reverence. It's been a long time since I've seen anything he's drawn. "What is this?"

He laughs a little. "You have to open it to find out."

I gasp as I take in his artwork. He doesn't draw as much as he used to, but when he does... wow. I have no words. Every page is so detailed, so full of life that I have to wipe my eyes as I flip through it.

"It's our story." His voice is unsure. "Do you like it?"

I nod as I take everything in. As I turn the pages, I can't help the memories that come with them.

"This is your old bedroom window." He points at the charcoal drawing. It's of his viewpoint from the ground, and you can see my silhouette through the curtain.

I choke on a sob. Every night, I would crack my window open for him. We spent the nights patching him up, doing homework, and talking. I both dreaded and looked forward to those interactions.

The next page is filled with stars, and underneath them, we're dancing. The lyrics to our favorite Coldplay song is weaved around us, almost as if the wind is singing to us as we dance. I was fourteen the first time we did exactly this.

I finally find my voice. "I don't understand," I say as I study the next sketch, which is a drawing of my sister handing me a piece of candy. She's dressed in her practice leotard, ballet shoes strung over her shoulder, and I'm dressed to go on a run.

"Hadley saw me sneaking candy into your bag one day, so I recruited her to help me. She had her own stash under her bed."

"She used to joke that I had a candy fairy and it wasn't fair that she didn't have one."

He laughs. "Yeah, and when she caught me, she bribed me into getting her some too."

The pain of my dead sister comes swift, robbing me of the moment Jax is giving me, just like her life was robbed from her too. As much as I don't want to go there, I can't help it. This, this bliss with Jax, feels wrong.

"They wouldn't want you to keep suffering, Ads. Sooner or later, you're going to have to forgive yourself."

I close the sketchpad. "You wouldn't understand."

"I understand more than you know. That raw pain you feel every time you enjoy even a second of happiness? As if your heart is tearing open, bleeding uncontrollably, and no matter how many times you try to fix yourself, nothing works? The blood, the pain keeps pouring out of you.

"I understand that sleep doesn't even give you relief. The second you close your eyes, you'll dream of them, of everything that happened, of everything you wish you could do differently. Then you wake up and go through the motions, praying that maybe today will be the day that it hurts a little less."

I still. Everything he's saying is everything I feel. It's as if he's stealing the words from my haunted mind.

"The worst are the days you forget. The sun kisses your cheeks, and everything is right in the world when you open your eyes. Then it all comes back and you're left more broken than the day before. Trust me, Adalynn, I know all too well what haunts you. I'm stuck in the same nightmare."

I want to ask him what his nightmares are about but I can't. The words won't form. His pain is different from mine. His childhood was stolen from him, just as the rest of my life has been stolen from me.

Wyatt changed the man that Jax could have been, robbed his son of so much by turning Jax into his personal punching bag.

My family changed me too. When you're forced to watch your family die in front of you, it changes you, and not for the better. Jax and I are the same.

Chapter Twelve

Kohen

Smiling at her assistant, I let myself into Olivia's office. We have an appointment after all. Just as expected, she's perched behind her mahogany desk. She doesn't glance up from her computer; she's giving me the silent treatment. I return the gesture, continuing the same song and dance we do almost every time Adalynn has an appointment with the good doctor.

She hates that I've forced her into this role, even more so now that she knows my endgame. She never anticipated how far I'd take this. She never thought Adalynn would drive me to this point. Heck, until we were at my house, I didn't think I would go this far either. I didn't think I would have to. I thought once I got her alone, out of the gilded cage Jax put her in, she'd see everything I've done for her.

I was wrong. She wasn't ready then, but she will be. I have a few more things to line up, but once I'm done, she'll see exactly the kind of people she's surrounded herself with.

Soon... Adalynn will be mine. I just need to bide my time, starting with her therapist.

Without acknowledging Olivia, I make a show of walking around her office, as if every little thing fascinates me. It doesn't. Still, I make the effort to appear as if I'm at home here, simply for the fact that I know it makes her uncomfortable.

She pretends that she isn't watching my every move but we both know she is. That's probably why I lean forward just a tad, on the disguise of checking out one of her books, but really I want her to see the knife in my back pocket.

Her sharp inhale fills me with warmth. She wasn't expecting it. Good, I need to keep her on her toes so she falls in line. She catches herself, though, because all too quickly her therapist mask is in place.

Tick... tick... tick... the clock on the far wall is the only annoying noise in the room now that she's gone back to ignoring me. I welcome the silence. I need more time to process what just took place in this very office. I'm on the verge of snapping.

I need to get Olivia to heel. I would really hate to have to put her down. She's been a better asset than I originally planned.

It's because of Olivia that I've even been able to get this close to Adalynn in the first place. It was Olivia who steered her away from Jaxon and into my arms. So instead of doing the only thing I've wanted to do since I watched today's session, I pretend to care about the books that decorate her office. I act as if I'm not consumed by pure rage at the very sight of her.

Just when I think it's all too much, that Olivia is more of a burden than an asset at this stage, I catch a whiff of Addie's unique fragrance.

Fuck, I can practically smell her as if she's still in this office. I lick my lips, pretending that it's her that I taste. All I can think about is her. She's all I want. She's all I need. I burn for her.

"Kohen—"

My reprimand is quick, my tone lethal. "You're becoming too predictable. That's both welcoming and annoying."

Just the sound of my voice makes her tense. Good, she's still afraid of me, as she should be. My smile is anything but friendly. "I thought we had a deal, Olivia."

"We do," she rushes out.

I huff. "I think I need to remind you of our deal. It seems you've forgotten."

She swallows. And I slowly inch myself towards her, loving the way her hands start to shake the closer I get.

"I thought we'd agreed that you would be her therapist and I'd be able to watch each session." Instead of answering, she nods like the good girl she is. "Then can you tell me how I could possibly watch her sessions if she's seeing a new therapist?"

"You have to understand I'm doing what is best for Adalynn."

What a fucking joke.

If she were doing what was best for Adalynn, then she wouldn't be illegally taping each session for me. She stopped doing what was best for her patient years ago. Fuck, at this stage, she deserves an Oscar for her performance. She has everyone fooled, even Ads's precious Jax.

If she wasn't making my access to her easier, Olivia would have been gone the second she decided her vengeance was more important than being a therapist. Olivia doesn't have to worry though. Soon it won't matter that she's betrayed Adalynn.

Just another thing Ads can thank me for.

Once I'm behind her, I place my hands on Olivia's shoulders, welcoming the way she closes her body into itself as if she can protect herself from me. She can't. Not wanting her to miss one single word I say, I lean down until my lips are brushing against her ear as I whisper, "If Addie isn't your patient anymore, what use will you be to me?"

Her whole body stills at my words. I doubt she's even breathing.

"Do you know what happens when you're no longer useful? What will happen to your family when they find out what you've done?"

Swallowing, she finally finds her voice again. "I did what was necessary, Kohen. She's back on my schedule. She'll be here next week."

My hands start to wander to her delicate neck. "And what happens if Logan forces her to see the other therapist and she likes them better than you? You made it very clear today that you come with too much baggage. It might be easier for her to start over."

She turns her head to face me directly, as if her spine has suddenly steeled. "You compromised my relationship with my patient when you fed her that lie. Sooner or later, she's going to realize that I was never there that night. I have to pretend that the lies you told are true. *You* forced me to put that baggage there."

How dare she take that tone with me!

Not so gently I give her neck a squeeze, reminding her who is in charge here. I welcome the panicked look on her face as she struggles to breathe. Slowly, I watch her face pale. She starts to thrash but I hold on as her lips lose their color.

When it comes to Adalynn, I need her to know how serious I am. Nothing will get in my way of having her. When it's clear she's learned her lesson, I release her. She's still gasping for breath as I make my way out of her office. The stuffed animal is right where Adalynn left him. I can still picture her clinging to it not even thirty minutes ago. I bet her scent lingers on it. Without a second thought, I grab the stuffed bear and leave Liv's office.

It's time to go pay my girl a visit. I don't want her to think I've forgotten all about her. Just the thought of being in the same room with her reminds me of the very first time I broke all the rules I set and finally started doing what I wanted.

Two years ago

Scanning the area, I make sure nobody notices me as I take the elevator to her floor. I overtook the security feed so all they'll see is a repeat of the last two hours until I cut it and release the live images. I couldn't risk being caught on camera. I know her brother is a tech genius, and I have no doubt that he has her floor monitored at all times. Fuck, it wouldn't surprise me if he's alerted to every coming and going from this building.

I check the live footage of her in her bedroom on my phone. She's still fast asleep. The urge to be close to her is almost overwhelming. I've never felt like this for someone, not even Em. Quickly, I use the copy of her key I had made. I just need to be in the same room with her.

I make sure not to make a sound as I move around her apartment. I know which places to step, which parts of her flooring squeak if you put too much pressure on them. At this stage in our relationship, I know her apartment better than I know mine.

This is the first time we're both here together. Fuck, my pulse is erratic. Just knowing she's here, breathing the same air as me, has all of my nerves on fire. I'm so close to her.

For months, I've studied every inch of it. I thought putting in cameras would help me get over my obsession. I thought if I could see her flaws, I'd get over her. All the hours of watching her, listening to her, have only fed into my hunger for her.

As much as I tried, I knew I wouldn't be able to just sit by and watch her. I need to be with her, to be in her life, to touch her, to hold her. Fuck, I'm hard at just the idea of being this close to her. I need to calm down. I remind myself that I'm just going to watch her, just like I do every chance I get, this time from the vantage point of her room. That's all. I won't allow myself anything more, I just need to be closer to her, to remind myself why I'm doing this in the first place.

I carefully maneuver around her apartment. I don't want to rush things. I know I need to calm down before I go into her bedroom. If I go in there in my current state, I don't know how much self-control I will have.

I spot a few dishes in her sink. I know I should leave them be, but I can't. I want to help her, to make her life a little easier. Besides, what harm will come if I put them in her dishwasher for her? Next, I go back into her living room and fold the throw blanket before laying it over her couch, just the way she likes it.

If only she'd give me a chance, she could see how much easier her life could be with me in it. She'd never have to hide who she is from me. I wouldn't lie to her like her precious fucking Jax does. Like everyone else in her life does. I'm the only person who can bring her happiness and give her the one thing she wants.

She doesn't know everything I've done for us.

She might not know it yet, but I'm the farthest thing from a stranger to her. Ever since the accident, I've been around. I've always checked on her because I wanted to make sure she was okay, but somewhere down the line, I fell in love with her and my obsession grew into something more.

I almost have everything in place, and once I do, I will no longer have to watch her life from the sidelines. One day soon, I'll be by her side, holding her hand. I'll be the man Jax could never be.

Glancing around the room to make sure nothing else needs to be fixed, I finally head towards her bedroom. I stop just outside the door to check my phone again. As much as I love the idea of her knowing I'm here, I know that waking up to someone she believes is a stranger would frighten her, and that's the last thing I want.

Once I know she's still asleep, I turn the knob and walk silently into her room. The door doesn't make a sound as I close and lock it. I don't think she'll wake up, but just in case she does, I don't want her to run from me before I can explain everything to her.

The light from outside her windows illuminates my path to her sleeping form.

Chapter Thirteen

Adalynn

When I woke up this morning, Jax was already dressed and had break-fast made. It doesn't escape my notice that since I tried to take things further with us the other day, he's always up before I am. I know he thinks we need to wait to take the next step, but I'm done waiting. I want my boyfriend. I need to lose myself in him.

I thought after moving into my new place, we'd take the next step, but we haven't. Every night I go to sleep wrapped in his arms, and I wake up on top of him. I can feel his need for me, but he never gives in, no matter how much I tell him I need him too.

I'm tired of waiting for him.

That's why, instead of getting dressed in the bathroom after my shower like I always do, I'm just dressed in a towel. I don't care what his plans are for the day. We're not leaving my apartment until he makes me his again. My plan is to seduce him. That's why I'm sporting what Harper calls sex hair, red lips, and only a towel that I plan on los-ing once I find him.

When I step out of the bathroom, Jax is leaning against the wall. I guess I won't have to go too far to look for him after all. He watches me as I close the distance between us. I'm done taking things slow. I need him.

"How did you sleep?" he asks when I'm a breath away. I don't miss the way his eyes caress my body, heating at the sight of me.

"Better than I thought I would." The lie falls easily off my lips. I don't want to worry him and tell him that I'm still plagued by nightmares of Kohen.

"What do you want to do today? I was thinking—" He stops talking when I brazenly drop my towel. I'm his sole focus. "Ads," he groans. "I thought we agreed to wait."

"No, you decided to wait. I'm tired of waiting, Jax." Biting my lip, because I know it drives him insane, I walk backwards to the bed and crook my finger at him. "Show me I'm yours." My fingers trail a path down my stomach. I love the way his pupils dilate as he watches me. I'm ready to beg him to *really* touch me.

That's all it takes before he's on me, making me shiver in anticipation as he slinks his arm around me and pulls me flush against him. "You've always been mine," he growls right before he tastes me. The feel of his lips against mine lights me on fire. He's barely touched me and I'm already burning for more.

This is what I need. I don't need sleep. I don't need therapy. All I need is him. Jax makes me feel safe. He makes me forget all the fucked-up stuff that's happening, all the ugly surrounding us, and everything else in the world. He's the only thing I need. His love for me, that's what I've been craving.

His lips abandon mine as he leaves a scorching path down my neck. I moan his name when he gets to the sensitive spot right below my ear. He's not done teasing me though. No, he gets off on this, on watching what he does to me.

"Jax,"

"What do you need?" He licks my naked shoulders. I arch into him, seeking more, as he sucks the water droplets off my glistening skin. I'm panting, my thighs quivering. I'm desperate for him. I yank his shirt open, and the buttons go flying. I don't stop there—no, I need these offending clothes off him.

New house rule: Jax can't wear clothes. I want him naked at all times.

I gasp at his deep, throaty laugh. Crap! I said that out loud. When he looks the way he looks, nobody can blame me for wanting to see his chiseled chest and the eight-pack he hides behind custom suits.

"Maybe." He kisses my forehead. "We should." He kisses each of my cheeks. "Both have." He kisses down my jaw, careful to avoid my lips. "That rule."

I'm smiling by the time he finally devours my mouth. My hands roam all over his muscles, down his abs to the button of his pants, making him groan deep in his throat. His skin is hot to the touch. I rub my palm against him, loving how hard he is. He moans into my mouth when I start stroking him through his briefs. Jax gets impossibly harder, the head of his cock poking up and wanting to be played with.

I lick my lips in anticipation. Jax stops me from exploring though. I pout as he drags me up the bed, his body following closely behind me. His lips brush against my ear as he whispers, "I'm going to take my time reminding you who you belong to."

I moan in response as he licks a path from my neck to my chest. My thighs squeeze together, desperately searching for some release. It's not enough though, so I wrap my legs around him, loving the feel of him against me. I rub against him, my efforts shameless as I roll my hips, making Jax groan into my neck.

"I need you," I say desperately.

"I need to taste every inch of you," he replies right before his tongue circles my nipple, and his hand comes up to caress the other one. Desperate for more, I arch into him. When his teeth graze my nipple, I lose it. I throw my head back and moan his name. "Fuck, I forgot how sensitive you are," he says as he continues his assault.

I'm getting lost in him, in him finally touching me, but it's still not enough. "Make me forget about everything but the feel of you inside me."

His mouth is hot on my already-scorching skin. I wiggle underneath him. His tongue is amazing but it's still not enough. "Jax," I pant while pushing his head farther south.

He doesn't go where I want. No, the sadistic Adonis above me just winks as he kisses my hip bones. I arch into him again, but he clutches my hips, stopping me. "I want you as desperate for me as I am for you." He circles my belly button with his tongue.

"Please, Jax."

Finally, his lips kiss a path down my inner thigh. Every time I move, he stops. He gets right there—I can feel his breath where I need him the most—just to switch to my other leg. "I'm going to mark you," he warns right before I feel him suck on my inner thigh. Fuck, it feels so good. I don't even care that he's leaving a hickey inches from where I'm desperate to feel his mouth.

"More," I beg.

"Fuck, I can see how much you want me," he says huskily, his fingers finally dipping into me.

I'm panting, moaning, mumbling for him, but still he just teases me. His mouth is right there, breathing me in as he watches what just the tip of his finger does to me. I'm on the verge of screaming at him. If he doesn't do something—

"Yes!" I moan as he sucks on my clit. "Please, Jax." I'm shamelessly riding his face, trying to catch the release that he keeps dangling in front of me just to rip it away.

"Patience."

He gets me to the edge, and right when I'm about to fall over, he slows his movements. His hands keep me pinned to the bed as he takes his time exploring me with his tongue. Over and over again. I'm crying out for him.

"Jax," I groan when he stops.

He kisses his way up to my ear. "Don't take your eyes off me. I want to watch your face when I finally slide home."

Holy hotness, his filthy words have me teetering on the precipice of ecstasy. The slightest nudge and I'm free-falling. He hovers over me, caging me in with his body, and leans his forehead against mine, watching me. I lick the seam of his lips and moan at the taste of me on him. That seems to be his undoing. Before I can take my next breath, he thrusts into me. We both groan at the feel of him finally inside me.

"Oh, fuck, Ads," he pants breathlessly.

I'm doing this to him. It's intoxicating.

He doesn't allow me to adjust to his size before he's giving me exactly what I want, what I need, what I crave. All I can do is hold on to his shoulders and claw at his back when he hits my G-spot.

"Yes, harder!" I moan.

I keep rocking with him, digging my nails into his shoulders, and he fucks me fast and hard, pulling almost all the way out to just slam into me again and again.

He devours my mouth, swallowing the sounds of my pleasure. "Squeeze me just like that."

I do what he demands. Clenching my pussy around him as he fucks me relentlessly. I use his shoulders as leverage, matching his thrusts. Needing to taste him again, I reach for his lips to kiss him. Only Jax isn't kissing me. He's fucking me with his tongue in rhythm with his thrusts. He starts rolling his hips, rubbing against my clit with each penetrating drive.

He sucks my lobe into his mouth. "Come for me, Ads." He's my undoing. He thrusts two more times until he follows me into orgasmic bliss, moaning my name as he comes. I've barely had time to catch my breath when he whispers, "We're going to do that again and again. I want you to feel me tomorrow."

I can only moan in response.

"Hey, you okay?" Connor asks as we leave the park. Since he's returning to Europe soon, he wanted to take me to lunch. Lunch turned into a walk around Central Park before we head back to meet up with everyone else.

Turning to look at him, I notice he's a few steps in front of me. I didn't realize I stopped walking. I shake my head. Kohen isn't here, and even if he were, Connor wouldn't let anything happen to me.

I'm safe.

"Yeah, sorry. I thought I saw someone."

Connor is instantly on alert, searching the area for him.

"It's fine, Connor, just my imagination," I tell him, even though my skin is still crawling. I can't shake the feeling of him being out here, watching me. It's like this every time I leave my apartment. One of the best things about New York is that almost anything can be delivered, so it's not like I *have* to leave for anything.

He comes back to me and wraps his arms around my shoulder. "You have nothing to worry about. He can't hurt you anymore."

I give him a weak smile. "I know."

He tips my chin so I'm forced to look into his eyes. Since he's a giant of a man, I have to tilt my head all the way back. "Kohen isn't going to get away with hurting you. He put his final nail in his coffin the second he laid his hands on you." His voice is eerily calm, as if he's not talking about what I know he's talking about.

"The police don't believe us," I remind him.

He rolls his eyes. "We don't need the police for justice, Adalynn. Don't worry, soon you'll never have to think about him again."

"Love your enthusiasm, but let's not get carried away," I tell the lets-set-free-every-spider-instead-of-killing-them man beside me.

"I won't allow this to go to court, neither will Jax."

I shake my head. "There's nothing any of us can do. Kohen wants to press charges. With the news around this, we're going to court."

"I won't let that happen. I won't allow him to try to paint you as someone you're not."

Is it really that hard to believe though? I am exactly what Kohen told the detectives. I have the medical history to prove just how crazy I am. "It's going to be fine," I lie. "I can handle whatever happens." Maybe if I say it enough times, I'll actually believe it.

"Can you honestly tell me that you're going to be fine if a judge orders you into a treatment center?"

It's the only thing I'm prepared for. I don't see any other outcome, but I don't tell him this. Instead I say, "It won't come to that." It's the same thing I told Logan the other day when we met with the lawyer.

He arches an eyebrow. "We both know it can."

"And you think if it does, I won't be able to handle it?"

"Do you?"

I remain silent and watch the kids on the nearby playground. Now that the temperature has dropped a few more degrees, their mothers are packing up for the day. Winter has swept through the city quickly.

"Do you think I should let it go?"

"Fuck no. I just want you to be prepared. Besides, it's not like I'm going to allow him to go down this path with you. He'll drop the case, Adalynn."

I shake my head. "Don't, Connor. Whatever you have planned, just don't..." I don't want to make things worse, and I don't want to watch another person I care about be dragged in the middle of this.

"Okay, Addie," he says in a way that makes it hard to believe he's going to listen to what I said.

He leads me over to a nearby bench and we watch the ducks in the pond. In a few weeks, this whole place will be covered in snow. The trees are bare, all of their colorful leaves on the floor. There's one left, barely hanging on to the branch to my right. The softest wind threatens to bring it to the ground.

I'm the leaf and Koehn's the wind. He's going to blow straight through me, ruining the lives of everyone I care about. He's my destruction.

"I know you blame yourself," Connor says after a while.

I raise an eyebrow in silent question.

"For the accident. Is that why you didn't tell anyone?"

I hate that I don't need him to explain. He's talking about all the other times that Kohen hurt me, all the other times I stayed with him, hiding the evidence that I was in an abusive relationship. I nod, the guilt weighing heavy on my chest. I've played the 'what if' game so many times in my head I've lost count. The end result is always the same. I would have stayed with him because it was easier than being alone. Being with him, even as volatile as Kohen was, gave me that release I craved. Instead of turning to my hidden blades, I had him to hurt me, to leave bruises that I would later poke to inflict more damage on myself.

For six long years, I've grown accustomed to using any form of self-harm.

He reaches out to turn my head towards him. "Nothing you did or will do in your life will ever justify a man hitting you. Nobody deserves to feel terrified of their partner."

My eyes water.

"You didn't deserve this. This wasn't penance for surviving." He wraps his arms around me. "This won't break you. Don't give him that kind of power."

Easier said than done. I wish I could be who they think I am.

"You're stronger than you realize, Adalynn," he says when he releases me. He uses the sleeve of his jacket to wipe the mascara from my cheeks.

"Thank you," I whisper once he's done.

"Now, let's get back. It's freezing out here."

This is one of the many reasons why I love Connor. No matter what is going on, he always treats me the same. He doesn't try to coddle me like everyone else in my life. One day, when he gets his head out of his ass, he'll make the best husband. I almost choke on air. There's no way Connor is settling down anytime soon.

"What is all this?" I ask Harper, who was waiting for me when I got back to my place. She was all secrets while she helped me with my makeup, hair, and even picked out an outfit from my closet that I've never seen. Now we're standing in the waiting area of an empty restaurant with candles everywhere. There's only one table in the middle with two empty wineglasses.

"Um, I think this is a little much, Tinkerbell." I force out a laugh.

"I think it's just enough," Jax says from behind me.

I gasp, surprised to see him. Harper told me we were having a girls' night, but when I look around to find her, she's nowhere to be seen.

Jax is wearing a black three-piece suit; his hair is styled in that way that makes it look like he just spent all day rolling around in bed, and his eyes are heated as he takes in my cherry-red full-length dress, with the sweetheart neck that's just a little too indecent. It fits me as if it's painted on. It leaves nothing to the imagination. I thought it was too much but Harper insisted that I wear it. Now I'm glad I didn't chicken out and wear the modest blue number I originally planned.

"What is all this?"

Instead of answering, Jax saunters over to me, closing the distance between us. He cups my face. "This, my beautiful girlfriend, is me winning you back."

Before I can tell him that he doesn't need to win me back, that I've always been his, his lips are on mine. I arch into him, seeking more. I use his suit jacket to pull him closer to me. He has a hint of whiskey on his tongue. His hands slip through my coat and he traces the outline of my dress. His tongue dances with mine in a soul-shattering kiss that makes me never want to come up for air. His fingertips leave a blazing path of heat in their wake, my need for Jax growing as I get utterly lost in him. His hands tangle in my hair, and he angles my head back, deepening the kiss. With Jax's lips on mine, everything else disappears. He's all I see, all I feel.

It's intoxicating. He's intoxicating.

The kiss quickly transforms into something more. I can feel his desperation. It's almost as if he's trying to show me how much I mean to him. It reminds me of all those other times. The times when I would completely surrender myself to him and he'd pull away, leaving me before we could really get started.

Is this him saying goodbye?

As if sensing where my head is, he slows the kiss. With a quick peck to my nose, our signature gesture that always steals my breath, he rests his forehead on mine.

"You're it for me," he whispers, his lips brushing my mouth as he speaks.

For how long? He tells me that I'm his, that he's done pulling away, but I know there's something holding him back. Maybe it's our past.

Maybe it's something else. I hate that I feel that I'm on borrowed time when it comes to him.

We're standing in an empty restaurant, my favorite flowers in the middle of our table and candles scattered around. It's all very romantic, yet I still can't help the thoughts that run through my head. We've spent years playing a stupid cat and mouse game. Whenever I felt like this was finally it, he'd pull away again, running from us.

"This is different. I'm not letting you go again," he says as if he has the power to read my mind.

With vulnerability that I usually try to hide, I tell him, "I won't survive losing you, Jax. I need you." I know he loves me, but is that enough to save us? I don't know why, but recently I've felt like I'm going to lose him. I've never been this happy, and when something is too good, it's gone... It's the story of my life.

"You'll never have to. I'm not going anywhere."

I force the dark thoughts out of my head. I don't want our past to keep ruining our present. I want this. I want him. As hard as it is, I have to learn to trust him again. That's the only way we'll be able to move forward. If all I have is right now with him, I'm going to live in the moment. And if there comes a time when he leaves me again, I want to remember this. The way he looks at me as if I'm all that he sees.

"I love you."

"I love you, Ads."

After Jax helps me out of my coat, I turn around to reveal my naked back. The red dress stops right above my cheeks, my dimples on my lower back on display along with everything else.

His fingers trace up my spine, and he groans, "You're going to be the death of me."

My smile is wicked.

"I can't believe you're mine." He pushes my hair over my shoulder and places a kiss at the pulse point in my neck. "I love you, Ads," he whispers in my ear again before turning me around and grabbing my hand.

Instead of leading me to the table, he guides us to the empty dance floor. It isn't until he spins me around in a perfect twirl that I finally notice we're not alone. To our right sits a pianist, who immediately starts to play our song.

The opening cords of "Sparks" by Coldplay have my heart nearly stopping. The last time we danced to our song, I was just *Logan's little sister*. It's the first song we ever danced to. I thought *that* last time was going to be *the* last time I would ever be in his arms again.

I guess not much has changed. I'm still clinging to him, wishing I could keep him forever.

"*My heart is yours.*" Oh my gosh, is he...? "*It's you that I hold on to. Yeah, that's what I do.*" Yes, he's softly singing to me as he twirls me around the dance floor.

I don't think I breathe for the entirety of the song. I'm in awe of this man, of everything that he is, of his love for me.

Please let me keep him.

He tells me I'm strong, that I'll survive anything. It's a lie. I'll never survive losing him.

Please let me keep him.

CHAPTER FOURTEEN

Jax

When we were younger, we made so many promises to each other. I knew then that she was it for me. That's why I tried so hard to keep my feelings for her a secret. If my dad knew how much she meant to me, he'd take her away from me.

After my mom left us, Adalynn was all I had. My dad never let me forget that I was the reason we were abandoned. I thought if I was the best in school, did all my chores, and made as little noise as possible, my mom would come back. I tried to be better so that when she finally came home, she'd want to stay. I thought she'd save me from Wyatt.

Each night, my dad would remind me why we were alone. He always thought hurting me was the worst thing he did. No, his words hurt far worse than his beatings. Those were the marks that stained my soul. Everything else healed over time. Addie is the only one who knows most of my tattoos aren't because I wanted them. They became a necessity... to hide the reminders of my childhood.

That first night Addie found me, I knew I shouldn't have gone into her room, but I couldn't not go there either. I've always been drawn to her. I promised myself that I just needed that one night with her to finally break whatever hold she had on me.

I've always been afraid of becoming my father. I didn't want to be the one who destroyed her, didn't want to give her the power to do to me what my mother did to Wyatt. I know how much he loved my mother. When she left, she destroyed him. He never once raised his voice, or hit me when she was there. He loved me, and that all changed when she left.

The one night turned into two, and then slowly it became a regular thing. I told myself that I kept going back to her because I wanted to prove there was no way someone in this world could be so pure and still love me. After years of hearing my father tell me how unlovable I was, I started to believe him. I spent so much time pretending that she didn't mean the world to me. I allowed her to think she was my dirty secret because of my loyalty to her brother. It was never because of Logan; it was always because of Wyatt.

I wish that I could go back and redo everything with her. I wish I could erase all the times I allowed her to believe that she wasn't the most important thing to me, that she was just my best friend's little sister. Fuck, sometimes when she thinks I don't notice, I see the way she watches me. Almost as if she's waiting for me to pull away again. I want her to know that no matter what happens, I'm not going anywhere.

I just came back from telling Logan that I was going to marry her.

Logan's hand pauses midway to his mouth. He's swirls the amber liquid around in the glass, and I'm sure he's contemplating if it would be worth throwing it at me.

"*That's a $40,000 bottle of whiskey,*" *Connor says as if sensing the same thing.*

Logan sets the glass down harder than necessary. Maybe I should have done this in a more normal setting, but I knew if I asked him over, he'd say no. That's why we're all currently in Connor's office. He's the referee.

"*You didn't even have the decency to ask me?*"

I swallow the smooth, smokey liquid in one go. I have a feeling once I answer him, I won't be able to drink properly without remembering what his fist feels like on my jaw. It's okay though, because after this, I'm meeting Adalynn at a restaurant that I rented out for the evening.

"*Asking for your permission would imply that I'm going to respect you enough to leave her alone if you say no.*"

Connor chuckles silently beside Logan. "*I told you to just ask him.*"

Yes, he did. But I don't care what anyone thinks. I'm going to marry Adalynn. I'm giving him a warning, since we all know he isn't going to be thrilled with this news.

"*Would it make you feel better if I do?*"

"*She's all I have left, Jax.*" *Pushing to his feet, he pours himself another glass at Connor's bar.* "*I can't lose her too.*"

"*She's all I've ever had, Logan.*" *I need him to know how serious I am. I take her ring out of my suit jacket. I've been carrying it with me since I followed her to Kohen's. When we made our first million, I started looking into getting something custom made. It took years for me to design the perfect ring for her.*

She thinks I've spent this time running from us, but all I've done is waited for her to be ready. Everything I've ever done has been for her. She thinks she's damaged, unlovable. She couldn't be more wrong if she tried. She's everything to me. She's... fuck, Adalynn is the air I breathe. I'm done acting as if she's anything less than everything to me.

Logan glares at the ring. "*If you think that I'm going to sit by while you make all these promises to my sister before she knows the truth, you obviously don't know me."*

I'm already shaking my head. "Not yet. Right now I'm going to date her, ensure she knows she's my priority." I don't ever want her to feel as if I'm with her just because of what she did for me when we were children.

"I meant what I said at the hospital."

I put the ring back in its place before I turn to face him. Connor is also standing. It doesn't escape either of our attention how he moves so he's somewhat in the middle of us, ready to stop us if we get into another fist fight. "I'm not going to sit here all night and debate the reasons we belong together. Your sister loves me, I love her, and I'm going to marry her." He opens his mouth but I speak over him, "I'm not going to ask her until she remembers everything, because you're right. That would be unfair to her, but I am going to ask her one day. It would be better for her if we could all get along."

"And if we can't?"

I shrug. "I stopped caring about your feelings at the hospital. All I care about is her."

"And what happens when she remembers, Jax? Do you think she's going to forgive you, forgive us?"

I take my time grabbing my jacket and putting it on. It isn't until I have it buttoned that I finally answer him. "One day she's going to remember. I've done everything I can to make it right, and I'm hoping when she's ready, we can grieve together."

"So you're giving up?" Connor asks.

I can't answer that. Instead, I give the only answer I can. "It's been almost seven years. I think it's time we all start living our lives again." Then I leave them both in his office while I go to surprise our girl. Glancing at my watch, I have just enough time to pick up her favorite cupcakes before meeting her and Harper at the restaurant.

I wish Logan would have given me his blessing, but I'm not giving up. By the time I finally ask her to be mine, he and I will have worked things out. For the first time in years, I have hope, and a lot of that has to do with my sessions with Liv. I'm finally starting to forgive myself for everything that happened. I never thought that could be possible. I thought I didn't deserve her, didn't deserve happiness. Now? I'm hoping that we can finally put our past behind us and move forward.

I haven't forgotten who was stolen from us. I'll never stop searching for answers. I'm just starting to realize that I can have her and be okay. We can save each other from this hell. With Adalynn by my side, we can get through anything. Soon we'll grieve together. Soon we can start our lives again. I refuse to allow the loss of our son to be the destruction of us.

CHAPTER FIFTEEN

Adalynn

The next day, I'm sitting on the balcony waiting for Harper to come over for lunch. The heaters give off just enough warmth. It's a surprisingly tame November day. We have to take advantage of the almost 50 degrees outside. Since things have been hectic at work for her, I had Henry grab lunch at Harper's favorite restaurant to save her time.

My phone beeps to alert me that she's inside. "On the balcony," I call out as I set my phone down. I'm itching to dig into our tacos. I'm starving since I skipped breakfast this morning. "Hope you're hungry! Henry may have gone overboard with lunch." I wave at the spread as I laugh at all the food in front of us. She doesn't laugh with me. "What's up—" The rest of the words die on my tongue when I realize it's not Harper.

He's not here. I fell asleep. Wake up, wake up, WAKE UP!

I rub my eyes, certain they're playing a horrible trick on me. They're not. That's really Kohen taking the seat that my friend should be in. "Harper had to cancel. Something came up at work," he says nonchalantly as if he has every reason to be here.

My phone chimes with another text that goes ignored. It takes too long for my brain to kick in to gear. When I finally realize the situation that I'm in, I'm reaching for the knife before I even think about it. Kohen easily captures my wrist and twists it until I'm forced to let go.

His jaw tightens before he makes himself relax. "I think it's best for the both of us if I forget that happened."

"You need to leave. Logan is on his way," I lie. I keep talking, trying to distract him from my intentions. "He and Connor ran out to get... juice." I use them instead of Jax because I know what will happen if I utter his name right now. Without making any sudden movements, I start to reach for my phone. "They're probably almost here."

Right before my hand comes into contact with my lifeline, Kohen shakes his head in a way a parent silently lets their child know they're misbehaving. "Are you trying to anger me? Do you know what it took to finally get you alone?" He snatches my cell from me and pockets it.

My phone chimes again.

I need to keep him calm. Someone will come for me. Just keep him talking. "Why are you here? I thought your lawyer recommended keeping your distance until the trial?"

He frowns. "They don't know I'm here, Adalynn. You don't have to pretend anymore."

"Pretend? Are you crazy? I don't want you near me. I don't want you to touch me. I want you to forget all about me!"

He reaches a hand out to mine. I'm paralyzed as he caresses my skin as if we're lovers. It isn't until his thumb traces my bottom lip that I finally snap out of it.

"DON'T TOUCH ME!" I yell.

Before I can process what's happening, he grabs me and hoists me over his shoulder. I thrash against him, fighting every second of being his prisoner again. I kick, bite, and punch his back. Nothing I do slows him down as he heads to my bedroom.

No, god, no... the memory of that night comes swift. I remember him leading me to the stairs at the beach house. I hid the scalpel, and when he turned, I stabbed him.

This can't be happening. Not again.

"Please, Kohen, just leave," I beg.

With more gentleness than I knew he could possess, he lays me down on my bed. His body follows. "I'm not going to hurt you. I just want to talk, Adalynn." He brushes my hair out of my face as he hovers over me.

I refuse to be a victim again. Using as much strength as I can in this position, I head-butt his face. It barely fazes him. I think it hurts me more than him.

Slowly, he smiles, showing his bloody teeth. "Tsk, tsk, Addie. You know what happens when you misbehave."

"So you do bleed," I mock, spitting in his face.

He leers at me, a giant of a man compared to my broken self. And in this moment, I realize how much power he has over me. I have no way of fighting him. His vile smirk says it all.

I need to play this smart if I want to make it out of this alive.

After he wipes my spit from his cheek, he reaches into his pocket and pulls out a knife. I whimper as he holds it to my throat. "I don't want to use this on you." He waits a second to see if I'm going to try anything. I don't. "I tried visiting you in the hospital but they didn't leave your side. You have to know I didn't mean to hurt you."

"This coming from the man currently holding a knife." With each word spoken, I feel the blade press deeper against me.

"Are you going to behave?" he asks as if I'm a dog.

Swallowing my anger, I bite out, "Yes."

"Good girl." He pockets the knife again.

I can't call him crazy a second time. I don't want to see that knife ever again. *Think, Adalynn. Think.*

"Kohen, you need to go before they come back." I try to rationalize with him. "We can't be together anymore. We're not good for each other."

He caresses my face. "We're perfect together, Adalynn. Nobody can keep us apart. I won't let them. We're meant to be." He's unable to see how irrational he's being. It's as if he's flipped a switch and became this madman in a blink of an eye. The once-helpful doctor is gone.

"I don't want to be with you."

He leans back as if I struck him. "You have no idea what I've done for you... for us! We're going to be together! We're a family!"

Does he realize how insane he sounds? I can't even force myself to ask him what he means. I'm afraid of what other ridiculousness will fly out of his mouth.

"I WISH I NEVER MET YOU!" I scream.

"You don't mean that. I know you love me!" He leans down and sniffs my hair. I cringe at the closeness. "If it weren't for Jax, we could all be together!"

"I could never be with you. You put me in a hospital!"

He continues to talk as if I haven't spoken. "Once he's out of the picture, everything will go back to normal. I'll make you so happy. Once you see everything I've done for us, you'll understand how much I love you. Nobody will ever love you more." He resumes tracing my lips with his thumb. It takes everything in me not to bite him. "Don't worry, my love, he won't be a problem anymore."

My eyes widen in fear. I think I stop breathing. "What do you mean? Where is he?"

Kohen's smile is anything but charming. "I don't want to worry you about the details. Soon, he won't be able to ruin our lives anymore."

I hate that he's still poisoning my life and those of the people I love. He's not the god he thinks he is. I refuse to let him have any more control over me. I won't let him hurt me or anyone I care about. The days of me cowering in fear are over.

"You'd be dead if I didn't stop him," I remind him. "You think he's going to be lenient again when he realizes that you didn't stay away?"

"I'm not afraid of him."

"Yes you are." I can't help but laugh at the coward caging me in.

"I'm not afraid of him," he repeats, as if saying it twice will somehow make it true.

"The fact that you're here when you know he's not speaks volumes."

Instead of responding, he checks his Rolex as if he's pressed for time. It's an obvious risk for him to be in my apartment but he's willing to risk everything for me...

Why? I'm nobody special.

Leaning in until his breath mingles with mine, his lips brush against my mouth. I try to turn my head but he grips my chin, halting my movements. "Remember that everything I've ever done is for our future. Once you come to your senses, we can be a family again." He licks his lips before slamming them against mine, attempting to rape my mouth with his tongue.

When he finally pulls away, all I want to do is erase every single memory of him. Kohen makes me feel dirty. "We will never be a family! I HATE YOU!" I scream.

He doesn't take his eyes off me as he slides from the bed like the snake he is and slinks out the bedroom door. With a sad smile that doesn't reach his eyes, he says, "Ask your precious Jax what really happened when you were taken to the hospital after the accident."

All self-preservation gone, I jump off the bed, chase after him, and yank on his arm. "What do you mean?"

"If he really cared about you, he wouldn't have spent the last six years lying to you." He opens the door. "Everything they've ever told you has been a lie. You can't trust any of them... especially Jaxon." He sets my phone on the foyer table before leaving, taking all the warmth with him. I keep calling out to him, desperate to know more, but he's long gone.

My veins fill with ice, and my body shakes uncontrollably. I sink to the floor and wrap my arms around my midsection to protect myself from the memories that bombard me.

"It's going to be okay, Ads," Jax whispers in my ear after he helps me to my feet.

I stare at the three graves. My family. Gone. All because of me. There's an empty spot next to my dead sister. The blood drains from my face as I imagine the hole that's yet to be dug. How long before I give up and force them to etch the last name in stone too?

"It's never going to be okay again. They're...gone... I can't... do... this... anymore." Jax clutches me in his arms as I look up at him. "How are we going to get through this?"

"Together."

I shake my head as I step out of his embrace. "That was stolen from us too. We have no future."

Jax moves towards me, and I step back. "We're not over. I came back to make things right between us. I don't want a life without you. You're it for me."

The thread that I was barely holding on to snaps. I close the distance between us and bang my fist against his chest. Over and over again. I don't stop. I can't. I'm possessed. "This is what you wanted! You left when I needed you the most! This is all your fault! You let us down. I hate that I ever loved you!" I scream at him until my voice becomes hoarse.

Tears I thought were long dried up fall. Fuck, how is it possible that someone can have this many tears in them? You'd think it would be an impossible task, yet here I am. Drops cloud my view as I bang my fist on him. Still, he doesn't once make a move to stop me from hurting him. He stands immobile as I take everything out on him. He did this. He deserves this. I can't see anything past my grief.

"I promise I can fix this!" he pleads once I lower my hands to my sides. "I love you."

His wet face enrages me. "I hate you! My whole world collapsed that night and you did nothing! I feel like I'm dying. Every day I wake up and pray that it was a horrible nightmare. No matter how much I wish things could be different, they're not. It's your fault. I can't breathe, Jaxon! I don't want to live anymore!"

"I know! Don't you think I know that, Ads? I would trade places if I could. I had to stay with you."

"I wasn't the one who needed you!" I scream.

"I needed you to live!"

I point to the spot next to Hadley. "That won't stay empty for long. Every second, for the rest of my life, I'll wish it was you. You're dead to me too."

"I'll fix this. We'll be whole again," Jax vows to me as he looks up to the sky. "You won't be lost forever. I'll bring you back to me."

I watch as he bows his head before I turn on my heels. "Your love destroyed us," I whisper over my shoulder.

As the car pulls away, I turn my head and watch Jax. He's fallen to his knees. I clutch my chest at the sight of him. Maybe I should let go of everything before I'm gone too. I hold on to the very same blanket Jax brought to me a year ago and lift it to my face. God, I swear it still smells like him. Something inside me breaks, reminding me that the pain is never ending.

I thought I only visited their graves the one time...

I was wrong. What else have I been wrong about?

I have no idea how long I've been glued to the entryway floor, but eventually I force myself to get up. As much as I wish that Kohen was trying to get inside my head, I know what he said means something. He knows something about me, something that I've hidden so deep within myself I can't even remember what it is.

Yet he knows. That's what kills me the most.

With shaky legs, I grab my phone and send off a single text to the only person who can help me unlock the truth.

Me: I need you.

I don't bother saying anything else to him. There's no need. Powering down the device, I grab a throw blanket off the back of a chair, head outside, and wait for him.

After today, there's no more hiding. After today, I'll finally know the truth.

Chapter Sixteen

Jax
Five months ago

It takes everything inside me not to throw the freshly wrapped present against the wall. Instead, I settle for punching the hardwood floor over and over again. Nothing can control the anger radiating off me. Fuck, I messed up!

She thinks I'm pulling away again. I'm... fuck, I don't know what I'm doing. As much as it kills me not being with her, I can't. It's not fair to her. I'm being selfish by going back to her. I just... fuck, I wish she would remember! I need her to remember him, to remember what we lost.

I can't help but blame myself for all of this. I know she blames me too. All of my actions have led us to this point. It's because of me that he's gone. And her scars... every single one of them is because of me and what I allowed to happen. Every time I notice a new mark on her skin, I wish she'd use my body as her canvas. I hate that she continues the battle and harms herself because of all of those feelings locked inside her.

The grief she feels is too much for one person to bear. It kills me. The realization that for her to remember, she'll remember everything. She'll remember how much she wanted him, how I left them. She'll remember what really happened to Hadley. As much as I want her back, I wish that particular memory will stay lost forever. She doesn't need to relive that night.

If I could take all her pain, I would.

Every time I think she's coming back, she retreats to her shell again. Still, I always find myself trying to push her just a little bit so she's forced to remember. As much as I tell myself to leave her alone in the blissful lie she lives, I can't. It's not fair to her.

That's what I tell myself at least, but sometimes I think I'm just being selfish.

I want her to remember so she can come back to me, so we can finally grieve together, so I'm not in this alone anymore. When I'm at my lowest, I find myself so angry with her, which is unjust and unfair to her. It's not her fault that the grief of what happened was too much for her. I know that, but on days like today, when I'm wrapping a present for Asher, I can't help the little flicker of resentment I feel towards her. Of course, then I feel worse, because I would rather suffer alone than have her here with me. I'm in constant agony. With each passing day, I hate myself a little more.

Logan made me start seeing Olivia, suggesting it would help me get closure. Olivia warns me what will happen if I force Addie's hand, but I still have hope.

These days, hope is all I have left.

Connor can't believe I'm okay with her dating Kohen, but I don't have a choice. I can't be honest with her, and as much as it kills me to see her with someone else, as long as she's happy, that's all that matters. Maybe one day she'll remember everything we've been through and she'll come back to me.

But, fuck, when I see him with her, all I want to do is slam his face into the nearest wall. Sometimes, I think she wants me to tell her to leave him, to be with me instead. I can't though. Not when I can't be who she needs, when she can't be what I need.

Sometimes it gets too hard to pretend that she's not the most important thing to me. Sometimes it just gets too hard. Loving her is too hard.

Even though it's not her fault, I can't help but blame her for forgetting him. Why was she so easily able to give up on him while I'm forced to live in this perpetual hell?

Logan was right. I want her to remember because then I won't be living like this alone. I should want her to stay in her blissful ignorance but it seems... wrong.

Wrong for me. Wrong for Asher.

In this moment, I'm fucking angry with Adalynn all over again. I hate that she forgot him when I'm constantly reminded of him. I hate that she can give up. She never gave him a chance... gave me a chance.

I don't know how much time passes, but I finally find the strength to get off the floor and put Asher's present with all the rest of them. Half of the walk-in closet is full of the presents we've never been able to give him. The other is filled with what I hope are clothes in his size.

One day we'll get him back...

When that day happens, I want him to know that we never stopped searching for him. I refuse to let him think he was forgotten. As much as Addie tries to live her lie, I know deep down she knows the truth.

She has to, right?

Fuck, I hate this. Connor and Logan always try to convince me that I need to stop, that this isn't healthy. They don't understand that I have to keep buying him things. I have to do this...

This is my way of keeping his memory alive... Because his mom had to forget him.

Chapter Seventeen

Adalynn

"Ads!" Jax shouts as he rushes into my apartment.

Before I have time to respond, he's already barging outside and dropping to his knees in front of me. Jax runs his hands all over my body. "Are you okay?"

No. "Yes." My voice sounds flat.

"Your phone is off."

I pat the seat next to me. "We need to talk, Jax. It's time." I don't need to elaborate. We both know what I'm referring to. For the past five weeks, we've been living a blissful lie with whatever ties us to our past hanging over our heads like a dark storm cloud. Not anymore.

Slowly, he takes a seat beside me. His hand finds mine, and I cling to him as if he's my anchor.

In the back of my head, I know that he's the only one who has the power to pull me all the way down, drowning me in our past that's filled in agony... the very past that I chose to forget because remembering is too... everything.

As I cling to him, acting as if just his hand in mine has the power to save both of us, I pray that I'm finally strong enough to know the truth.

We've come so far. I can't lose us. Not again. I won't survive it.

His knee bounces. He's nervous. "What happened? Why was your phone off?"

I refuse to tell him about Kohen. I can't. Not yet. After. I'll tell him after. First, I need to know what everyone, including my ex-boyfriend, knows. "For the past few weeks, I've had the same dream. Every night, I close my eyes and I dream about that box in my parents' living room."

He gulps.

"Whatever happened to us, I know that box is a part of it."

"Yes," he answers the unspoken question.

I turn so that my back is against the arm and I'm facing him directly. He can't escape me, not this time. "Tell me what was in the box."

"I can't."

"I'm remembering more." I take a deep breath when he tenses. "We were at the cemetery again. I told you I hated that I ever fell in love with you. I blamed you." With everything in me, I hated him. Even now, I struggle with that knowledge. Because it's has to be a lie. I love him. He's a part of me. I can't think of any reason I'd feel that kind of to-my-core hatred for Jax.

We're soul mates. We belong together.

He drops my hand. I feel the loss immediately. "I hated you, Jax, with everything in me." I was consumed by rage. I wanted him to feel just an ounce of what I felt. He remains silent as I collect myself. "I didn't care what happened to you."

"I know, Ads. It's okay to hate me."

I shake my head. I refuse to believe that. "Why, Jax? Why did I hate you?"

"I can't, Addie." His voice breaks as he pleads with me to stop, to not do this, not ask this of him.

In the back of my mind, the worst fear takes hold. No, this can't be right. I hate that I voice my deepest, darkest fear out loud. "Tell me you didn't cause the accident." He stills, becoming a statue. "Tell me that my family isn't dead because of you!" My voice gets louder with each word, until I'm screaming, "Tell me, Jax! Tell me you didn't cause the accident!"

He shakes his head. "I had nothing to do with any of it." He grips my hand. "Emily Hayes was the driver. I was on the plane going back to New York," he reminds me.

I release the breath I didn't realize I was holding.

I know I lost my family because of her, but there's something that happened that night, something I'm missing, something everyone knows but me. "Then why did I hate you?"

Jax's silence reminds me that he has the keys. He's keeping my secrets to himself. I can't believe I thought today would be different. I thought he'd finally open up to me. Maybe Kohen was right, and Jax's just going to keep lying to me.

"Trust me enough to still want to be with you once I find out."

"You just explained to us both how much you used to hate me." He sighs in frustration. "I wish that hate was misplaced, but it wasn't, Ads. I don't deserve your love."

"I know that's not true, Jaxon." I pick up his hands and kiss the tips of his fingers. "Trust our love. We can get through anything together." Even though everything in me is begging me to drop it, I can't. I need to know. "There's not a world where I could ever hate you. That world doesn't exist, Jax."

He does nothing but stare at me. His gaze traces over each part of my face, trying to memorize every inch of me as if he's not sure how much longer I'll be here.

"I'm not going anywhere. I love you."

"You're the love of my life, Adalynn. I breathe for you. When I thought I was going to lose you... I don't exist without you." He kisses my nose. "You, Adalynn, are my life." He kisses the left side, then the right side of my cheek. "I thought I lost you."

"I'm right here. I'm not going anywhere."

"You don't understand. We didn't know about the accident until *after* we landed in New York. They refused to tell Logan anything over the phone. We had to wait. For the entire flight, I died a thousand times over."

A sob escapes my throat as I think about how I would have felt if our roles were reversed. Agony. I would have been in pure agony.

"When I finally saw you lying in the hospital bed, my entire world stopped. Every moment we ever had flashed through my mind. It wasn't enough. I wanted more time with you."

"Jax, I—"

"I was helpless while you lay there, fighting for your life. I knew I couldn't live in a world without you in it. That night, I promised to not leave your side until you woke up." His eyes start to fill with unshed tears. "I didn't break that promise, Adalynn."

"I know." Connor told me.

"I was frozen... waiting on you to come back to us. Nothing else mattered."

My breathing speeds up. "Something happened while I was in the coma." I don't ask. Deep down, I know. I feel it in my bones.

"Something happened when you were in the hospital."

Whatever happened is what shaped the person I am today. It's the weight I always feel. "Tell me Jax. I need to know."

Silence.

"Why did I hate you?" I feel like I'm shouting but the words are barely audible. Somehow he hears them though, and he stills.

That's when I realize the truth. Jax is broken too.

It's as if his world is falling apart around him, crumpling with each shaky breath he takes. "Are you sure you want the answer to that? Once it's out, Addie, I can't take it back. I need you to know I've been doing everything in my power to fix what I did."

Yes.

No.

Yes.

He looks as if he's going to be sick. I thought watching my family die beside me, while I sat helpless to do anything, was the worst thing that could ever happen to me...

I was wrong.

Jax keeps talking, but I can only focus on one word. The second Jax says our son's name, I wish I could take it all back. That heartbreak that's always been inside me, waiting to come out, is back. And with it comes all my memories.

Asher.

Asher. James.

Asher James Chandler.

I repeat his name over and over again, until the letters blur together in my mind. My lips are moving but nothing comes out.

Jax was right. Everything is different now. Love isn't enough. There are some things you can't come back from.

With our son's name, Jax opened the vault. All the memories are tumbling out. I was protecting myself and now, almost seven years later, the pain is still unbearable. I trace the scar on my stomach.

How could I forget I was pregnant?

I remember the first time he ever let me down. When he left me crying on the airport floor, I promised that I would protect myself and our baby from him. I would never let him disappoint Asher.

For eight long months, I excelled at avoiding him. I screened every one of his calls and locked my windows when he came to visit. His name was never spoken from my lips again. I lost count of how many nights ended with me screaming at my parents.

They tried to make me talk to him. The last few months of their lives were spent in a constant state of fighting. All because of Jax. The only bright side was Asher. He was the light in my life, and I failed to protect him.

I can't...

My head hurts. I'm not breathing right. It feels as if something is lodged in my throat, constricting my airway. It's too hard to fight for air. It's all too much...

Jax is saying something but I can't hear him over my screams. I'm finally remembering everything, reliving it as if the accident is happening all over again. All of my memories from before were a lie. All these years, the guys have been protecting me from my darkest memories, my darkest truths. They helped me form a web of deceit so thick I began to believe it too. And the truth disappeared.

I'm breaking and I don't know how I'll ever be whole again. Forgetting our son isn't the worst thing I've ever done...

Chapter Eighteen

Kohen
Six years ago, May 21st

The entire drive home from the hospital, I played out how the evening is going to go. I've planned out everything so tonight is perfect. I know that she's going to be grateful for all of the effort I've gone through to make her happy. Once she sees all of what I've done for her, she'll forgive me.

She has to.

I took the time out of my 24-hour shift at the hospital to make the evening special. I even spent my lunch picking up her favorite chocolate and the purple hydrangeas that she loves just so much. Personally, I can't stand the smell, but for her, I'll allow them in the house... at least for the night.

I've already picked out what movie we're going to watch after we eat the dinner she has waiting for me. Right before the opening credits start, I'm going to surprise her with a weekend getaway visiting the Redwoods in Northern California.

Instead of taking a much needed nap at the hospital, I spent the time *practicing my speech. Just to make sure it was perfect, I went through it one more time before I pull up to our house. Everything has been thought of—tonight it supposed to be perfect.*

Pulling the visor down, I practice my smile one more time. I need Em to see that I'm not the same person I was before I went to work.

"Flawless," I mutter to myself. Grabbing the flowers and chocolates, I go into the house to have a perfect night with my fiancée before I whisk her away. I try to keep the anger out of my voice while I call out, "Babe, I'm home," to the empty kitchen.

Em usually has the table set, dinner at the ready for my return. The oven, microwave, and fridge are all empty. I crack my neck, a habit I've learned to help relieve any sudden bursts of anger coursing through me. It's at the tip of my tongue to remind her of our rules, but I decide to save it for another time. Tonight is supposed to be about us; it's supposed to be perfect.

As much as I hate improvising, I do what I must to keep the evening running smoothly. I'll take her to her favorite place by the Santa Monica Pier. I'll tell her to get dressed. I'll wine and dine her. Then we can come back and watch her favorite movie, and she'll be so thrilled that I'm taking her away we won't even make it to the end before we're wrapped in each other's arms.

All plans of going out are obliterated when I finally find her on the couch. Her face looks worse than I imagined. The butterfly stitches I put on her eyebrow do nothing to mask her black eye. Her cheek is still swollen from when I had to remind her of her place. I'm sure her makeup would do a decent job of covering the yellowing around her forehead, but that's not what concerns me the most. No, it's the clear handprints around her neck. It's Southern California. There's no way she'd get away with wearing a scarf.

Okay, so we'll have dinner delivered. I can't risk being seen with her in her current state. I don't want to chance running into anyone from the hospital while she's like this. They'll ask too many questions. They'll immediately jump to the conclusion that it's my fault. All they'll see when they look at Em are the shiners I left her. They won't even question what led to it. They'll be on her side like the last time. No, we definitely won't be going out this evening. I still remember how long it took me to find another placing during my residency because of what happened last year. Not again. I can't risk my career for her. She's just going to have to learn to fall in line, or she won't be stepping foot out of our home.

Wearing my practiced smile from the car, I grin down at my fiancée. "How does—" Words escape me. Her mother's urn is missing from our fireplace.

My fingers twitch at my side. Tap... tap... tap... tap... tap. Keeping my eyes trained on her, I give nothing away. If she's going to try to leave me, she can grow a pair of balls and tell me that she's about to break my heart.

Slowly, I walk around the couch until I'm crouched in front of her. I run my hands over her eight-month belly just as I do every night. I pretend I don't notice how she scoots back into the couch as if she's afraid I'd hurt our unborn son. I would never hurt an innocent child.

"Were you nice to Mommy today?" I ask my boy.

Discreetly, as if I don't know what she's doing, she stands and pretends to fix the already perfect pillows on the other couch. "You're home early."

Ah, she thought I wouldn't be back until tomorrow. It's all falling into place. She wasn't going to be here when I came back. She was going to attempt to leave me. I thought she'd learn her lesson from last time. I guess I didn't hit her hard enough. I won't make that mistake again.

Grabbing my phone out of my pocket, I make sure the house is armed. "I was thinking of ordering in tonight," I say as I try in vain to engage the security system. Wow, she somehow shut it off without it alerting me.

If I wasn't so blindingly mad, I'd almost be impressed with the lengths she went to.

This wasn't a spur of the moment decision. She's been planning this.

"*That... so... sounds... gr... great.*" *She stumbles over her words, her nerves giving her away.*

Ever so slowly, I move to the mantel. My smile is all teeth. Her blue eyes widen in fear the closer I get to the spot her mother's urn should be. I stop when I'm inches away. Now is a better time than any to let her in on my year-long secret.

Just picturing what my secret is going to do to her has a laugh escaping me.

"*What's so funny?*" *she asks.*

How fucking stupid you are. She's inched herself farther away from me and closer to the front door. As if I won't catch her before she even reaches it.

"*I wasn't going to tell you this but I don't think we should keep secrets from each other.*" *I take another step in her direction. She takes a step back. The cat and mouse game we're playing is getting a little old. "Do you remember the bonfire we had last year? The one right before we moved here?*" *I wanted to purge ourselves of the bad memories from our last place. I thought if we were really going to start over, we should start with new things that wouldn't remind her of the time when I cracked her skull against our dining room table.*

"*You mean the house fire?*" *she sasses back.*

I nod, a smile firmly planted on my face. In my head, I'm seething over the fact she thinks she's earned the right to disrespect me in the home that I provide for us. She just earned another slap for the attitude.

I burnt the house down along with her passport, license, and anything else she could try to use to leave me. "Last time you left, it took almost two weeks for me to find you. I went mad looking for you. I thought the worst had happened."

She gulps.

"I was sick with worry. I didn't know if you were lying in a ditch somewhere... if someone kidnapped you... So imagine my surprise when I realized you faked a burglary and left."

"I'm so... sorry, Kohen."

She's not, but she's about to be. I take a tiny step in her direction. "You needed to be punished." She still does.

"You did... I... le... learned my lesson." If she did, then I wouldn't be imagining all the ways I'm going to hurt her. She's no longer the mother of my child. She's now the surrogate. I only need her until she births my son. At thirty-six weeks, I won't have long to wait.

I think I always knew this would happen. That's why my trunk is currently stocked with everything we'd need in case she ever goes into early labor. It's not like we go on vacation a lot. My job would never allow it. No, I always knew this would be a possibility.

She's just a surrogate. Soon I won't need her. I'm already thinking of all the different ways to plan her death, so it doesn't put a stain on my record. There are so many possibilities.

"I'm so... sor... sorry."

"You know the one thing I hate more than stuttering is lying, Em." Another step closer. "I wanted to really hurt you but I couldn't tell you what I did. I knew you wouldn't forgive me."

"You don't have to tell me." Her voice is barely above a whisper. Her hands shake, showing me her fear. I shouldn't enjoy it but I do. I really, really do.

"Oh, but I have to. I want to watch your face when I take the last piece of your old life away from you."

Tears are already falling down her face. "I'm sorry, Kohen." She knows that I know she was going to leave me. Good.

I hate punishing someone when they don't know the reason. No, that's a lie. I think I enjoy it more. It gives me a reason to hurt them just a lit-

tle bit worse. Because I don't tolerate ignorance and stupidity. I can't wait to remind her of all her misdeeds. I can't believe this is where our night has gone.

She has nobody to blame but herself.

On the outside, I'm sporting the charming smile I show the world. On the inside, I'm yearning to finally tell her the truth. I've lost count of how many times I've imagined this moment. I hope she tries to fight me. It's so much more fun when she does.

"I flushed your mom down the toilet before I came to get you, Em." I point to the spot the urn should be. "Those precious ashes you wanted to take with you when you left me are nothing more than remnants of a bonfire."

She gasps, horrified. I'm so happy I finally told her the truth and that I'm here to witness her crumble to the ground with the knowledge she will never escape me. I will always be one step ahead of her.

"I told you what would happen if you ever tried to leave me again."

She cradles her stomach. "Kohen—"

"He's not going to save you this time, Emily."

Chapter Nineteen

Adalynn
Six years ago, May 21st

"Don't talk, Mom. Save your strength. I know you love me. I love you so much. I'm so—"

"You have nothing to be sorry for... Be the person... I raised. I'm so proud of the mother... you're becoming."

I'm paralyzed, stuck in the back seat. I stretch towards my mother with the only hand that seems to be working, the one that was trying to get Asher to kick back. I haven't felt him move since our car went off the road. It's too dark outside, the rare southern California storm raging on and making it impossible to tell how long we've been here. How long it's been since my baby stopped moving...

"Mom." The blood dripping into my eyes is making it difficult to see. "Asher isn't moving. I think he's—"

"Addie, are you bleeding? Any... contractions?"

I touch my wet thigh. It's covered in blood. "No." I lie to my mom. I don't want her worrying about me. There's nothing she can do, nothing any of us can do. It's too late.

When my mom speaks again, I can hear the fear she's trying to hide. She's scared. She's going to die and her grandson might already be dead. Oh god, I can't do this. I need to get out of here. I can't be here when she dies, while my baby stays unmoving inside me.

"Everything is... going to be... okay. Deep breaths. You need to... remain calm. Someone is coming."

"Mom, what if he—"

"No, Addie, you have to... stay... positive... for Asher."

She starts coughing, the kind of coughing that sounds like she's choking on a lung. That realization makes my heart stop. It's the red dots flying on the dashboard that have me screaming in terror. Blood. My mom is coughing up blood and the only thing I can do is sit here and watch her suffer.

When she finally stops, she whispers. Somehow I know this is the last time I will ever hear her voice. I can tell how much pain she's in and how much effort she expends to say the words that most people take for granted. Nobody ever realizes how much they take for granted until it's too late. Even words. There's so much I wish I could take back. Especially over the past eight months. I've made everyone around me miserable. I've made my parents hate me, and now I'm the cause of... this. I'm the cause of their deaths.

"Hadley will... need... you. Be st-strong for her. Be strong for... Asher. Tell Logan... how much I love him. Never forget... how much I love... you... three. I'm sorry."

"Mom!" I cry, my stomach cramping and the pain causing me to pass out. I don't know how much time passes before I'm coming to again. "Mom?" I ask. I'm met by the most terrifying silence.

Our parents are dead. We're orphans. It's all my fault. I did this.

I turn, trying to find the source of all the wetness. I rub my head on my shoulders, to wipe away the blood so I can see. The driver's side window is broken, and the wind is blowing all the rain into the car, soaking us even more. I try not to think about what caused the glass to shatter. If I do, I'll break, and I don't have the luxury to fall. Hadley and Asher are counting on me.

"Hadley, can... you... hear... me?" My teeth are chattering so much, making it difficult to talk. I reach out and check her pulse. It's there. She must have passed out from the pain. Like me, *I tell myself, refusing to believe anything else. Today is not going to be the day I lose everyone. "We're going to... be... okay... someone will... find us," I tell Asher and Hadley. Being trapped in the back seat means I can't do anything to help shield either of us from the cold. I rub my pregnant belly, begging Asher to move. "Come on, baby, give me a kick. Remind me who's in control of my bladder."*

The stillness of my stomach frightens me.

He's sleeping too, I tell myself.

I try in vain to reach for the swim bag on the floor. My legs aren't listening to my brain. Every bone in my body screams in protest as I attempt to maneuver. If I can get free, I can save them. I have to keep trying. I whimper as I use my only working limb to get my other arm out from the locked seat belt. Blood is steadily pouring from my face, making it even more difficult to see in the darkness of the wreckage. It takes everything in me to lean forward and stretch out my arm. I scream at the top of my lungs as I clutch the strap. The second I try to pull it to me, my hand spasms and my grip releases.

"FUCK!" I say as the blackness takes over again.

The flashes of lightning wake me. I'm disorientated. It takes a few moments to realize that I'm still trapped in the car. There was an accident. Both of my parents are dead. I turn to my still-sleeping sister. Just like the baby inside me, she lies motionless.

"Hadley, I need you to wake up now," I say louder as I start to tap on

her arm. "Hadley!" I shake her enough that I can see her eyes start to open.

"Addie?" Her voice is barely above a whisper. At first, I think I imagine it.

"Hads?" I ask again, to be sure I'm not going crazy.

"Wh... what... happened?" She cries out in pain when she tries to get up.

"Shh, don't try to move, okay? We've been in an accident but it's okay... We're okay."

"Daddy!" She screams out to him.

"Look at me, Hadley! Hadley, look at me!" Holding her gaze, I take a deep breath. "We're o-kay. It's go-going to be okay."

"Is he...?"

"They're just sleeping," I say, panic rising in my chest. Now is not the time to tell her the truth.

"I'm so tired."

"I know, but we have to stay awake until help comes, okay?"

Hadley squeezes my hand. "I'm so... co-cold."

I cry, "I know, Hads. We ha-have... to... hang on. Help is com-ing."

"Addie, I don't... I don't want to... die," Hadley cries, breaking my heart. She's only thirteen. She's barely lived. Now is not her time. We're going to survive this. We have to. I can't lose her too.

"Help is coming! We just have to sit here and wait for someone to rescue us. We're not dying. No, we're all going to live long, healthy lives. You're going to grow up and dance at Julliard! Asher is going to paint like his dad." I need to keep her talking.

"Jax?" She guesses, my last comment giving it away. I should care, but I don't. Claiming Jax as the father seems so insignificant compared to what is happening right now.

"Yes," I admit for the first time out loud. "He's going to need you so you have to stay alive, okay?"

"*K,*" *she says softly, too softly. Her hand goes limp in mine.*

"*Hadley!*" *I choke out.*

She's unresponsive. It doesn't matter how many times I shake her, she's not waking up. She still has a pulse. I can see her chest rising and falling with each shaky breath she takes. I tell myself that we're going to be okay, that help is coming.

Just a little longer. We have to hang on just a little bit longer. *I keep repeating the mantra, switching from rubbing my unmoving stomach to feeling Hadley's pulse on her wrist.* Just a little longer and someone will find us.

"*Come on, Asher, move for Mommy.*"

We're going to be fine. Hadley is still breathing. Just a little longer, and someone will find us.

Something flashing catches my attention right before sleep takes over again. I blink the fuzziness away and use my broken left hand to wipe the stickiness from my eyes. I don't need to feel the cut on my head to know I'm in bad shape. I'm losing a lot of blood. I see another flash and hope blossoms in my chest. Help is here.

Finally. "*We're going to be okay,*" *I tell Hadley and Asher. Just as my eyes are closing, another flash goes off. That small glimmer of hope vanishes as quickly as it came. Nobody is here. Nobody is going to save us. It's my phone.*

Phone!

I try to move towards it, but my feet aren't responding. I can't feel them. I haven't been able to feel them since the car hit us. I refuse to tell myself what that means. I can't be paralyzed. If I'm paralyzed, then I can't walk to the road to flag down a car.

My sister stirs right before she lets out a whimper that will forever haunt my soul. Hadley and Asher need me to keep fighting. I'm all they have left. I gulp as I stare at Mom's lifeless body slumped over the passenger seat. The flash goes off again, alerting me to a new text. It's exactly what I needed. That little flash illuminates my surroundings, allowing me to see where I dropped my swim bag and attempt to reach for it. I wrench the bag onto my lap. Every cell in my body tells me to close my eyes, that the pain will go away if I close them. I can't. I need to cut my way out of here.

"It's okay. I got us," I say to Hadley and Asher as I begin the slow task of sawing through my seat belt with the nail clippers.

I don't know how much time goes by before I'm free. It feels like hours. The angry sky has long since settled. Moving quickly to my sister, I check her pulse. I need to make sure I'm not crazy and I wasn't imagining her breathing this entire time.

Thump... thump... thump.

It's there. Faint. But there. I'll settle for faint over nonexistent.

"Hadley, open your eyes. Please. Open your eyes for me. We're all going to be okay," I plead with her.

Pulling my unmoving legs onto the seat so I can lean over, I search for my phone on the ground. It's gotten lighter outside, making it easier to distinguish different shapes in the car. When I finally pull my phone out from under the now soaking-wet jacket, I waste no time calling 9-1... and the battery dies before I can press the last number.

"FUCK! FUCK! FUCK!" I scream over and over again.

"Ads?" Hadley chokes out.

My head whips around so fast I feel faint. "We're okay. I'm going to get us out of here," I vow as I grab the nail clippers and start the agonizing task of cutting her out of her seat belt too. "You have to keep talking, okay. Tell me about the boy in your class." I don't need to elaborate. Hadley's had a crush on him for the past few months. He recently transferred and my sister can't seem to stop talking about him.

"I'm scared." She hiccups.

Careful to not hurt her swollen face, I wipe at her tears. "We're going to make it, okay? Do you hear me, Hads? NOTHING is going to happen to you." I wait until she nods before going back to the task at hand. "Just keep talking so I can focus on getting us out."

It takes a few seconds, but she does what is asked of her. She talks about nothing important, and with each word that leaves her bloody lips, I say a prayer to a God I didn't know I believed in until tonight. By the time the sun starts to rise, I'm almost done. Just a few more cuts and I'll be able to tear her seat belt apart like I did mine. Forgetting about the pain, I work faster.

"Adalynn." Her voice is full of terror as she clutches my hand.

I look up to find her staring straight ahead. Crap, the sunlight breaking through the clouds is enough light for her to see Dad. I wish I could take it all back. I wish she wasn't seeing something that I know is going to haunt her. I don't need to turn around to look for myself. Our dad's lifeless body, glass piercing every inch of his face, isn't something either of us is ever going to forget.

I grip her head in my hand, forcing her eyes on me instead. "Watch me."

She's struggling to breathe, and her pupils are too wide, panicked.

"We're okay. Slow, deep breaths," I tell her.

"Ads... I..." She doesn't get to finish her sentence before she starts choking.

"Hadley!" I scream as her body goes limp. I put my ear to her chest and check her pulse. She's not breathing. "FUCK!" With strength I didn't know I possessed, I tear apart her seat belt and angle her lifeless body so she can lie across the seats. I hear a snap of a bone breaking. I don't have the time to check if it's hers or mine.

With the only hand that seems to be working, I start compressions, breathing into her mouth every fifth set. As I press on her chest, using my bodyweight to help, I scream at her, begging her to come back to me.

"YOU'RE NOT DYING. I'M NOT LOSING MY FAMILY ON MY BIRTHDAY! HADLEY, COME BACK TO ME!" I attempt to *breathe life back into her still unresponsive body. I repeat this process over and over again. Sweat mingles with the blood on my face and drips onto her. I don't give up. I can't. "COME ON, HADLEY, BREATHE!" I scream at her as I lean down to offer another breath of air. Leaning back, I check her wrist. "Hadley?" I ask, terrified that I'm imagining the steady pulse under my fingertips.*

The seconds it takes for her to open her eyes feels like a lifetime. My body sags with relief, tears falling freely, as I hug her.

"Don't ever scare me like that again."

"It hurts," she cries out in pain.

"We're getting out of here." I try her door. "Just keep talking, Hads." Gritting my teeth, I slam my body against her door, trying with every-thing left in me to pry it open. "Fuck!"

"I don't want to die."

I turn back to her. "You're not going to die! You, Hadley, are going to survive this. You're going to live a long life. You just have to keep talking. Can you do that for me?" I refuse to let her die. If there's a God, he can't have her. It's not her time. She has so much life she needs to experience. No, He can't fucking have her. He can have me instead.

Hadley is pure. The world needs her in it, not me. Logan will take care of Hadley. I caused this. If anyone else dies tonight, it's going to be me. I'm the only one who deserves this.

Not her. Please, God, not her. Don't take her from us.

"I love you," she mouths before her eyes roll to the back of her head and her whole body seizes.

"HADLEY!" I cradle her head as I watch helplessly, begging God to save her. "Take me instead!" I'd rather be with my parents and Asher than live a life without her.

The second she stops, I check her pulse. She's not breathing. It takes twice as long to bring her back. As her eyes flutter open again, I vomit onto the floor. I ignore the taste of copper in my mouth and wipe at my lips.

"Keep breathing. I'm going to find a way out."

She moves her mouth but nothing comes out. My body feels like it's filled with cement, making each movement harder than the last. Still, I don't give up. I can't. Hadley needs me.

"Save us," I pray. The second I try to move Hadley, she screams in pain. "Shh, you're okay," I say as I check her body. Her foot is pinned to the door. Vomit forgotten, I sag to the floor, and any fight I had left in me evaporates. There's no getting Hadley out. She's trapped. She's going to end up just like my parents... like Asher. "Someone is coming for us," I tell her as I brush her hair out of her eyes.

She clutches her chest as her body starts to seize again. My eyes widen in horror. I check her pulse. Nothing. Just like all the other times before, I start doing compressions. I have no idea how long I stay like this. I keep going, breathing for her, refusing to let her die. My hands feel as if they're broken but I don't give up. I refuse to give in to the pain.

Hadley needs me. So, as much as I want to give up, I can't. It's time for compressions. My teeth bite through my lip, the pain so intense I'm afraid I'm going to pass out. Still, I somehow find the strength to keep going, to keep fighting for her.

"You can't have her!" I scream. "Take me instead!"

Minutes tick by. The sun is shining bright, illumining the horrors within, all while my baby sister tries to die in my arms. I continue to push, telling myself that help is coming. The more time that passes, the slower and weaker my movements are.

"I'm so sorry, Hads," I say over and over again through my weakening compressions. I keep breathing life into her until I know it's too late, and even then I don't stop. I check her pulse. Still nothing. It's time to let her go. I can't, not yet. I'm not ready to lose another person I love. Not today.

I don't know how much time passes, but eventually it all becomes too much. I can't go on. I can't even lift my arms anymore. They seem bro-

ken. It's too late. I can't save her. I check her pulse one more time, praying that the last breath was enough.

Nothing. She's gone.

Somehow, I'm able to maneuver my body so I'm cuddling Hadley's. I lie with my head on her chest, silently begging for the impossible. I beg for it to beat. I beg for Him to take me instead. If possible, I'd give her my beating heart.

I did this. It's all my fault.

Today is supposed to be my seventeenth birthday. I'm responsible for all of their deaths. I'm cuddling my lifeless sister's body, while my unborn baby lies motionless inside me. I'm just turning seventeen and I've already lost everything.

"Take me too," I beg Him. "Take me too."

Chapter Twenty

Jax
Six years ago

It's been three days since my world ended. Seventy-two hours since I learned that if Addie lives, and that's a big if, she is never going to survive the grief of losing her family. She will forever be haunted because of the carelessness of one driver. It's been 4,320 minutes since I left her side. I promised her I wouldn't leave her no matter what, but I need a moment.

I need a moment where I'm not surrounded by the constant grief of everyone around us. By my friends begging me to "step up." By the constant beep... beep... beep of the monitors, reminding me she's barely holding on. Each breath she takes seems as if it might be her last. I can't sit here for one more second and wonder if this beep will be the last one until she flatlines again. What if they can't bring her back to me?

I need her to survive. There isn't a world where she doesn't exist. There can't be. If there's a God, there's no way he's that cruel.

Stepping into the hospital chapel, I see an elderly man on his knees, his hands pressed together, his eyes closed, and his mouth mumbling words only he can hear. I take the last pew at the back. Sliding to my knees, I mimic the man in the front. Hands pressed together, eyes closed. That's where our similarities end. I'm sure he's praying for a loved one to get better... He's praying for a miracle.

I'm praying to a God I don't believe in. I'm praying for revenge. I'm begging, pleading, to the unjust being upstairs to give back what He's taken from us.

As I sit here on my knees, I think about all the people who are more deserving of His wrath. I think about all the murderers, the rapists, the disgusting animals who should have been wiped from this planet, and all the unfairness in this world.

Why is it always the innocent ones who suffer? Why are they the ones dealing with so much loss, so much heartbreak, when there are more deserving monsters in this world?

I can't help but think about Wyatt... my father. He should be the first in line, not my sweet, innocent Ads. I pray that it's Wyatt lying in the morgue instead of the Maxwell family. Out of everyone I know, my father is the most deserving of death. Yet, here I kneel, surrounded by all the unfairness, while someone like my father is tucked safely in his bed for the night.

My lips are moving, but I'm not praying. No, I'm naming everyone I know who is more deserving of this fate. I beg Him to take it all back... to take me instead. I beg and beg for so long that my knees scream in protest.

"Jax, you need to—"

I shake my head at Logan. I'm tired of him and everyone else telling me what I need to do.

"Jax—"

"Leave me alone."

They don't understand. They expect me to carry on as if my everything isn't lying unconscious in a hospital bed, fighting for her life. They don't understand. Without her, I'm nothing. I don't exist without her. I can't. She needs to live. If she doesn't, I can't go on either. No matter the cost, I refuse to live in a world without Adalynn in it. I'll follow her into the next.

This can't be her fate. No, I need more time. I'm not ready to say goodbye. So, instead of doing everything that is expected of me, I will keep praying to a God I don't believe in and remind Him of all the people who are more deserving of this fate than she is.

Present

"Just breathe, Ads. It's going to be okay." I try to talk her through her panic attack. I lay her hand over my chest and mimic taking deep breaths with her. "You just have to breathe."

Fuck, maybe Logan was right. Maybe I am pushing her too hard. She's my whole world. I can't do this without her. I won't lose her again.

"That's it. Deep breath in... slowly out." I kiss her forehead.

I don't know how long we stay like this, wrapped up in each other, while I remind her to breathe. That's all I need. I don't need her to be strong. I'll be strong enough for both of us. I just need her to be here with me. I don't need much... just her... just the other half of my soul.

I rub my hands over her body, down her arms, more to make sure she's still here with me, that I haven't fucked up completely. My mind is racing. I can't stop the images of all the times I've seen her at her lowest. I can't lose her again.

"It's going to be okay," I promise, my arms wrapping tighter around her.

Chapter Twenty-one

Adalynn

He's staring at me as if he can't believe I'm real. I lean into his touch, welcoming the warmth he gives me. He keeps stroking my face. "What do you need?"

My chest feels as if it's filled with cement. Just inhaling small puffs of oxygen seems to take everything out of me.

I remember it all.

I look at my arms, regarding the scars differently now. There're three pins in my wrist from when I broke it in four places and contin- ued to perform CPR on Hadley. I shredded my tendons trying to save her. The paramedics did everything they could. Her internal bleeding was too severe; she died in route to the hospital. I'll never forget forc- ing the paramedics to take her first, to save her. I chose her over myself. I thought I already lost Asher. I couldn't lose her too. I didn't know that he was still alive until it was too late. He died because I made them choose her and she still died. I lost them both.

This can't be real.

"Talk to me," Jax begs.

"Asher." My voice breaks, saying our dead son's name. It doesn't sound like me at all.

This isn't real.

My eyes glaze over as I stare at my son's father, the father who didn't forget him. He's been mourning what we lost alone, all because I was too weak. I didn't protect our son... I didn't even have the strength to remember him. I took everything away from us. I'm the reason we're broken.

His gaze is cautious, as if he doesn't think I'm really here. "Do you want to talk about him?"

Desperately. I just don't know how. What could I possibly say to make it okay? I had one job as a mother. To protect our son. And I couldn't do it. If I'd gotten out a little sooner, would he had made it? How could I forget everything about him?

"I'm so sorry, Jax."

Bringing my hand up to his lips, he presses the most delicate kiss to my skin. "You have nothing to be sorry for."

"You had to mourn the death of our son." His eyes squeeze shut from the pain of my words. "You were all alone with your grief. I'm so sorry, Jax."

"Ads," he says, his voice hoarse with emotion. "There's something I—"

"Asher... he's the reason you've been pushing me away?" I rub at my chest. The ache is almost unbearable. "Because I forgot about him?"

"No, you didn't choose to forget him, Ads. Your mind was protecting you from the loss of him. Nothing that happened is your fault. I've never blamed you."

I keep crying, until the tears dry up and I'm sobbing uncontrollably. Still, Jax holds me, never once letting go as I mourn our son all over again. Jax promises it's going to be okay, even though we both know it's not. How could it be?

Everything I've ever known has been a lie. When the pain of losing him became too much, I tried to kill myself. I remember Jax visiting me, helping bathe me when I was in the psych ward. I forced everyone to stop talking about him. I couldn't stomach hearing his name, being reminded of what we lost.

Eventually my mind closed him off to me for good. Until now.

Time continues to move forward while we're stuck in this painful bubble, each of us remembering our boy in silence.

Needing to know everything, I finally find my voice. "What was in the box?" For some reason, I know there's more. It still doesn't make sense why I blamed Jax. Was it my grief after losing them? Was Jax my verbal punching bag? Did I force myself to hate him because it was easier than remembering the life we created together?

He sighs. "It doesn't matter, Ads."

"It does. It matters to me." I shut him out for the entire length of my pregnancy. He never got to see what Asher looked like, hear his heartbeat. "I'm sorry I shut you out," I say aloud, realizing I kept him from knowing his son. I don't know how he can stand to even be in the same room as me. I'm the worst kind of monster.

Jax wipes his eyes. "You have nothing to be sorry for," he says again.

"You wanted to be there for us and I wouldn't let you."

"It's okay, Ads."

No, it's not. "Will you tell me what was in the box?"

"I got him a New York onesie and taped to the card was a key."

I'm almost too afraid to ask. "A key?"

He closes his eyes while he answers. "A key to the place I bought us."

Jax bought us a place together... He was trying to make amends and I was too stubborn to let him in. "I'm so sorry."

"Shhh, you have nothing to be sorry for," he repeats, lacing our hands together. "I need you to tell me what you remember of that night."

I don't want to relive it again, not anymore. "I can't, Jax."

"What happened to Asher?"

The pain in my chest amplifies at just hearing his name. "He died."

Seconds turn into minutes before Jax speaks again. "How did you get that scar on your stomach?"

Insecurity has me tracing my fingers along the raised skin. "It wasn't from internal bleeding?"

Jax shakes his head. The mark is about five inches long, running right above my pelvic bone.

"What happened to Asher?" he asks again.

No. "Stop. I don't want to do this." I cover my ears. *I can't do this.*

"What happened to our son, Adalynn? Why did you hate me?"

No. No. No. I take it all back. I don't want to do this anymore. I want to forget. I can't do this. I can't be here anymore. I need to escape. I need... I need to bleed. I need to feel anything but this. This emptiness.

CHAPTER TWENTY-TWO

Jax

I can't listen to her apologize. She doesn't know that every time she utters those words, I die a little more inside. She's blaming herself because she doesn't know the truth. Hesitantly, I pull away from her so I can find the news article from six years ago.

She doesn't hate me, not yet. She doesn't remember everything. She doesn't remember all the things she's said, all the things she blames me for.

Since the accident, she's tried to leave me and I won't let her go. I don't care how selfish that makes me. I won't allow her to give up. Every time she tries to end her pain, I'm there. I'm always there, saving her, bringing her back to the world she's desperate to escape.

But I wasn't there when she needed me the most, because I thought I was somehow saving her. I thought the only way to protect her from Wyatt was to pretend I didn't care about her or our son. I let her go through the pregnancy all alone. I told her I didn't love her.

I could have fought for her then, but I didn't. I made up a lie and all of us went back to New York instead of staying. We should have been following them home that night, not making our way to the airport. Would the car accident even have happened if I wasn't such a coward? No, it wouldn't have. Somehow she found out about the lie. The lie that cost her and Logan everything.

And how did I make it up to her? I chose her over our son. I wasn't there for him when he needed me. I shut everyone out while I waited for her to wake up. I thought nothing else mattered but Adalynn. I was wrong and it cost me everything.

She keeps saying sorry, as if anything is her fault. The fault has always lain with me.

Once, about a year after the accident, she told me to stop. She begged me to let her go. There was nothing left in this world for her. It was too hard. She didn't want to keep going. Ads believes she should have died that night too. She was wrapped in my arms, pleading with me not to call the paramedics as she slipped in and out of consciousness.

I almost didn't. I almost let her go. I saved her and she hates me for it.

Every single time I see her paint a smile on her face, as if she doesn't have a care in the world, I die a little more. Every single time I see her look longingly at a playground, searching for him, I die a little more. I've lost count of how many pieces of me have crumpled away since that night.

The night of her seventeenth birthday...

The night I ruined us...

May 21st

"Why are you here?" She spits the question at me. "You came today of all days?"

I move towards her, and she takes a step back. "Please, Ads."

She looks as if I slapped her. "You lost the right to call me that." She wraps her hand around her body, as if protecting him from me. "You need to go. I don't want to see you."

I can't let her go. She's everything to me. "I'm sorry. Let me explain." I grab the letter from my back pocket. I knew there was little hope that she'd actually talk to me so I resorted to writing in all down, telling her everything I should have told her months ago. We used to write each other letters all the time. I wonder if she still reads them like I read hers. Adalynn stares at it as if she's afraid it will bite her. "Please, Ads, I just need one chance to explain."

"Wow, I honestly thought he'd tell you." She glances at Connor. "I went back to New York."

I'm almost too afraid to ask. Yet, somehow, I'm able to make my mouth work. "When?"

When she faces me again, I wish she'd stop talking. With each word out of her ruby-red lips, I can practically see her heart breaking. I did this. There's nobody to blame but myself. I thought leaving her alone while she was pregnant was the worst thing I ever did. I was wrong. This is the worst thing I've done to her. I thought I could keep this from her.

I want to beg her to stop, but she doesn't listen. The more she speaks, the more distant she becomes. I'll never make this up to her. I've truly lost her.

"Imagine my surprise when I came all the way to New York to fix this, and you weren't alone."

No, I wasn't. I think I'm going to be sick.

"Imagine my surprise when I saw the pink panties on the floor, the bra on the table."

The letter slips from my hands. I've lost her for good. It doesn't matter that it didn't get to that point. It practically got to that point. I can't even remember her name. I'd laugh if this weren't so tragic. I know if I try to tell her that nothing happened, she won't believe me. Why would she? If she saw the trail of clothes, I'm sure she also heard me trying to forget her.

"I hope she was worth it."

She wasn't.

"Leave. I want to celebrate this day without you."

"But—"

"I want you all to leave." She wipes at the tear that finally escaped, her nostrils flaring and her jaw clenched. "You owe me this. I want to be alone."

All I can do is nod. I want to tell her it was a mistake, that nothing really happened. As much as I tried to pretend that the blonde wasn't Adalynn, I couldn't do it. In the end, I stopped. It doesn't matter though. I still tried to forget her by getting between someone else's legs while she was in California, pregnant with our child.

Instead of telling her all of this, I finally let her go.

Today's her seventeenth birthday. I thought I could make it all better... I thought I could have them both...

My hands shake as I search for the article that has the possibility of taking her from me forever. It's what I deserve. Deep down, I think I've always known...

She's always been too much. Too much brightness. Too much everything. I've never deserved her.

When I turn back to face Adalynn, I pause, phone pressed to my chest. If I do this, I might lose her. I could send her back into a catatonic state. Logan's warning haunts me. *"Does remembering Asher help you or her?"*

I'm doing this for her. I hate what I'm about to do, but I have to. I know she's not remembering it all. She doesn't know the worst part. I can't keep it a secret anymore. She deserves to know what really happened to our son and who's to blame. I let her believe the lies. I made everyone else lie to her.

"Jax?" she prompts.

Her voice is hesitant as if she somehow knows that this, the lie, is what truly broke us. I should do what Logan wants, what Olivia urges. I should keep pretending. I can't though, not anymore. I can't keep pretending that every new scar I find on her body isn't because of this lie. She thinks she hides them from me but I know. I see them every time were together. Each and every mark that covers her skin is because of me and what I've done to us.

She blamed me for everything all those years ago, and even though I know I deserve it, I hope this time it's different. I hope this time doesn't take her away from me for good.

Taking a deep breath, I hand her my phone, having pulled up the article with the headline: *"Fatal Car Crash, Two Survivors."* I continue to read over her shoulder. *"Fatal crash on the 101 took five lives. The driver, Andy Maxwell (46) died on impact alongside his wife, Quinn Maxwell (42) who died before EMS arrived. Hadley Maxwell (13) died in route to the hospital, while Adalynn Maxwell (17) and 32 weeks pregnant is in critical condition in the ICU. Doctors had to perform an emergency C-section to save the life of her premature son. Doctors are optimistic that the baby boy will survive. The other driver, Emily Hayes (24), was also eight months pregnant. Mom and son are remembered by fiancé..."*

Adalynn tosses the phone to the end of the bed. "I don't understand."

I know. Staring deeply into her eyes, I watch as my next words sink in. "Asher is alive."

Chapter Twenty-three

Adalynn
Six years ago

"Are you ready to meet him?" Jax asks softly as he kisses the inside of my palm.

I should pull away from him but I don't. The girl in New York doesn't matter anymore. Nothing but our son does. "Who does he look like?"

Logan left a few minutes ago with a nurse to get our boy. After everything, everyone we lost, he's still here. Asher James Chandler is our miracle baby.

Jax scratches at the heavy scruff on his face. "I don't know... I couldn't... not without you."

I wish I could say I would have done the same if the roles were reversed. I can't though. I wouldn't have been able to stay away. I'm surprised I'm not angry with him anymore. I guess, after you're forced to watch your family die, everything else doesn't matter.

I let Jax hold my hand. He keeps touching me, kissing me as though *he's afraid if he looks away, I'll disappear again. His touch used to set me on fire. Now, I feel nothing. I'm numb. No, numb isn't the right word. I feel as if I'm dead, hanging in the balance.*

This is my new reality and I have to pull it together. I can't keep wishing I was taken too, when I have someone who needs me.

I can't believe that they're gone. "Hadley?" I ask again. I've lost count of how many times her name passes between my dry lips. They keep telling me she didn't make it, and as much as I try, I can't believe she's gone.

I didn't save her.

He presses my hands to his mouth. "I'm so sorry, Ads."

Everyone keeps telling me that. That they're so sorry. It doesn't make any of this easier. Fuck their sorrys. I'm so fucking angry at everyone, at the world, at them. They all died, leaving me here to pick up the pieces. I yelled at Logan. I couldn't stand to see his puffy eyes. I couldn't stomach him hugging me. He doesn't know that I gave up on her, that I was too weak to save our sister.

I'm taking my anger out on everyone around me. I hate this. I hate this person I'm becoming. I used to be happy. Now, it seems like a distant memory, another life, something I'll never be again.

Somehow we survived and everyone else died. I didn't even get to attend their funeral. They were buried while I fought for my life. I can't believe Logan said his goodbyes without me. How could he do this to me? How could any of them think that was okay? They should have waited for me.

Well, I guess Jax did wait for me. Connor told me he didn't leave my side, not even to attend the service. I didn't think it was possible to break any more. I was wrong. Hearing that he stayed here... it crushed me. I know how he felt about my parents. Because of me, he didn't get to say goodbye.

Maybe we can go together.

I can't believe this is my life. When I first woke up, I knew they were gone. Jax, Logan, and Connor didn't have to say anything. It was written on their faces. Still, I had to ask. I had to have them confirm I was an orphan, that my baby sister was dead.

The sounds I made... I didn't know those sounds could ever come out of a human. When Logan whispered, "I'm sorry, Addie," I broke. Hearing that we were all alone crushed me.

Hadley died because I gave up. I was too weak to save her. I let her die. Somehow I have to find the will to live, not for me, but for our son.

For Asher, I'll stay strong. For Asher, I'll keep going.

Jax kisses my knuckles. "I'm never leaving you again."

I can't find the will to respond. It seems as if all the joy has been sucked out of the world. I have to get it together. I'm about to meet our son. No matter how hard I try, I can't. It's as if everything in me has shattered. I'm still there, in the car, trapped, listening to them all die around me.

Why me? Why did I survive?

I'd trade places with Hadley if I could. She deserves to be here, not me. It's all my fault. How am I supposed to be the mother Asher needs me to be when it's taking everything in me to just keep... breathing?

"What's taking so long?" I ask just as an alarm starts to ring throughout the hospital.

"I'll be right back." Before I can say anything else, Jax is already running out the door. From my vantage point on the bed, I can see doctors and nurses running around.

A security guard shouts into his walkie-talkie. "Code Pink. Lock it down!"

Code Pink... Why does that sound familiar?

Before the panic can take hold, Jax is back. "I'm... he's... Ads... I..." Jax falls to his knees. "He's gone."

I'm already ripping wires off my body. "Gone? What does that mean? Where is he?" Jax tries to stop me but it's too late, and I yank the IV out. "WHERE IS HE?"

"Some... someone... to-took... him."

NO. NO. NO. NO.

I was unable to help my family. I was forced to watch them all die, one by one. I thought that was the worst day of my life.

I was wrong. This is.

"Ads!" Jax screams just as my world goes black.

CHAPTER TWENTY-FOUR

Kohen

"How do you know this?" Olivia asks me from where she's perched behind her desk.

There's no need to tell her that I have cameras in everyone's penthouses. They think they're smarter than me. Logan thinks he's a tech genius. He is. However, I've found someone better. Someone who's willing to look the other way for the right price. I've been a step ahead of them for the past two years. And thanks to a twenty-something college dropout, I now know that Jax finally told Adalynn the truth. She remembers their son.

"I want you to keep her sedated." I hand Olivia the prescription. I used to be able to switch out Adalynn's pills for her, but now that she's in a new place, it's too risky. The good doctor is going to have to help me keep my girl numb for a little while longer.

My plan is already in motion. I'll be able to come for her soon.

"I'm not putting her on this." Olivia tosses the paper into the trash.

I place both palms on her desk, caging her in while I get as close to her as possible. "You're going to encourage her to talk about Asher, steer the conversation away from me, and you're going to prescribe those pills."

"She's never been on those before. It's too high of a dosage."

I almost laugh. "Do you really think that other stuff was working? I upped her prescription a year ago. She can handle it."

"She doesn't need to be on medication anymore, Kohen."

No, she doesn't, but I need her on these. I need her to be numb, to be unaware of everything around her, so that when I come for her, it will be too late for her to fight. I don't say any of this to Olivia though. The less she knows, the better.

"She just realized that her son's missing, most likely dead. Trust me, she's going to need all the medication she can get." The lies fall easily off my tongue.

I don't bother sticking around to see if Olivia is going to obey me. We both know she is. There's no way out of the cage I've put her in. Once Adalynn and I leave New York, I'll set her free. I thought I would have to kill her to keep our secrets, but thankfully I still have my insurance policy.

Checking my watch, I notice I have an hour until I'm due back at the hospital. I know that Jax and Connor are at the office, since my phone alerted me to their presence when I first arrived at Olivia's. That means Adalynn is alone, and just like clockwork, I also know she's going to go to the bakery for a treat before she visits the park. I have just enough time to say hi and ask her how she is.

I hate that I had to leave her like that the other day. I hated watching Jax tell her what really happened and not being able to comfort her.

Nobody knows the extent of my love for Adalynn Maxwell, but soon she will.

"Flat white?" the barista with blue hair says cheerfully.

"For Kohen?" I ask as I move around the teenagers to pick up my order.

She slides my coffee and Adalynn's tea in my direction. "Enjoy!"

Instead of telling her she reminds me of a Smurf, I throw some cash in her tip jar, take my drinks, and wait at the table beside the door. From my vantage point, I can see down each direction of the street. If Adalynn came from Jax's, she'll be on the farthest side. If she came from the park, she'll be on the sidewalk closest to me.

My girl is a creature of habit. She'll be on this side. That's why I chose the coffee shop. It's easier for me to "accidentally" run into her. I'm vaguely aware of the table of women staring at me. It's the scrubs. I always draw unnecessary attention in them. Usually I'd smile at them knowingly, but I'm too anxious to be polite. It takes everything in me not to roll my eyes at them.

After what seems like forever, I finally catch a glimpse of her and my breath catches at the sight. She's in yoga pants and a winter jacket that reaches the top of her boots. She's not even trying, and still she's the prettiest woman on the sidewalk. Her hair is in that messy bun I love so much. A few strands have come loose. They keep blowing in her face. Her glove-clad hand moves to tuck the ends behind her ear but the wind just blows them back. My heart threatens to beat out of my chest. My legs are shaky as I stand. I think someone says something when I open the door, but I can't hear them over the ringing in my ears. It's been weeks since I've been able to see her in person.

She must hate me for leaving her like that. I hope she can forgive me. I just need a chance to explain everything to her. I'm sure she has a lot of questions. Hopefully, with tea and cupcakes, I'll have enough time to tell her the truth before I have to let her go back to them. As much as it pains me, I'm not ready for us to be together. I have a few loose ends to tie up before we can leave. I need to make sure nobody follows us first. I can't risk someone ruining us before we even have a chance to begin.

She's on her phone when I step outside. The smile on her face makes it difficult to breathe. Fuck, she's beautiful. Soon, she'll be all mine.

A gust of wind hits me and I swear it brings her smell with it. Holding the warm drinks to my chest, I breathe deeply as I head in her direction. She's at the light, about to cross. Just a few more minutes and we can be together again.

I hope she doesn't blame me for keeping everything from her. I wanted to tell her. I... I couldn't do it. As much as I wanted to, I knew it had to come from *him*. Thankfully, she knows it's because of me. That if it weren't for me, she never would have pushed *him* enough to uncover the truth.

Please don't be mad, Ads.

Her attention is still on her phone. I wonder who she's texting. Probably Harper. It can't be *him*. Fuck, I never even considered the situation she's in now because of me. She's stuck living with *him* because of me. He's spent years lying to her and now she has to keep up this charade for us.

It just shows how much she loves me.

"Ads," I say when she's within hearing distance.

Her smile lights up every part of me. "What are you doing here?" she says, her voice full of awe.

The cups fall from my grasp. It's not my lips she's leaning up to kiss. Those aren't my hands cupping her face.

Fucking Jaxon Chandler! He's supposed to be at work! FUCK!

Chapter Twenty-five

Adalynn

It's been almost a month since my memories came back. I've spent that time locked in my new apartment. Jax resumed his role as my caretaker. He's been bathing me, forcing me to eat and drink. He's even helped me go to the bathroom. I'm almost catatonic but not. I'm here. I just don't want to be. Our son was stolen from us. It's been almost seven years. I know what that means, what Jax refuses to believe...

Connor is in Europe, overseeing the expansion. He's due back in the next few days. Logan handles everything here since Jax has been with me. It's almost as if he's in mourning too. He hasn't left my side since my memories returned. Except when Harper decided we were having a girls' night. She threw on Netflix and painted my nails while I silently cried in bed. She never once asked what was wrong or forced me to talk about it. The only thing she did was force me to eat. She said she promised Jax that I'd eat. So I ate a breadstick. I think I dipped it in the sauce too.

"I'm a good listener when you're ready," was all she said, while she filled me in on everything I've missed at the office, and told me how much she hates my replacement. I couldn't remember a word she spoke if I tried.

I've been lost... stuck in the past.

Today, Jax told me that it was time for him to show me something. We left my place and Jax is bearing all my weight, as he hugs me to him while we wait for the elevator to reach his penthouse. I hope the thing he has to show me is his bed. All I want to do is lie down. Nothing else matters, not anymore.

I told him our love could survive everything...

It can...

I can't.

I want to turn the lights off permanently. I want to give up. I don't want to be here anymore.

This is what they've all been trying to protect me from... myself. I wish I could go back to not remembering him. This is too much. Our child was stolen from us when he was five weeks old. Logan and Connor are the only ones who ever got to meet him.

When we step off the elevator and into his foyer, Jax hands me one of the pictures of Asher that he keeps in his wallet. It's worn. You can easily tell he looks at it every chance he gets. Our baby is covered in tubes, his eyes are taped shut, and he's still the most beautiful thing I've ever seen. The pain I feel every time I see a photo of him is all-consuming. I'm drowning. There's no way up.

"Logan took a lot of photos for us. While I stayed with you, he stayed with Asher."

Then how come he was stolen from us? How could they let this happen? It's hard not to blame everyone for the loss of our son. Now that I remember everything, I'm also remembering how much I blamed every single person for his disappearance.

It's not fair to them. The only one responsible is the person who took him from us.

"Are there any leads?"

Jax shakes his head, his eyebrows knitted and his lips downturned. "Nothing recent but I haven't given up." Hand in hand, I follow him into his home office. "I need to show you something," he repeats as he leads me into the closet. Only it's not a closet; it's an office within an office.

"What is this?"

"Every piece of evidence I've been able to find since that night."

I'm stunned. Each wall is covered in information. One wall includes all the employees from the hospital. I go over to what appears to be the timeline of Asher's abduction.

"I've had the entire list of staff looked into, even their family members," Jax says as I leaf through all the documents. He comes around my side to point to a few stills. "This is who took our son, Adalynn."

The grainy photo shows someone in a hospital uniform pushing Asher's incubator to the elevator. The person's face is obscured by a mask, and a surgical cap covers his hair. But the way he carries himself and his overall frame tells us he's male.

"Our PI determined he wasn't a current employee at the hospital."

I turn away from the photo to Jax. "What does that mean?"

He shrugs. "We think he may have worked there at some stage. That's the only reason he knew where all the cameras were and how to leave the hospital without getting caught."

Jax explains each wall, goes through every piece of evidence he's collected over the years. There are hundreds of newspaper clippings with age progressions of Asher, begging the public to give any information they have. I stop at an image of what he'd look like today and commit it to memory, hoping that one day I'll be able to find him in a crowd.

"We're going to bring him home, Ads."

I wish I could share the same conviction I hear in his voice. It's been six years, almost seven, and we're no closer. Still, I let Jax lead me around the room. The more Jax shows me, the emptier I feel.

For six years, Jax has done everything in his power to give us answers. For six years, I've done everything in my power to forget.

I don't deserve to be a mom.

It feels like hours go by while Jax shows me every little piece of evidence. He wants to set up a meeting with his PI and me. For some reason, Jax thinks that now that I remember I can help bring our son home.

It kills me that I have nothing to offer.

"Can I show you one more thing?" he finally asks as he closes the door behind us.

I nod. My hands are still cradling one of the photos Logan took of Asher before he was abducted, as Jax leads me up the stairs of his penthouse and stops at a door across from his bedroom. He seems to gather strength from somewhere before he unlocks it. He hands me the key.

"I didn't want you wandering in here before you were ready." He steps out of the way so I can see.

I gasp. My eyes can't stay in one place for too long. They jump from the blue-striped walls, to the twin bed with a light grey comforter and matching pillows, to the desk in the far corner. My gaze lands on what would be Asher's bookcases. They take up an entire wall and there's even a little ladder so he can reach the ones at the top.

"Jax—"

"We're going to find him, Adalynn. I'm going to bring our son home."

I didn't think it was possible to love Jax more. I was wrong. This selfless man created a bedroom for the son he's never met, the son that could very well have the same fate as my parents and sister.

If there's a heaven, at least he wouldn't be alone. Somehow, that thought brings just a sliver of happiness.

I spot something on the nightstand that nearly takes my breath away. Without a second thought, I'm already stepping towards Jax's worn copy of *The Giver*—the last book Jax's mom gave him before she walked out of his life. I hold the precious gift to my chest.

"Sometimes I read it out loud in here." Jax says in explanation.

I thought my heart couldn't break anymore. I was wrong.

Jax points above us. "Look up." And then he switches off the lights. The black ceiling is bathed in constellations. The night sky dances just out of reach. "I know you wanted a skylight, but this was the best I could do with the building regulations."

After all these years, he remembered. When we were younger and life became too hard, we would lie out and count the stars. One night, I told him I wanted to have skylights in every one of our kids' rooms so they could fall asleep under the stars. We've made so many secret promises to each other... promises I thought would never come true. Jax and I always seemed like a dream that I couldn't quite reach.

Until now.

Tears stream down my face as I walk over to him. Neither of us says anything as I wrap my arms around him and bury my head into his chest. He holds me while I cover his shirt in tears. Jax presses his lips to the top of my head and squeezes me tighter. His body starts to shake as he finally lets the unshed tears he's been holding in fall. I cradle his face in my hands, my thumbs wiping away the traces of his pain.

"We're going to bring him home," he vows.

We stand in the middle of Asher's room, crying for what feels like hours, while each of us grieves for the child who was stolen from us. I rest my head against his heart, listening to the steady beat thumping beneath the surface. We're going to get through this.

We have to.

"Thank you for doing this, for being a father to our son." My voice is raspy from lack of use.

He wipes the end of his sleeves over my tear-stricken face. "I have one last thing to show you."

Oh god, I honestly don't think I can take any more heartbreak tonight. Still, I place my hand in his and follow him to the walk-in closet.

"Ever since I found out you were pregnant, I've been buying gifts for him." He turns the knob. "I've bought him a present for every holiday, every birthday, and just... just because I was thinking of him."

The entire closet is filled with unopened presents. I see tags that read: from Santa, love Daddy, love Mommy. There's even some from Logan and Connor.

I rub at my chest, trying to soothe the pain there. Every time I notice something new, it feels like someone is slowly ripping my heart from my chest. No, that's not accurate. It's more like someone has my heart in their hands and they're taking a cheese grater to it. It's a pain that permeates all the way to my very being, something I hope I never have to feel again.

All these years of willing blindness, and Jax has done everything he could for our son.

My knees buckle. Jax catches me before I collapse to the ground. Eventually he leads me out of our son's room and into his.

How is this man even possible?

For years, he's been suffering alone. I was so lost, locked away in my head. And here Jax was, being the best father he could possibly be to a son he hasn't met.

Before my memories returned, there was always something holding me back. Always a wall that I couldn't quite take down and let Jax in, and now I know why.

I've never deserved him. I still don't, but I'm going to do everything I can to keep him.

"Don't ever leave me," I beg as I get under the covers with him.

He pulls me over so that my head rests on his bare chest. "I'm never leaving you, Ads. You're it for me."

I lean up on my tiptoes. "Promise me that no matter what happens, you won't help me forget him."

Jax nods. "I promise."

Kissing his chest, I rest my lips over his heart and silently pray that he doesn't leave me. Not that I'd blame him if he did. I've spent the past few years hiding, while Jax has spent the time searching for the son I forgot.

I don't deserve either of them, but I'm going to try to be worthy of them both.

Chapter Twenty-six

Jax

"Why do you keep looking at me like that?" Ads snaps after taking a sip of orange juice.

Because I'm waiting for you to break. I'm waiting for you to lock yourself in Asher's room and try to kill yourself. I'm waiting for you to tell me this is too much. I'm waiting for you to lose yourself... just like every other time before. Most of all, I'm waiting for you to leave me alone in all of this again.

I don't say any of this. Instead, I shrug as if I haven't been watching every move she makes since she found out the truth. "I just like watching you."

It's been two days since I showed her Asher's room. She's started taking naps in his bed. To say I'm worried would be an understatement. Logan hates me. He thinks we're going to lose her again. I'm afraid he's right.

At night, when she's sleeping, I search her body for new marks. She told me she's not hurting herself anymore but we both know that's a lie. I've seen the inside of her palms. Thankfully she hasn't resorted to anything else yet. I just have to stay with her, keep protecting her from herself.

My phone chimes with another text, most likely from Logan. Every hour on the hour, he's asking for updates. I ignore this one and focus on cooking.

I can practically hear her mind thinking while I plate our breakfast. Each day is the same. We get up, she spends time in Asher's room, and I pretend that I'm working while I wait for her to join me in the kitchen as I cook for us. I drink coffee; she drinks orange juice. And just like the days before, we'll finish our omelets and she'll immerse herself in trying to figure out what happened to our son.

I wish I could tell her to stop, but I'm afraid of what will happen when she realizes that he's never coming home, that we'll always be parents without a child. I've spent the past six years searching for him and I'm no closer.

Logan thinks it's unhealthy, and even though I agree, I can't make her stop. She's processing. As long as she's processing, she's still here. She still remembers. So while she processes, I pretend that I'm not studying every item in my home, trying to figure out if I left something that she can harm herself with, all while I watch her.

Please don't let this be too much for her. Don't take her away from me again. I don't know if I'll survive it. I'm hanging on by a thread.

"I'm fine."

She's said the word "fine" so many times in the past two days that I have no doubt that she's anything but fine. Her palms are still red from all the abuse she's given them this week. She didn't even notice last night when her nails dug a little too deep and she started to bleed.

"Just a paper cut," she said as if it were no big deal.

It is a big deal. Instead of arguing, though, I just held her hand while she sifted through the endless paperwork I've collected on each and every hospital employee.

My phone chimes with another text, then another. He'll just show up if I keep ignoring him.

Logan: 911! We need to talk!

Logan: Answer your fucking phone!!!

Logan: You have two minutes to answer me before I come over.

Logan: ANSWER YOUR PHONE!!!!!

Logan: ...JAX!!!!!

The last text has my heart stopping.

Logan: Kohen was at her place.

My hands shake as I type out a response.

Me: When?

Logan: The day you told her about Asher.

WHAT THE FUCK?

That's why she asked. He must have known. How could he know about Asher? The pictures! He's been stalking her for years. Sure, the cops think that it's me but we all know it's him. If he's been stalking her for this long, then he definitely was able to find out about our son. All he had to do was Google her name. It's one of the first things that pops up. Well, now it's the story about the beach house, but it wouldn't take someone long to realize that Asher Chandler is related to Adalynn.

Fuck!

Her phone pings with Harper's ringtone. She puts her on speaker. Never once does Adalynn stop reading the document in front of her. "Harper, I'm going to need to call you back."

"Fine, but we're hanging out tomorrow. I'm forcing you to go outside. I'll text you the spot."

It seems like an eternity passes before Adalynn finally hangs up the phone. Much calmer than I think I'm capable, I ask, "Did Kohen get into your apartment?"

This has her eyes rising to meet mine. "How d-did... you—"

"Know?" I supply for her. "Your brother told me. Why didn't you?" I try to keep the hurt out of my voice, but it's nearly impossible.

She may not remember every detail of the beach house because of him, but I do. I've never experienced anger like that. If it weren't for her, I would have killed him. Fuck, I should have killed him. As much as I try to turn a blind eye to Connor, I know he's not the saint he's perceived to be. He could have made sure that none of this would have fallen on us.

I should never have stopped. Once again, I feel like no matter what I do for her, it will never be enough.

She glares at me. "Why didn't I tell you? Are you kidding me, Jaxon?" She waves her hands around the paperwork in front of her. "I don't care about him. Kohen doesn't matter!"

"Don't, Adalynn. Don't say his fucking name!" I'm seething by this point. He somehow forced my hand in telling her something that deep down we all know she isn't ready to hear. If she was, I wouldn't be con-stantly filled with dread, wondering what she's going to use to end this.

Logan was right. I'm selfish for sharing this with her. I could have done what I've always done and pushed her away again. I could have lied to her. What's one more lie when I've told her so many that I've lost count? Seeing her like this... it's so much worse than when she was in the dark. I wish I could take all of her pain away. I hate watching her break, especially when there's nothing I can do.

I used this as a chance to force her to remember. At least she was happy when she was blissfully unaware that we're parents. If I'm being honest with myself, it's because I didn't want to keep it up. Looking for him without her help kills me. I hated that she didn't even know she's a mother.

I didn't want to do it alone anymore. I'm hoping that there will come a time when we both know we've done all we can and move on.

But how can I tell her all of this? She just found out she's a mother without a child. I lied to her when I said I wouldn't help her forget him again. I don't know if I can keep that promise. All I want is for her to be happy. Watching her lose herself all over again is too much.

She's still here though. She hasn't tried to leave me. That gives me hope. We can get through this. We have to.

"Remember... the important thing is that I'm safe," she says hesitantly.

"Adalynn, why didn't you tell me? How can I keep you safe if you keep things from me?" I wish I could take the words back. I know the second they land. Her face crumbles as if I've struck her.

"Maybe the same way you've kept EVERYTHING from me!" She knocks the chair over in her haste to stand. "Why did I have to find out about our son from *him*?"

Fuck.

In two strides, I close the distance between us. "I'm so fucking sorry, Ads." Thankfully, she doesn't push me away when I wrap my arms around her.

"Would you have told me if he didn't come by?" she asks as she pulls away to look at my face.

No. If he didn't give me the opportunity to finally have the courage to tell her, she'd still be in the dark. "Ads—"

She steps out of my embrace, taking half of me with her. "That's what I thought."

Before I can say anything else, the elevator alerts us to Logan's arrival.

CHAPTER TWENTY-SEVEN

Adalynn

To say my brother overreacted would be an understatement. What I wasn't expecting was Connor to come in with a portfolio of private security we'd be hiring by "end of day." I guess he's back from Europe. I can't believe my life has been reduced to hiring a team of bodyguards.

Since Kohen somehow gained access to our security codes and cameras that are installed at every entrance and exit in the building, he was able to delete any evidence of being there. The police weren't easily convinced that I was telling the truth. It also helped that he had another ironclad alibi.

Thankfully my family believes me.

A few hours later, we've gathered in Jax's office at the conference table. We've just finished interviewing another team and Connor is about to bring in the final candidates. Apparently, my family thinks I need a minimum of three bodyguards at all times. Everyone has drilled it into my head that under no circumstances will I be able to go anywhere without them.

Since my place is too small, Jax suggested that I move in with him. At first, Logan protested, but when he realized that meant that they'd be here, he was practically ready to leave and repack all of my stuff. Moving in with Jax... I... I want to... but I don't want it to be because of Kohen. I want Jax to ask because he wants me here and is ready to take the next steps in our relationship.

"We're already living together," Jax chimes in.

I shake my head. "We have our own places."

He rubs his chin as if deep in thought. "Right, and how many times have we slept apart, Ads?"

We both know the answer. Since the beach house, we've barely spent a few nights apart. When you think about it, Jax has a point. We're already living together.

"All I want is you, Ads. Let's move in together."

My answer is a kiss. A kiss that is quickly broken because my brother pulls me away from Jax, right as Connor returns. The first man to follow him in is massive. He's probably 6'4 maybe 6'5. He's close to Connor's height but his muscles rival my brother's. His red hair is cut short, a well-kept beard covering his face. He's sporting a perfectly fitted suit that's clearly custom made.

"You seem too pretty to be in this line of work." I say that out loud, so that everyone in the room can hear me. Oh my gosh, how embarrassing. My face is scarlet red. Jax growls beside me.

The redhead lets out a chuckle. "I get that a lot." He reaches out a hand to shake mine. "I'm Dawson." His voice sounds familiar, as if I've heard it before. I can't place his southern accent though.

"Adalynn."

He nods to everyone else on my side of the table and starts to introduce his team as they enter. The next man is wearing a similar suit to Dawson; his chestnut skin is smooth except for the diagonal scar that covers the right side of his face. I can spot his gun from here. Just like Dawson, he nods in the direction of my family but shakes my hand only.

"Nice to meet you—"

"Lucas," he supplies.

The next man is dressed in the now-familiar suit, probably reaching just 6'1, and has a runner's build. His nose is crooked, likely due to his profession, and his head is completely shaved.

"Hi—"

He smiles. "I'm Sawyer." His accent is thick, matching Dawson's.

"Mississippi?"

"Alabama."

Interesting, that's where Harper's from.

The last one to file in is a tiny blonde, who has to be maybe 5'2. Instead of a suit, she's wearing skintight black jeans, combat boots, and a black leather jacket. The side of her head is shaved; the rest of her long blonde hair is pulled into a fierce ponytail.

"I'm Reign." She hangs her leather jacket behind the chair across from me. It's then that I notice the two knifes at her hips. She catches my eye. "Not a fan of guns."

Well, okay then. Somehow I think she's the most dangerous of everyone in the room.

Before Connor can take control of the meeting, like he did the last one, Dawson stands and hands each of us a folder. "I insist on doing our own recon," he explains.

The first page is a detailed report about me, including the news article on the accident. Logan tries to shut my folder. "I remember everything," I say as calmly as I can. My hands shake as I push the document aside.

"Props to how detailed you are," Connor says. "You work fast."

Reign smiles. "Thanks, I like to know who we're getting into bed with."

Jax points to the other two men in the room. "What do they do?"

Dawson gestures to Lucas. "For the foreseeable future, he's her shadow." He nods to Sawyer. "We will rotate out, one of us being her far guard while the other rests."

I mock salute him. "Which one of you gets paid to wipe my ass? Is that extra, or do you guys have a package deal?"

Connor jumps in before they can answer. "Ignore her. This is going to be an adjustment."

"Ass wiping is extra," Reign says in all seriousness. And that's the reason I like her immediately—*that* and her weapons of choice.

"Now, if you can sign here." Dawson points to the documents in front of me. "We can get started."

"How do you know you're hired?" I ask.

"Because we've done our research and you need the best. That's why Connor reached out," he counters. Connor, Jax, and Logan all seem to have some sort of weird silent conversation before they try to take the paperwork from me, but Dawson stops them. "I don't care who pays us, but since we're protecting Adalynn, she's the one who's going to have to agree."

With a quick scan of the documents, I see that I'm going to have to wear a tracker. I almost laugh. Jax is already tracking me, so what's one more? I feel safer with the known killers here. I've read their background, and they're right. They are the best. Their hands might be covered in blood but that's what I need. I need a team willing to bypass laws to ensure that I'm safe. If Kohen ends up hurt in the process, I'll take that as a win.

The second I sign, Dawson hands me a necklace with a plain charm —it already has an A etched onto the front. Wow, I guess they really knew they'd get the job. "If for whatever reason we're not in reach and he approaches you, press this button." He turns and shows me the almost invisible button at the top of the charm. "It calls the police, gives your location, and alerts us, along with them." He nods to the rest of them.

The lifesaving device is about the size of a quarter. "Interesting."

"Keep it on," Logan and Jax say at the same time.

While Logan, Connor, and Dawson talk about the next steps, Jax helps fasten my necklace around me. His fingers brush over my skin, causing goose bumps to breakout in his wake. Ignoring the audience we have, he presses his lips to my neck before brushing my hair back into place. I shiver at the contact.

We spend the next hour going through everything. Dawson reviews the new set of rules and how I'm going to have to live the next few months. Hopefully, with the extra security measures we're taking, we'll be able to bring new evidence to the police. We're due to meet in court in a few months. Jax's lawyer was able to get an extension. She knows it's only a matter of time before Kohen messes up and then the judge will rule in our favor.

When I start yawning, Jax stands and holds his hand out to me. "We're going to bed." He looks to my brother. "Can you make sure they have everything they need? Get them access to our place?"

I love how he's been referring to his place as *ours,* even before he found out about Kohen. I guess it kind of is. I never noticed until he started pointing things out, but the space is decorated with my taste in mind. He remembered all the ways I used to decorate our make-believe house when we were younger. We spent countless nights dreaming of our future. Looks like we're here, we made it! It's not what we pictured, but when I look down at our clasped hands, I know that the only thing that matters is that we're finally in this together.

Once we say goodbye to everyone, we climb the stairs to his bedroom. Of course I stop right outside of our son's room. I still can't believe Jax did this. With a deep breath, I turn away from Asher's room and lead Jax into... our room. He locks the door behind us.

"Come here." His arms close around my hips when I'm within reach, and he drags me to him until I'm flush with his chest.

With a mind of their own, my hands wrap around his neck and pull him down to me, until his lips are a breath away from my mouth. We breathe each other's air as the space between us crackles with energy. My skin feels as if it's on fire and the only thing he's doing is resting his forehead against mine. His fingertips play with the hem of my sweater, and each caress leaves me wanting.

"Make me forget everything but you," I say, breathless and needy.

Chapter Twenty-eight

Jax

"Make me forget everything but you." Her words are breathless against my lips.

The need I have for her is too much... She's too much.

Gathering the end of her sweater in my hands, I slide it up, my movements painfully slow. My fingers graze each inch of exposed skin, and my smile is wicked as I squat down to kiss her bellybutton. She sucks in a breath, shivering at the contact. When I finally lift the material all the way over her head, it's my turn to groan. Fuck, the green lace of her bra barely covers her nipples. I know when I get her jeans off she's going to be in matching panties; she always has to match.

As much as I want to pick her up and throw her on our bed, I need to take this slow. I need her to forget about everything but what I can do to her. I want to erase every single memory she has of *him*. Sometimes, when we're like this, it's hard not to blame myself. I wouldn't have to help her forget, if I didn't let her go.

He never deserved her. I won't allow him to have another piece of her.

I lick my way up her body, causing goose bumps to break out across her skin. Smirking, I watch her face as I suck her nipple through the lace, and she arches her back, seeking more. Releasing it with a pop, I give her other nipple the same attention. When I graze my teeth against it, she pulls at my hair.

"Please." Her desperation fuels my hunger for her.

I wrap my arms around her and use her ass to pull her closer to me. Her fingers tighten in my hair. She's rubbing herself against me, searching for her release. Cheeks red, head thrown back, she's the very image of a wet dream. And she's all mine.

My tongue guides my movements as I work my way down her body. The sound of her zipper seems to echo off the walls as I make quick work of taking off her jeans. Just like I knew they'd be, her panties match her bra and do nothing to hide her arousal. I grab her ass cheeks, pull her to my mouth, and breathe her in, loving the evidence of what I do to her.

"Should I make you come like this?" Each word is whispered across her mound. She shudders as I taste her through the wet lace. I wait until she's close before I stop. My cock screams to be released, but I know once I do, this will be over far sooner than I want. I want to take my time with her. I want her panting, moaning my name, begging me to take her. I pin her arms above her head and tell her, "You move, we stop."

She groans in protest but when I take my hands off hers, she leaves them in place. Her eyes are darker; you can barely see their violet hue. When she drags her teeth over her lips, it's almost my undoing.

Fuck. Her pout drives me insane. "When you come, it will be all over my cock."

"Jax," she moans, squeezing her thighs together.

Clutching the lace in my hands, I tear it from her body. "Spread your legs," I order, and she obeys immediately. Fuck, I can see her need for me. Her pussy glistens, and my mouth waters at the sight. I told her when she came, it would be on my cock. But now I'm thinking she needs to come on my mouth.

She wants to forget. I'll make it where all she knows is me.

"Use the wall to support yourself." That's the only warning she gets before I finally taste her without any barrier. I'm not sure who groans louder, me or her.

I take my time sucking her clit. I use two fingers to work her pussy. She shamelessly rides my face as I fuck her pussy. My name is a plea on her lips. I worship her, making her as desperate for me as I am for her. I can feel how close she is. When she's right there, I use my teeth, mixing pain and pleasure, becoming her undoing. I make her forget everything but my name as she whispers it over and over again before she shatters on my tongue.

"You're incredible," I whisper against her skin. Her whole body is flush from her orgasm. This is by far my favorite look. I'm a very lucky man.

Standing, I quickly unclasp her flimsy excuse for a bra. She's still pressed against me, so my chest is holding it in place as my hands roam across her back. I take a step back and the scrap of lace drops to the floor. Ever so slowly, I circle one of her nipples with just my fingertips. She throws her head back at the contact.

"Jax," she pleads, her chest heaving with each raspy breath.

"What do you need?" My voice is deeper, filled with the longing I have for the goddess standing in front of me.

She's still panting from the orgasm I gave her, and I haven't really touched her yet... not in the way we both want. "Please." She moans as she squeezes her thighs together again. She's dripping with need, desperate for me to touch her.

"Please what?"

She tries to shift closer to my cock but I pull away. I love seeing her like this. I squeeze her juicy ass, savoring the moan that falls from her lips. "Kiss me."

I get lost in her lips. My hands tangle in her long hair as I move her towards the bed. I was supposed to be making her forget about everything, but it's me who's getting lost. My need for her is too much. It's all-consuming; she's all-consuming. She sits at the edge of the bed. My lips follow her, refusing to separate us, while her inpatient hands make quick work of undoing my slacks. We both pull them down, never once breaking the kiss. She rubs her thumb over the head of my cock that's poking through the top. It's my time to shudder.

"Ads," I warn when I pull back from her lips.

She looks up at me innocently. "Yes?" She works me through the briefs. I'm desperate for her touch but I don't rush her. I love when she's like this.

She hooks her thumbs through my briefs and slides them down my legs. Gripping her hair, I angle her head back so she's forced to look at me. My cock is lined up with her lips. It's practically bouncing for her touch. "Now that you have me naked, what are you going to do?"

She licks the precum in answer.

I grasp her jaw. Gripping my throbbing cock, I trace her lips with it. "Open." She obeys immediately. "Suck." She's reduced me to one-word requests.

She doesn't disappoint. Bobbing her head up and down, she hollows out her cheeks. As much as I want to take control, I let her go at her pace. I let her get accustomed to my size. She uses her hand to work the rest of my length that she can't quite get down her throat.

"Fuck," I hiss. She's going to make me come. With more restraint than I knew I had, I pull back, grip her waist, and drag her up the bed. My body follows. Hovering over her, I brush her hair out of her face.

"I need you." She reaches between us and lines me up with her entrance.

"You have me." I rub myself against her, and with every gentle brush against her clit, she moans.

"Jax." She's gasping as I enter her, taking her all the way to the hilt.

Fuck. She feels incredible. Her pussy clenches, already trying to milk me. Slowly, so she feels every inch I have to offer, I slide out, then in. Over and over again. I watch every expression on her face. When I hit her G-spot just right, I do it again and again. She claws at my back. Desperate. Seeking more. Still, I don't speed up.

It's like this every single time. We are made for each other.

Her name is a prayer on my lips as I finally let go.

Chapter Twenty-nine

Adalynn

A few weeks later, I wake the same way I have every day since I moved in. Jax is practically mounting me in his sleep. His upper body is lying on mine, his head in the nook of my neck, with one of his legs thrown over my thigh. He effectively traps me to the edge of the king size bed while he has all the room on his side. Typical man.

I wiggle, trying to escape.

"Stop moving. I'm sleeping," he grumbles in his gruff, semiconscious voice that's too hot to handle right now.

"Move over."

Jax lifts his head. His eyes sparkle with mischief as he climbs the rest of the way over my body. My legs open automatically, and I groan when he presses his hips into my already-wet center. That's all it takes. A look of dirty promises from Jax, and my pussy is ready for him and all the things he's going to do to me.

My phone rings from the bedside table. "Ignore it."

His lips are on mine before I can finish speaking. He slides the blanket off me, exposing my body to him, as his fingers dance along my skin. Teasing me. Then he nips at my jaw while his thumb finds my clit, rubbing in circles. I moan into his mouth.

Jax's phone goes off next. We ignore it too.

"Pull my dick out," he growls into my ear.

My hands are already reaching inside, grabbing my favorite appendage. I cry out when he stretches me with two fingers. I'm slick. His fingers move in and out of me easily, preparing me for his thick length.

"Please, Jax," I pant. He yanks my hips up and I feel his hard cock at my entrance.

"We'll be late if you don't move your ass!" Harper calls out from the other side of the door.

I yelp from a combination of surprise and the sensation of Jax thrusting home. The door rattles with the sheer force of my tiny redheaded best friend. Soon-to-be *ex* best friend if she doesn't leave us alone.

"Go away!" Jax yells, never slowing his pace. I bite his shoulder to keep from crying out.

"You have two seconds to open this door before I have the sex-on-legs man downstairs open it for me," Harper yells back. "I told you I had plans with her today!"

I laugh, and Jax glares down at me. "You can never laugh when I'm inside you."

Of course, all I do is break out in hysterics, causing him to roll his eyes before he flops down beside me. "I'm coming," I shout at Tink's new onslaught of knocks.

"No, you're not. That's the problem."

I kiss Jax's grumpy lips. "I'll make it up to you."

He pulls my wrist, stopping me from leaving the bed. "Have dinner with me."

"I thought we had plans at Connor's."

Jax groans. "Fuck, I forgot."

I peck his lips again. "I'll see you at Connor's. Eight o'clock. Don't be late."

He's mumbling something about Connor being a pain in his ass when I leave him to open the door for Harper. Her hand is raised as if she was going to bang on it yet again.

"Do I have time for a shower?"

"No! We're on a schedule. Get dressed. You have ten minutes or I'm going without you." Her southern drawl is more pronounced. Probably because she's irritated.

"Go without her," Jax says, coming up behind me. He rests his head on the top of mine.

She wiggles her dainty finger in his face. "You've monopolized my best friend for weeks. This is our day. No penises. You'll have her back tonight."

He kisses the top of my head. "I'll make a snack for you and let the guards know you're leaving."

Crap! How have I already forgotten about them? It's been almost three weeks since they became my newest accessories that follow me everywhere!

Harper barges her way into our bedroom. "No need. I already filled everyone in." She shoves Jax out the door, and before he can say anything, she slams it in his face. She rubs her hands together like a villain about to reveal her master plan. "Today is going to be perfect!" she announces, then proceeds to drag me into the walk-in closet where she tells me, "You have ten minutes before we leave. Dress fast!"

And because I know she really means I have five, I throw on the first pair of jeans I see, a blue sweater, boots, and a scarf before I hurry to the bathroom to brush my teeth.

"Any wedding bells in the future?" Harper asks the second we stroll out of the salon. After watching a comedy, we grabbed late lunch before she decided we needed to get a mani and a pedi.

I couldn't stop the smile almost splitting my face in two if I tried. "I've been waiting to marry him for as long as I can remember."

"So no more games?"

I shake my head as I link my arms through hers. Reign escorts us to the waiting car with Lucas at the wheel.

"You're happy," my best friend comments once we're inside the warm vehicle.

"I didn't think it was possible but I am. He makes everything better."

"Just promise you won't run off to Vegas and get married. You deserve a real wedding."

"He hasn't even asked," I point out, trying to calm my sudden nerves. I wipe my sweaty palms on my jeans.

"Yet."

I gulp. I want nothing more than to be his wife. I just don't... I can't do a wedding. It's too much. Before everything happened, I spent an embarrassing amount of time planning our perfect day. From the flowers, all the way to the color socks he'd wear.

That was before. Before I lost everyone. Before Asher.

Now, I don't care about anything other than having his last name. Everything else is just a bunch of details. Stupid, unimportant details. I don't need the big white dress that stands by itself, or the stupid four-tier red velvet cake, or the stupid wedding socks that match mine since I planned on having us wear matching Converse. I don't need my dad to walk me down the aisle, or my mom helping me into the stupid, unimportant, big white dress.

All I need is him.

"You okay?" Harper asks, sensing my mood.

"Yeah, just lost in my own little world."

"Love will do that to you."

"So who were you in love with?"

She looks at me as if I've magically grown two heads. When she realizes I'm serious, she laughs hysterically. Harper clutches her stomach, wheezing as she tries to calm down.

"I didn't realize I was so funny."

She wipes her eyes. "You've met me, right? Have you ever heard me talk about a man before or seen me with any?"

Wait. Is it because of her ex-husband?

She seems to know where my thoughts go. "I never want to be tied to anyone again."

"Have you been in a relationship since..." My voice trails off. We both know what I'm asking.

She shakes her head, and her red hair falls in her face. "I can't be in a relationship."

As much as I want to question her further, I know now is not the time. My best friend is many things, but someone who talks about her emotions is not one of them. Can't say I blame her. I'm just as bad. We all have our own issues.

"Come on, give me something. The sex has to be amazing. I mean, look at him. He's practically a walking orgasm ad," Harper demands as she opens the oven.

"Harper! Stop opening the oven!"

"I'm just checking on them! I don't want them to burn."

I've lost count of how many times she's checked on the cupcakes. Between her letting heat out and eating most of the frosting, I doubt we'll have anything to bring to Connor's. I've already had to mix more frosting since she kept "checking it" with greedy fingers. Hopefully the guys don't have a problem with sharing her spit, since she ditched the spoon after I told her no double dipping and has since been using her fingers. Yes, fingers, as in *plural*.

I slap her hand away while I start piping the first batch of raspberry vanilla cupcakes. "A walking orgasm ad?"

"Yeah. A walking orgasm ad. Don't tell me you don't know what I mean."

Oh, I do. That's why I nicknamed him The God years ago. He's a god among us mere mortals. "He's definitely above average."

She rolls her eyes. "Even though you have nothing to compare it to, I guarantee he's better than above average."

"Who's better than average?" Jax asks, stepping into the kitchen.

I scream. "You scared me! I thought you were out with the guys."

Coming up behind me, Jax wraps his arms around my waist and pulls me flush against him. I'm so focused on his lips on my neck that I miss him snagging the cupcake I'm working on until Harper yells, "Those are for after dinner!"

I push him back and reach for it... and I'm too late. He swallows it whole. "What am I going to do with the both of you?" I mumble under my breath.

"You love us," Harper sings, snatching a cupcake for herself.

"Harper!"

She points at Jax. "It's not fair he gets one."

"Oh my god. Can we please remember we're all adults here?" I'm smiling as I get back to work.

"Who's better than average?" Jax asks again.

"No one," I say at the same time Harper says, "You." Knowing there's no point in telling him to drop it, I let Harper explain her turn of phrase.

"I'm a walking orgasm ad?" His grin is smug.

"As if you didn't know," Harper tells him.

Jax jumps on the counter beside me. "Do you agree?"

I roll my eyes. "How does your head even fit in here?"

"So you're saying I give Addie orgasms by walking?"

The oven beeps. Harper grabs the chocolate peanut butter cupcakes and starts the quick task of placing them on the cooling rack. "I'm sure you're well aware of the effect you have on women."

He shakes his head. "Is this really what girls talk about?"

"And guys don't share their latest conquests?" she challenges.

"I don't."

Harper scoops the peanut butter frosting into a piping bag. She's a good assistant, even if she eats most of our work. Shaking my head, I try to focus on the task at hand.

"Probably because your best friends are Logan and Connor."

"And?" Jax raises a questioning brow.

"Logan is her brother, and Connor is...basically her sibling. I doubt they'd want to know *anything* about your sex life."

"You have to wait until they cool down," Jax says.

Pausing, I look over at Harper. She's already frosted two cupcakes and is picking up a third. Well, *frosted* is being generous. I honestly have no idea how she made them look so inedible in such a short time.

"Have you not done this before?" I ask, my gaze shifting from Harper to Jax when he hops off the counter.

"I saw you do it. Didn't look too difficult."

Jax kisses me on the cheek. "As fun as this has been, I have some work to finish." He grabs one of the peanut butter cupcakes before leaving the kitchen.

Harper's greedy hands take another one. "Nobody would want an ugly cupcake," she says with her mouth full.

"Classy." I grab her elbow and drag her to my station, where I spend the next thirty minutes showing her what to do when I could have finished in five. After the first few cupcakes, she finally gets the hang of it. Plus, it's just frosting. Super easy to wipe off so she can try again. Which I make her do until she finally learns how to do it properly.

It takes us another hour to clean up and get ready for dinner. Harper insists on helping me with my hair and makeup again. While we're waiting for Dawson and Reign to join us in the foyer, Harper's phone rings. "Crap, I forgot to send something for work. I'll meet you there."

Before I can remind her it's almost eight o'clock at night, she's already in the elevator on her way down.

Chapter Thirty

Adalynn

"I thought we were going to Connor's?" I ask when the car stops at one of the many entrances to Central Park.

"We are. I just wanted you to myself for a little bit." Jax holds out his hand for me to join him. "Walk with me?"

All I can do is nod as I wrap my scarf tighter around my neck. At this time of year, snow is all around us. Thankfully it's not currently falling from the sky too. It's too cold to snow. Jax wraps a blanket around me—I didn't even see him pack it—and pulls me to him so I can steal some of his heat.

I'm barely aware of our shadows as Jax leads me through the park. After a few minutes of strolling in silence, Jax turns to me with a blindfold in hand. Normally I'd put up more of a fight, but I'm too curious to see what he has in store. It's obvious we're not making it to Connor's tonight.

I turn around and pretend to grumble, "If you make me walk into a tree or something, I'll sic Dawson on you."

His breath washes over me as he laughs at my threat. Once he secures the blindfold in place, his fingers brush down my shoulders, to my forearms, and then he laces his gloved-clad fingers through mine. "Don't worry, I have you."

Taking slow, steady steps, I let him lead me to our destination. I'm already smiling, even though I have no idea what's going on. This is what happiness feels like.

Despite everything we've been through, we made it. Slowly, Jax has helped heal me. With him, I finally found myself again. When I'm swallowed up in our past, he's there, leading me to the light. Because of him, I'm not drowning anymore.

He's everything to me.

After what feels like forever, we finally stop. "Keep your eyes closed until I say." He removes the blindfold. "Okay, open."

I can already hear the excitement in his voice, and I gasp.

There are Christmas lights strung up on every tree. He's even made it appear as if there's a canopy above us. Candles flicker all around us. I'm in awe. It takes me a second to realize that he's turned my favorite place, Cedar Hill, into a bright Christmas wonderland.

I can't make my mouth work, and tears sting my eyes. I'm speechless. This is the most romantic thing anyone has ever done for me.

"You wanted the stars," Jax whispers against the back of my neck before placing a kiss on my racing pulse.

"Is this... are you proposing?" *Oh my god, stop talking.* "I... I... oh... my... god..." I clap excitedly as I spin around and take it all in.

He laughs as he drops to a knee in front of me. "I should have known asking you to marry me wasn't going to be easy."

"YES! YES! YES!"

Jax groans. "I haven't even asked you anything yet."

"It doesn't matter—*yes!*" I jump up and down.

"Stop talking, Ads, so I can do this properly." Jax grips my trembling hand in his.

This is really happening. I can't believe that, after everything, we're finally here. Jaxon Chandler is about to ask me to marry him! The ring box in his hand makes a loud *pop* sound that breaks the silence.

Oh my god!

My eyes are solely on Jax's. Everything I've ever wanted is coming true. He's finally going to be mine! *Deep breaths. Pull it together. He hasn't even asked you yet!* I don't try to fight the tears stinging my eyes.

"From the first moment I met you, I knew you were different than anyone else. I think it takes a special someone to spray a complete stranger with vinegar." I laugh through my tears. "I've loved you before I was ready, before I knew what love was. There's no one in this world I want to be forever tied to, besides you. You've always been it for me Adalynn Grace Maxwell.

"You're my soul mate, the person I want to spend this life and the next with. I don't know if there's anything beyond this life, but if there is, I promise I'll always find my way back to you. Because you and me, Adalynn, we're written in the stars. We're tied to each other, now and forever. Marry me, Adalynn Grace Maxwell."

I'm sobbing as I give him my left hand. "Yes!"

He slips the beautiful sapphire ring, with a starburst of diamonds surrounding the oval of the gem, onto my finger. Once it's in place, I throw my arms around his neck and he fuses his lips to mine. This kiss feels like nothing we've ever experience before. It's so much... more... everything...

"Surprise!" Everyone yells when we step off the elevator and onto Connor's marble floors. I was staring at my ring again so they caught me off guard.

Harper's face is mischievous. "So... I didn't have a work thing," she says in explanation and takes my hand in hers to study my ring. "Tell me everything!" Harper begs as she follows everyone else into the dining room, where there are chilled bottles of champagne waiting for us.

As I start to recount everything that took place in the past hour, Jax pops a bottle and pours each of us a glass. He wraps his arms around me when he reaches my side and kisses the top of my head. "Here fiancée," he whispers as he hands me my glass.

My smile is so wide I worry that my face may break in two.

Dinner is filled with delicious food, laughter, and so much joy. I'm afraid I'm going to wake up and this will all be a dream. I can't believe we're actually here. We made it. We're finally engaged.

"Do you have a date picked out?" Harper asks after a bite of one of the cupcakes we made together.

"He just asked her," Connor points out.

I shake my head as I look at my fiancé. I don't want to wait too long to be tied to him. It feels like I've been waiting for this my whole life. I would go down to the courthouse right now if it were up to me.

"Tomorrow?" he asks.

I'm already nodding my head, but Logan squashes that idea quick. "You're not marrying him in a courthouse. I'm walking you down the aisle."

"How quick can we plan a wedding?" Jax asks.

"Grab a seat and join us," Connor says to the person behind me before I can answer. I don't have to turn to know he's talking to Dawson. Reign went back to our place while Dawson stayed with us. Since there's not a chance Kohen could get in here, Jax and I insisted they both leave. But when Dawson refused, Connor let him use his office to finish up whatever he had to do while we all ate dinner.

Harper's fork is frozen halfway to her mouth as she stares in shock at the man behind me. Her eyes never stray from my bodyguard as he takes one of the empty seats across from her, his penetrating stare trained on Harper. Looking around the room, I notice that everyone seems to be watching the two of them watch each other. Connor is glaring at Dawson, as if his presence is suddenly offending him.

"Wine?" I ask, trying to divert the attention from Dawson, who's blatantly staring at Harper while she ignores him as if he's not even there.

Nodding, she reaches for the Pinot Noir I was attempting to pour for Dawson and pours a hefty amount into her own glass. She downs it all before refilling it again, taking a much smaller sip. Dawson has yet to look away from her.

Holy fuck, this is awkward. It isn't until now that I realize Harper has met almost everyone on my team except for the man in question and Sawyer.

Connor starts typing away on his phone. I'm sure he's trying to piece together whatever this hot mess express is in front of us. I take a healthy sip of wine, barely tasting it with all the tension in the room.

"Do you two know each other?" Connor asks, breaking the silence.

Neither of them answers, which clearly pisses him off. Before he can demand the response we're all dying to know, Harper turns to Dawson, "How long have you been with Glass House?"

He pulls on his collar. "Going on four years now, since I opened the doors."

She stabs at her cupcake. I have no doubt she's wishing it was him instead. Why though? "Your *family* must be so *happy* you're back."

He loosens his tie, his face a darker shade of red by this point. "I haven't told them yet."

Interesting.

"How do you guys know each other?" Connor asks again.

Dawson breaks their stare down and turns to Connor. "I thought I recognized her, but I'm wrong. The person I thought she was is dead."

He shrugs, as if this isn't a big deal, then picks up his glass of water and takes a sip.

"Tell me more about yourself, Dawson. I'm sure everyone is *dying* to get to know you more."

Yup, they definitely know each other. They have the whole jaded lover thing going on. I wish everyone would hurry up and finish their cupcakes, so I have an excuse to get her alone.

"I'm a hired gun. Not much to tell."

"I'm sure there's more to you than that." She keeps going, poking the lethal bear across from her. "Wait, if you're a 'hired gun' wouldn't Kohen be able to match your price? For all we know, you could be biding your time until you deliver Adalynn to him. More money for you, right?"

Everyone stops what they're doing. All three men are glaring at Dawson now. Jax grips my knee under the table.

"I would never betray a client. Or take money from someone like Kohen Daniels."

Harper mumbles something under her breath that I can't quite hear. From the way Dawson's body tenses, it's clear he did though.

"Harper. Explain," Jax grunts. She remains silent. "Now, Harrison!"

"Harrison, is it?" Dawson hums. "Interesting choice for a last name."

She shrugs. "Can't choose the name you're given."

"No, I guess we can't. Tell me, Harper, what are you doing here?"

She doesn't answer him. Instead, her panicked eyes search mine.

I'm about to rescue her but Dawson's words stop me. "How is having dinner with the Maxwell family keeping a low fucking profile?"

Low profile? She's not related to the mob.

"Just like you can't choose your *family*, you can't choose your friends."

He shakes his head. "Sawyer will be in contact." With that, Dawson pushes to his feet. "I'll be waiting in the office when you're ready to go," he says to me as if he didn't just leave us all with more questions.

"Really? That's all you're going to fucking say to me?" Harper starts to clap. "Bravo, you made it almost ten minutes in my presence before you're running away again." She throws her knife at him. He spins around and catches it with one hand before it lands its target... his face. Her accuracy is deadly. "*Sawyer will be in touch*? Why won't you?"

"We're not discussing this here, *Harper*." He sneers her name before marching out of the room.

Harper doesn't let him go though. No, she follows him, her heels clicking away on the marble floor. "When would be a better time? After Sawyer hides me away again with a new identity? I'm tired of running!"

We all stay where we are, each of us looking at the other as if someone knows what they're talking about. Their voices carry through the penthouse since they're screaming at each other in the next room. Logan, Connor, and Jax look at me as though I know what to do. I'm at as much of a loss as they are.

My mind is still reeling. New identity?

"Char—"

"It's Harper now!" When Dawson tries to talk, she yells over him. "I haven't heard from you in years! And you have the audacity to tell me that Sawyer will be in touch? Fuck you!" Something crashes to the floor, breaking when it makes contact. Connor jumps to his feet. "Let's forget this reunion ever happened and get back to tradition."

"You're supposed to be dead! How can you be dead when you're best friends with *her*!"

What in the actual fuck? I'm out of my chair before I even register that I'm moving. Harper has Dawson pinned against the wall as she hits him over and over again with her tiny fists. He doesn't make a move to stop her.

"Do you know that while I was there, I prayed every single fucking night that you would come back and rescue me? I knew once you found out what had happened, you'd make it right! But eventually, I stopped praying. You never came back for me!"

"I'm—" His voice is filled with utter despair.

"I don't need your apologies, Dawson. Too much has happened! You can't fix what you've broken!" I hear her sniffle as she tries to fight back her tears. "YOU FUCKING LEFT ME!"

"Char—"

She slaps him across the face. He doesn't move or rub his flaming cheek. "Don't ever call me that again!"

"I—"

"How long have you been stateside?"

He hesitates for a moment before he finally whispers, "Four years."

Jax tugs on my arm, nodding in the other direction, and pulls me with him. Right, we should give them space to deal with their issues. Connor and Logan are waiting at the entrance of the hallway, positioned to the side. Instead of giving them privacy though, we all stand immobile as Harper continues to yell.

"Did you know?" She gets quieter with each question. "Did you know who he really was?" Her next words are barely above a whisper but they somehow echo off the walls. "Did you know what he would do to me?" The way her voice breaks at the end... I feel it to the very core of my soul.

Oh god, what did he put her through?

We don't hear his response.

"I'm done," Harper whispers quietly.

We're all straining to hear what will happen next when the elevator arrives. We glance around, wondering what to do. I can't wait. My friend needs me. I rush to the foyer. When Harper sees me, she sticks out a hand, holding the elevator open.

"What can I do?" I ask, desperately wanting to pull her into my arms. I don't though. Her expression is telling me the last thing she needs is a hug. As if one touch will break her.

"I have... to... g-get... out of... here." Harper swipes at the tears falling down her face.

I nod, totally understanding her need to flee. With one final look at Dawson, she lets the doors close. Everyone shouts at the bodyguard, demanding answers, while he refuses to answer them, his eyes glued to the elevator.

Chapter Thirty-one

Adalynn

Putting my hands on my hips, I glare at my bodyguard. "Connor's office." I don't wait for him to follow me as I lead the way. Jax reaches out a hand but I shake my head. I need to talk to Dawson privately.

I lean against Connor's desk as I study the man across from me. There's not one sign that he just got into a heated argument with Harper. Well, if you can ignore the small mark on his face from her hand, that is. We continue to stare at each other. When it's obvious he's not going to spill any secrets, I sigh. "Just tell me one thing. Are you in love with her?"

His face contorts as if he's disgusted by the thought. "Not in the way you think." Before I can ask him to explain further, he drops a bomb. "I'm her twin."

What? Twin? How is that even possible? The more I study Dawson, the more I see it. They have the same hair, nose, and even their eyes are the same shape.

"Without the beard, it's easier to tell." He runs a hand over his jaw-line almost subconsciously.

I'm going to need a bottle of wine, maybe two, to digest this. My brain is overloaded with all this information. How did I not know she has a twin? Or that I've been working with that twin for the past few weeks?

That's why I've felt so comfortable around him from the start. It always felt as if I already knew him, but now that I know he's a part of Harper, I get it. I recognized him without even realizing it.

"Her real name is...?"

He nods. "Charlotte Murphy, up until a few years ago."

"Why?"

Silence.

Feeling a headache coming on, I groan. This is not how I thought tonight was going to go. "You cannot tell me that one of my best friends isn't who she says she is and think I'll be okay with that answer, Dawson."

"You already know too much. The sooner you forget all about her, the better."

My heart almost stops. "What do you mean? What are you going to do?"

"Exactly what I've been doing for years. Keep her hidden." He sighs, long and slow, as if he holds the weight of the world on his muscular shoulders. "I'm sorry. I know you must be confused, but it's better this way."

"Being friends with me makes it easier for him to find her, right?"

He nods.

"So let him find her."

Anger radiates off him in near-tangible waves. "If you knew what he did to her, you wouldn't be saying that." His fist clenches at his side. "You have no idea who he is, what he's capable of."

I march over to him until I'm standing right in front of him. "I don't think either of us knows exactly what he did to his wife. All I know is that she's scared and she's tired of running. Let's make it so she never has to run again."

"It's not as simple as that."

"It never is."

He runs his hands through his hair again, in obvious frustration. "Don't you think if it were that simple, I'd have already taken out the trash?"

"Your sister says you're a trained killer. I think we both know you have the resources to 'take out the trash' so why haven't you?"

He shakes his head. "Some people are beyond even my reach. I won't use her as bait. You need to say your goodbyes, Adalynn. Sawyer should have never allowed you two to become friends. By tomorrow, she'll be just a fading memory."

"No! You can't take her away from the life she has! She has a job, an apartment she loves. She won't give it up."

"She doesn't have a choice here."

I finally ask him the question that's been in the back of my mind since I found out he's her brother. "If being my friend is so dangerous for her, why are you even my bodyguard?"

"I wasn't aware you two were friends when I took this assignment. It's better for everyone involved if I don't know anything about her. When Sawyer set her up with a new identity, I never knew where she went or what name she chose." He scratches his beard. "Makes sense that he hid her in a place with a population of almost nine million."

"But Sawyer knew?"

Dawson nods once. "He and I are going to be speaking after I drop you off. I'm going to make it crystal clear what he's meant to do."

"Who is he?" My tone tells my bodyguard what I'm really asking. *Who is Harper's ex-husband?*

"Someone you never want to cross."

I gulp, instantly scared for her. "Wouldn't she be safer here, with you?"

He shakes his head. "I'm the first place he'll look. I'm sorry, Adalynn. I know you don't understand but you have to say your goodbyes. Being friends with you is putting her in unnecessary danger."

I stare into his eyes; it's eerie how similar they are to my friend's. I can't get over the fact that he's her twin, or everything else he's told me since coming into Connor's office. "Just promise me that you'll make it so she doesn't have to run anymore."

"That's my only goal in life, Adalynn." He sighs, his downturned lips telling me what he's going to say before he says it. "I failed her once. I won't do it again."

I only have one more question for him. "Can I trust you? You were hired to protect me, but your sister, your twin sister, insinuated that you're easily bought."

"Kohen couldn't buy my loyalty. I don't care how deep his pockets are. I don't protect abusers." Taking a step back, Dawson tilts his head, studying me just like I studied him. "There's nothing my sister wouldn't do to stay away from him. If she's fighting me on this, you must mean a great deal to her."

I hate that I know I can't fight him when it comes to her safety. No matter how much I wish she could stay, if her ex-husband is as dangerous as Dawson is making him out to be, I don't want to help him find her. Dawson's right. Harper needs to disappear. I just wish this wasn't her only option.

His voice is haunted when he admits, "I couldn't protect my sister when she needed me, but I will protect you."

"I wish there was some way to help." I have a lot of money. Usually money can fix anything, but I doubt that's the answer.

"Don't worry, one day she'll have her life back."

Of that, I have no doubt. I read Dawson's background. He's lethal. Harper wasn't exaggerating when she called him a hired gun. His hands are covered in the blood of his enemies. If there's anyone who can save her, it's him.

"Did you teach her that knife trick?" I ask, recalling how she threw it with deadly accuracy. "That was pretty impressive."

His face goes hard. "Yes, and it did her no good."

When we finally leave Connor's office, he's nowhere to be found. Jax and Logan are waiting near the elevator. Logan is on the phone, while Jax is typing away on his. He stops what he's doing when he sees me. Ignoring Dawson, he closes the distance between us and cups my face. "Are you okay?"

I almost lie. Hiding my emotions is second nature to me. Instead of painting a smile on my face, however, I tell Jax, "No, but I will be." I will be okay, once Harper or Charlotte no longer has to look over her shoulder. I hate how similar our stories are.

Not caring that we're not alone, Jax presses his lips to mine. The kiss is short and sweet but I feel it all the way to my toes. I'm not sure why, but just knowing that I have Jax…. It feels like everything is going to be okay. We're going to get through this. He's going to help me help Harper.

With a quick peck to my nose, he asks, "Are you ready to go home, fiancée?"

I nod. "Where's Connor?"

I don't miss the way Jax looks at Dawson before answering, "He had to run an errand."

I don't bother pointing out that Connor doesn't run errands. He has people for that. He's probably doing some digging, trying to find out what Dawson and Harper are hiding. I'm sure that 160 IQ brain is running faster than normal, trying to figure out the puzzle. I want to tell him to stop, that it's unnecessary, but what if he's able to find out the truth? Maybe we can do something that Dawson has never been able to do.

When Jax goes to grab our coats, I quickly fish out my phone and text Connor.

Me: Save her.

His text is instant.

Giant: I will.

CHAPTER THIRTY-TWO

Adalynn

After everything that happened last night, I didn't get much sleep. Not wanting to wake Jax, I ditched our bed in place of the chair across the room and have been watching him sleep while I write in a journal. It's something that I used to do before the accident, but like many things, I forgot about the peace it brings me to write down all the little things.

I've been up since right before two a.m. writing to a son I may never meet. I tell him how much we miss him, how much Jax has done, and how no matter what, he'll never be forgotten. I tell him the story of his parents, how we got together, and how much love we have for each other. I'm hoping one day I'll be able to give this to him.

"Come back to bed, fiancée," Jax whispers, his voice deepened by sleep.

I hear him getting out of bed, walking towards me. Finishing my last sentence, I set the notebook down and quickly wipe the tears before he sees them.

"What's wrong?" he asks as he kneels in front of me, naked.

He rests his hands on my thighs as he studies my face. I run my fingers through his soft hair and nod towards the notebook. "It's for Asher."

"Oh, Ads." He presses his lips against mine. "Are you okay?"

No. "I think I'll get there." *I hope.* "What are we going to do about Harper?" I ask, to change the subject.

"How about, after I surprise my fiancée with a romantic breakfast, you go spend the day with her?"

It hasn't escaped my notice how I'm no longer "Ads" to Jax. Any chance he gets, he calls me his fiancée. I love hearing it. There was a time not so long ago that I thought this would never happen. I thought we were doomed.

I press another kiss to his willing lips. "I'm all yours, fiancé."

Jax stands and holds his hand out. "Perfect. Get dressed and come with me."

I throw on a pair of yoga pants and a hoodie from Jax's side of the closet. He's dressed similar; the only real difference is I'm sporting a blindfold.

"One of these days, you'll be the one with the blindfold," I mutter as he carries me into the elevator.

"Kinky. I like it." His lips trail over my exposed neck. "Don't worry, you won't be in it for long."

"At least I'm not barefoot," I say with a grin, remembering the last time he had me blindfolded in here.

"I promise you'll stay dry this time."

The bell chimes. That was too fast. With Jax's penthouse being on the top floor, that only leaves one destination. The roof. I've been up here a few times with him. In the past, whenever I really needed him, he would take me up here. We wouldn't talk, just lie on the chaise lounges and stare up at the sky. Being near him helped.

I snuggle close to him when the cold morning air hits me. "We've had quite a few memories up here."

"I love all of our memories."

"Even the bad?" I ask.

He sits down with me in his lap. "I wouldn't change anything."

He finally removes the material covering my eyes. We're sitting on one of the many lounges, with a fire already roaring and a beautiful table setup in front of us. There's a single pink peony with a note attached to it and two flutes of mimosa waiting for us. I don't know how he did it, but I'm glad he did.

I reach for the stemware and hand one to Jax. "You think of everything." I don't know how he was able to have this ready at this hour, but I'm not complaining. I hope the rest of our lives are filled with these wonderful surprises.

"To many more sunrises, sunsets, and everything between," he says.

"To many more smiles, laughter, and everything between." I clink my glass to his.

We sip our drinks as the sun starts to rise over Manhattan. I've seen lots of sunrises in my short life, and one of my favorites is the present view. The way the sun glitters off the buildings is magical. All the way up here the city seems peaceful. There're no sirens or horns blaring to break the blissful morning.

The ride back down from the rooftop is filled with sexual tension. All through breakfast, Jax kept touching me. Kept trailing his fingers back and forth on my thigh, always getting closer and closer to where I needed him the most. But at the last second, he'd venture south. Wanting to ensure he was getting teased just as much, I made an effort to show my appreciation for breakfast. Every bite I took had his eyes darkening, or maybe it was the moans coming out of my mouth that had the desired effect.

"You've been playing with fire," Jax whispers as he pulls me flush against him so my back is pressed to his front. I can feel how much he wants me. I grind into him.

"I don't know what you mean," I say, my voice husky as I turn so that I'm facing him. His arms wrap around me. I didn't get to explore my fiancé last night like I wanted. I think it's time to see if anything is different now that I'm finally wearing his ring on my finger. Leaning up on my tiptoes, I tease his earlobe with my teeth. "I can't wait to taste my fiancé," I admit boldly, just as the elevator opens to our place.

Jax doesn't waste any time as he lifts me up by the back of my thighs. I wrap my legs around his waist and moan at the feel of him. "Fuck, you drive me insane," he growls.

"Please stop!" Logan's voice breaks through the heavy, lust-covered fog we're in.

I bury my face in Jax's chest. I'm so embarrassed. I'm sure my face matches the red hoodie I'm wearing.

"What are the chances he's going away?" Jax whispers as he sets me back on two feet.

"Slim," Logan answers. His back is to us, which only makes it worse. He clearly saw something no older brother should see. Hopefully he didn't hear me. I'd die.

"Why are you here? Don't you have anything better to do than coming over here this early?" Jax asks as he heads to the kitchen, to get much needed coffee I'm sure.

"Connor needs you in the office ASAP, and since you weren't answering your phone, I decided to drop by," Logan says as we follow Jax.

Jax groans. "You two realize that I just got engaged, right? Crazy thought, but I wanted to spend the morning with my fiancée."

Logan playfully messes with my hair. "Well, I have a surprise for my sister and Connor needs you."

Jax is going through his phone, no doubt checking all the missed calls and texts from Connor. He swears, then looks up at me. "I'll be back in an hour."

"Don't worry, I'm going to go check on Harper anyway." Ignoring the fact that my brother is in the kitchen with us, I walk around the island so I can snuggle with Jax.

He opens his arms for me and kisses the top of my head. "I'll let you know when I'm on my way back."

I smile up at him. "If you don't want to see your little sister kiss your best friend, I suggest you turn away," I warn Logan, right before Jax's lips descend onto mine.

I get lost in him. I forget about everything else but the feel of his mouth on mine. He licks the seam of my lips and I arch into him, seeking more. His hands tangle into my hair as he angles my head back and deepens the kiss. I'm not the biggest fan of coffee, but when I taste it on his tongue, it's intoxicating.

He's intoxicating.

Right when it's getting good, his phone rings. Jax groans into my mouth. I can't help but chuckle as he glares at the offending device. "I'll be back before you have a chance to miss me."

Doubtful. I already miss him and his arms are still wrapped around me. "We should take a trip this weekend, just the two of us."

He bites the tender flesh under my ear, making my toes curl. "How does a private beach sound?"

Jax, shirtless, on a beach... Where do I sign up? "Perfect."

"Great, I'll get everything organized." He glances at his phone again. "In two days, I want nothing in my hands except for you and a margarita."

"Okay, lovebirds," Logan says, reentering the room. "I'm not even a little sorry to interrupt, being that's my sister and all." He glares at Jax, though his expression is mocking. "Connor is about to lose it. Can you please at least attempt to hurry up and get some work done today?"

I practically have to shove Jax out of the kitchen to get him to leave my side. "Only pack bikinis," he calls over his shoulder.

"I don't think I've ever seen you this happy," my brother comments once we're alone.

"I don't think I've ever been this happy," I admit.

It's taken everything and then some to get here today. I've lost count on how many obstacles we've had to suffer through to get to this moment. Was it easy? No, surviving our love has been one of the hardest things I've ever had to overcome.

Jax was right. Our love did destroy us. But it also brought us back together. There's nothing we can't do together.

"I'm glad. Mom and Dad would be so happy for you two. Hadley would have been jealous; she always claimed she was going to marry him."

I can't help but look away. I know Jax and Olivia don't believe her death is on my hands, and even though I've read the report over and over again, it's still hard not to blame myself. Especially after finally remembering what actually took place that night.

I force out a laugh though. "She would have made the best maid of honor."

Thankfully, Logan doesn't comment on the fact that all the happiness I was feeling moments ago seems to have disappeared with just the thought of our sister and parents. I hate that they're not here. I hate that Asher isn't here. I hate that we're living our lives, trapped by all these ghosts of our past.

Logan knocks his shoulder into mine. "Stop that. Mom and Dad would kill me if I make you sad because they're not here. They would want us to be happy, to be loved as much as they loved each other."

"Does that mean you're going to start looking for that?"

"Maybe I found her, and she just doesn't like me."

At this, I laugh. "That, my dear brother, isn't hard to believe."

We're standing in one of Jax's spare bedrooms, the one I used to sleep in whenever I spent the night. It feels like a lifetime has passed since the last time I stayed here. I'm staring at the garment bag presently hanging on one of the iron rods of the canopy bed.

"What is this?" I ask, my voice as shaky as the rest of me.

"Mom always wanted you to have it." Clutching my hand, Logan leads me over to the bag. "After Jax told me that he was going to marry you, I took it out of storage and had it cleaned for you."

We take a hesitant step forward, then another, until we're both standing in front of it. I'm on the verge of tears. I always imagined our mother giving me her dress, going with me to get fitted, helping me plan everything. She used to promise me that everything would work out in the end. She knew how I felt about Jax, knew that we were it for each other. She even joked that when we got married, her speech was going to have "I told you so" in it.

I never thought this day would actually come. Now that it's happening, my mom isn't with me. All I have left is her memory and her wedding dress.

"Logan." I turn to my brother and give him the biggest hug. "Thank you," I choke out before my emotions get the best of me.

"I have one more thing to give you." Reaching into his suit jacket, he pulls out two sealed envelopes. The second I spot the elegant handwriting, the tears that I was desperately trying to hold inside come pouring out. My chest feels as if it's caving in. I know exactly what those letters are and who they're from. I have several of the same ones stored away, with a different milestone written on them.

"I...Logan..." At a loss for words, I concentrate on breathing, because right now that seems like an impossible task.

Quinn Maxwell was a constant worrier. I think losing her own mother at such a young age, so suddenly, caused her to be the way she was. I always thought Mom was paranoid. Now, while I stare at the sealed envelopes, I'm glad she did this. It's like she's here.

He hands the first one to me. It's blank on the front except for my name. "They made me promise to give this to you when enough time had passed and you could listen to what they wanted to say."

This isn't the first instance where I'm holding this letter in my hands. Back then, I almost destroyed it. I was so angry at them for leaving us, for dying, that I didn't want anything from them. I tried to burn it. Thankfully Logan stopped me.

He swallows loudly. "I've carried this with me since that morning. I've been waiting for a sign that you were ready to hear what they had to say. I think it's time, baby girl."

"Did you read yours?"

He nods. "It gave me peace." He closes my hand over the envelope. "It's time to let all the anger go. They wouldn't want you to hold on to this guilt any longer."

"And the other one?"

He places it in my still-extended hand. Written in her beautiful cursive is: *When he finally proposes.* I flip it over, and on the back above the seal is: *I told you so.* Despite the emotional turmoil I'm battling, I laugh through my tears. She knew.

"I have similar ones for you too," I admit when I can finally speak through the sadness.

"I figured as much."

Clutching both envelopes to my chest, I look up at my brother. "Thank you," I tell him. He has done so much for me. If it weren't for him, I don't know where I would be. He's always been my rock. When I was at my lowest, he'd be there leading the way out of the darkness. He's spent countless nights at my side while I was crippled by the weight of the guilt.

Leaning down, Logan kisses the top of my head. "It's time to finally put the past behind us, Adalynn. We can't continue to let that night define us."

"I know," I admit, even though I have no clue how to do that.

He glances down at the Rolex on his wrist. "Your tailor will be here soon."

"What?"

"I'm having a tailor come to help you with your dress. She's also bringing everything else you could possibly need for your wedding." He taps my chin up to close my mouth. "Harper is coming too, so if you want to read those before everyone arrives, you have about thirty minutes."

"I don't even know how to say thank you."

"I wish I could take all of the credit, but it was Jax. Once he knew about the dress, he had everything else set up."

I cannot wait to marry him.

After making sure I'm going to be okay, Logan leaves me to my own devices... well, my own devices and three bodyguards.

Sitting on the bed, I lean back against the headboard and stare at each envelope. I'm afraid of what they're going to say. There's been other milestones that have passed where I purposely didn't open the letters. I couldn't find the strength then. I know once I read them, it will feel as if she's here right beside me. I'm afraid the pain will be too much, almost as if I'm losing her all over again.

"Everything is going to be okay," I whisper to myself as I gently peel the first one open.

Bringing the thick paper up to my nose, I can almost smell her perfume. So I close my eyes and let the memories wash over me. I don't bother wiping my tears away. I know more will follow. My hands shake as I unfold the letter.

Our dearest sweet girl,

First, we'd like to explain these letters. When my mom died, I never thought I'd get over losing her. Your grandfather couldn't cope with the loss. He buried his pain in the bottle, until eventually that took him away from me too. We never want that to be your life.

Your father came up with a plan. Each year, we'd write these letters to you three, in hopes that if something ever happened to us, you all would be able to eventually find peace. Don't let our passing consume you, like it did for me. We hope you never have to read any of them, except for this one, because that means we didn't miss out on your life.

It took me too long to get over being an orphan. I almost missed out on your father's love because of it. As much as we hope that you're read-ing this when you're old and gray, we also know life isn't promised.

This is our goodbye letter to you, in case we don't get that chance.

Cry, get angry, scream... heck, even break things. Just let it out. Do not bottle up our passing. Whenever we do leave this world, know that we do so without any regrets. You three are the light of our lives.

We want you to live your life without regrets, have a love that never fades. We want you to have a life that's been lived to its absolute fullest.

Most importantly, don't shut your siblings out. They're going to need you. Logan may act as if he can take on the world, but he can't, at least not by himself. Hadley is going to need you to remind her to smile. If she forgets how, pull her off the floor and get her to dance again.

You, our sweet girl, are the glue that holds them all together.

This is too hard. Losing them was too much. They never imagined that I would lose them both the night I turned seventeen, that I'd lose by baby sister too. My hands itch to let it all out in the only way I know how. The ring on my finger catches my eyes, stopping me from going to that dark place.

Taking a deep breath, I work on all the stupid tricks Liv has taught me over the years. As much as I'm craving to feel anything else but this, in the end, I know I will only feel guilty. Especially if Jax finds out what I did. I've put him through too much already. I need to be stronger for him.

We know that our passing will crush you. You'll try to shut yourself off from the world, not letting anyone in. You'll pretend that everything is fine to make it easier for everyone else around you. You've always done that, since you were a kid.

The world is brighter with you in it, Adalynn. You, our darling sweet girl, are stronger than you realize.

Don't ever forget how much you mean to us, how much we love you.

We'll always be watching over you,

Mom and Dad

I let their words wash over me. I don't try to bury the pain this time. Despite all the years that have passed, it hasn't gotten any easier. They're gone and they're never coming back.

Another sob racks through me.

They're gone... Asher is gone...

I'm still sobbing as I reach for the second letter. The temptation to tear into it now, though it's meant for my wedding day, is overwhelming. Just like the last one, I bring it up to my nose and inhale. I swear her perfume still lingers on it.

Chapter Thirty-three

Adalynn

"You shouldn't be crying before you try on your dress!" Harper says when she comes into the room.

Dropping the letter, I run towards my best friend. "You're here."

She hugs me back just as tightly. I hate that I know today is the day she's leaving. I don't know where she's going or when she'll return. This might be the last time I see her. It's amazing how quickly someone can come to mean to you. You don't really realize how much until you're forced to say goodbye.

"I hate this," I tell her when we pull away.

"Me too, but I'm glad I get to see you in your dress at least once."

At least once... She's not going to be at my wedding? Of course she isn't. I can't believe that bastard still has so much control over her. I don't know how, but I'm going to help her. I won't let my friend's life be like this. She deserves so much more.

"Now, we both need to stop crying. I promised your brother that we'd be happy." She walks over to the garment bag and pulls it down. "It's time to try on your dress."

I shake my head. "No, we need to talk. This can't be—"

She sighs. "I don't want to talk about it. I want to pretend that I'm just a girl helping her best friend get fitted for her wedding." I wipe my face as she adds, "I know I'm not who you thought would be here, but let's make the most of it."

As much as I want to question her, find out what I can do, I don't. I know that it will just make it harder for her. So instead of interrogating her, I paint a smile on that I know is as fake as I feel and nod in the direction of the bottle of champagne my brother left chilling. As I pour us each a hefty serving, I make a promise to myself that this won't be the last time I see her. We clink our glasses together. She downs hers in one go. I follow suit and pour us another. I have a feeling that we both need a little liquid courage today.

Setting the glass down, she turns towards the door. "Okay, so now that we got that out of the way, let's get you fitted."

I arch an eyebrow in question. I don't have to wait too long before she's opening the door to an older woman, with long legs, stylish grey hair, and a tape measure hanging around her neck. She claps her hands and points to the middle of the room. "Set up there. Have my pins ready." Her thick Italian accent is curt. A young brunette, probably close to my age, pushes in a cart full of the supplies she'll need.

"Did you guys pick a date?" Harper asks once I'm in my mom's dress, while Alessia (as she introduced herself) takes another measurement.

This is so hard. I hate that I have to pretend that this is okay. It's not. I hate that this is her life and there's nothing I can do about it. With a deep breath, I answer her. "Yes, the first weekend of March." Just a few months away. We both didn't want to wait too long.

As Alessia and her assistant Serena finish, I tell Harper all about our plans. I explain how we want to go back to California, to the place we always dreamed of getting married. We're going to rent a villa on the beach, so we'll have the whole place to ourselves. Instead of a big affair, we're going to keep it simple. Just family.

"So she's just going to disappear? What about her job?" I ask Sawyer once Harper is in the other room. Sawyer had a hair stylist come by. I was naïve in thinking Katie was here to help decide how I'm going to wear my hair for my wedding. No, she's here to change Harper's red hair.

When Katie was putting foil in Harper's hair, I finally stepped away. I hate that she's forced to change herself. How many times has she done this? When will it stop?

"Don't worry about it. I'm very good at what I do."

"You can't just make someone disappear. People are going to wonder where she went."

He nods. "Yes, but after a while, she'll just be a girl who lived in the city. Don't worry, Adalynn, it will be as if she were never here."

As I'm about to respond, Dawson comes into the office carrying a black backpack. He tosses keys to Sawyer. "You guys need to be on the road in the next twenty minutes."

Sawyer nods once but Dawson doesn't see it because he's already gone.

"Twenty minutes? That's too soon!"

Sawyer takes in a deep breath and releases it on a sigh. "I'm sorry, Adalynn."

I'm so tired of everyone being sorry. Things shouldn't be this hard. Harper should have a choice in her life. I hate it. I don't bother telling them how unfair this is. They know. We all know but we have to do what's right. I leave Sawyer in the office and go in search of Harper.

With only five minutes left until she's forced to leave the life she has, I'm a mess. I'm staring at my best friend, and it's as if I'm staring at a stranger. Gone are her red locks. Katie has transformed Harper into a blonde with a short bob and bangs. She's in jeans, a sweater, and black Chuck Taylors. I can count on one hand how many times I've seen her in anything but heels. Heels are her drug.

"Don't worry, Adalynn. I'll see you soon." We both know she can't keep that promise.

If she wants to pretend, if it makes it easier for her, then okay. "I'll see you soon." With one last hug, we say our goodbyes.

"Take care of her," Harper says to Jax.

"Always." He holds his arms open to give her a hug. "I'm going to miss you throwing water at Connor."

She laugh-cries into his shirt. "Do me a favor?"

"Anything."

She's looking at both of us when she tells us, "Let him believe the lie. It'll be easier this way."

"For him or for you?" my fiancé asks.

Dawson interrupts before she can answer him. "Everything you need is in here." He hands her the backpack. "Sawyer will help you get settled."

She stares at the bag for a second too long, before finally reaching out and slinging it over her shoulders. "I hate you."

"I know."

Without another word to her twin, Harper gives me one last hug. Her eyes are filled with unshed tears when she pulls away. "We got to go," Sawyer says as he calls the elevator.

"I'll see you soon."

"See you soon," I choke out on a sob.

"Where is she?" Connor roars as he runs into our apartment.

"She's not here," Jax says, but Connor ignores him and jogs into the office that Dawson's team took over.

There's a loud crash. "WHERE IS SHE?"

"Fuck," Jax says as he jumps off the couch and runs after Connor. I'm quick to follow them. By the time I make it into the office, Dawson is on the ground and Connor is punching him over and over again. Dawson does nothing to stop the blows that Connor lands in his face, his ribs—ugh, his face again.

I've never seen my gentle giant ever hurt anyone. I didn't think he had it in him. Logan and Jax were always the hot-tempered ones growing up, never Connor. It's as if I'm seeing a stranger.

"Get off him, man." Jax tries to pry him off Dawson.

"Tell me where she is!" Connor yells, shoving Jax away and hitting Dawson in the jaw again.

Reign skids to a stop when she sees the scene in front of her. Lucas is hot on her heels. He goes to grab the gun at his hips, but Reign beats him to it. Before I even know what's happening, she somehow overpowers Connor and flips him—yes, flips him—over onto his back. The next second, she has a knife pressed against his throat. "If you do that again, I'll have to hurt you."

"Enough, Reign." Dawson has barely raised his voice, but everyone is so quiet it's as if he shouted.

She shoots him a glare before complying. With a talented twirl of her blade, she puts it back in its place at her ankle. "Next time, I won't be so nice." Then she spins on her heels and points at Dawson. "Letting him hit you isn't going to bring her back."

"Where is she?" Connor asks again.

I wish I could tell him that she's okay, that she'll be back, but I can't. I don't know if she's ever going to be free of him. For all I know, this afternoon is the last time I'll ever be able to hang out with her. While Sawyer was making sure she was unrecognizable, Dawson was covering her tracks. He made it where her picture was no longer in the company directory. Her place has already been leased out to someone else. Everything she had... gone.

I've stayed at her place. I know how messy she is. I don't know how he did it, but somehow Dawson was able to get it cleaned out and a new occupant in before her hair was even cut.

"I don't know," Dawson admits. He wipes his bloody nose with the sleeve of his shirt. "You need to forget about her. Harper Harrison doesn't exist anymore."

"I'll find her!" Connor promises.

Jax shoves his way between them. "You have to let her go, Connor."

He's already shaking his head. "I can't."

Last night, when I begged him to save her, I didn't think it would invoke this kind of reaction. No, this is something more. In all the years I've known him, I've never seen Connor like this. He attacked someone, and not just someone, but Dawson, a trained killer.

"Whatever you think she feels for you was a lie." Dawson wipes at his mouth. "She left you without saying goodbye."

This is why he was so quick to help her. I thought he was putting his differences aside for me. I was wrong. "Did you..." I can't even finish that thought. No, I would have known if my man-whore of a best friend slept with her. One of them would have told me. Right?

Connor keeps glaring at Dawson. I swear he's one second away from attacking him again. "You were the one that warned me about her!" I remind him. "You two weren't even friends!"

"I know!" He yanks at his hair.

"How long have you been fucking my best friend?"

He throws his hands up in defeat. "Not now, Addie." He focuses on Dawson. "Where is she?" he repeats.

I turn to Jax. "Did you know?" He looks away, giving me my answer. How did I not know this? How long was this going on?

Dawson told me that if Harper was fighting to stay here, I must mean a lot to her. It wasn't me she was fighting for. It was him, for Connor. That's what she meant when she told Jax to let him believe the lie. She wants him to leave her alone, to not try to find her.

"She didn't bother telling you anything real about herself. Forget about her. I know she's already forgotten about you," Dawson tells Connor.

"Fuck you!" He spits at him. "I'm not you. I will never forget her!" His words land the blow that he knew they would. He looks down at me. "Do you know anything?"

"None of us know anything. Drop it!" Dawson growls.

That's not true though. "She's blonde. They left a few hours ago."

"Adalynn!" Dawson yells. "You think you're helping but you're not."

"She can't spend her life running, Dawson."

Glaring at the bodyguard, Connor says, "I'm going to find her, and when I do, I'm going to do what you can't."

Dawson laughs. "Not even you can save her."

"Watch me," Connor says before storming out of the room. The door slams, echoing off the walls.

Dawson looks at Lucas. "Put someone on him. I want him watched 24/7."

"That's unnecessary." I turn to Dawson. "He's not a threat."

"24/7," he repeats to Lucas as if I haven't spoken.

Chapter Thirty-four

Adalynn

A few weeks later, I'm making dinner while I wait for Jax to come home. I've finally stopped asking for any news on Harper. Reign reminded me that we can never be too careful. We need to stop mentioning her, in case someone is listening.

"We need to talk," Jax says when he enters the kitchen.

I turn off the stove and grab plates from the cabinets. "Okay, one second and dinner will be ready," I reply with my back to him.

"Adalynn," he says in a way that makes my whole body freeze.

"Where have you been?" I ask, the scent of a campfire overpowering his natural musk. "And what's in the folder?" I nod my head at the manila file on the island beside him.

He pulls it closer to him. "I have to tell you something," he states, ignoring my question. "I'd keep it from you if I could, but unfortunately I need your help bringing my son home."

I swallow the lump in my throat. My hand goes to my chest, to see if my heart is still beating. It is. Home? Does that mean... No, it can't...

It's been too long. Even though I know I shouldn't hope, somehow I am.

It feels as if I'm barely breathing as he explains, "Dawson recommended that I reach out to someone he knows. He's the best, even if his tactics are not something I agree with, but all I care about is finding my son."

"He thinks we're going to find him?" I whisper, then add, "Alive?"

He nods. "Asher was living in the city a year ago."

How is that possible? "This city?" I ask too quickly, my words jumbling together.

His voice shakes when he says, "Stephen was able to track down a nanny who was looking after Asher for three years."

"How do we know it's him?"

Jax pulls at his hair. "The reason Stephen was even able to find Mandy is because she started looking into who Asher's mother really was."

"How long have you known about this?" I ask, my outrage evident in my tone.

"A week," he says without an ounce of remorse, as if he weren't purposely keeping me in the dark yet again.

"I thought we were done lying to each other. I'm his mother! How could you keep this from me?"

"I was trying to protect you!" he shouts back.

"That's always the reason though, right, Jax? I'm too weak to know everything, so let's only tell her the good parts! I'm not going to fucking break!" I throw the plate that I forgot was still in my hand across the room. Spaghetti goes everywhere, staining the white rug. "What else are you not telling me?" I ask, knowing there's always more with him.

"Whoever has him knows we're close. Maybe he saw the news about you and Kohen? We're not sure at the moment, but for whatever reason, the guy got spooked and covered their tracks."

I use the kitchen island to steady myself. If I let go, I'm afraid I'll sink to my knees and never be able to get up again.

"I'll explain everything." Jax takes a deep breath, and the look he gives me is absolutely gutted. "He killed Mandy. He burnt down her house with her in it."

"That's why you smell like smoke..." It's hard for me to have sympathy for anyone tied to our son's kidnappers. Then I remember what Jax said at the beginning. She started digging deeper; she must have known something was off. Suddenly, the distance between us feels wrong.

Before I can reach him though, Jax takes a step back. "There's something else I need to tell you. It's going to be difficult to hear."

My voice is calm, masking the fear coursing through my veins. "Okay."

My gut is telling me that whatever Jax has to say, the reason he's keeping his distance from me, why he continues to call Asher his son and not ours, is going to break us somehow. Whatever it is, I know it's going to be worse than finding out that he was in New York all this time. What if I've passed him on the street, or saw him at the park? Would I have recognized my own son?

"When Stephen tracked her down, she didn't want to cooperate until she heard your name." He waits for me to connect the dots. When it's clear that I'm as lost as he is, Jax continues, "Mandy said Asher started talking about you, saying that you were his mom. Apparently, when your face was on the rags after what happened at the beach house with Kohen, he recognized you and told her that you were his real mom but it was a secret. Mandy showed Stephen a picture that Asher had of the both of you by the ocean."

Jax keeps talking but I can't focus on anything he's saying. I've met our son...

Holy fuck. Our son knows me! How?

I search my useless mind and come up empty. It's almost as if the memory is right there, right below the surface, begging to come out. I can almost hear the waves crashing as Asher laughs in the distance. But just as quickly as it comes, it's gone. There's no way I would have spent time with him and not known he's my son. And if I knew, why wouldn't I take him back? Why would I allow him to remain with his kidnappers?

"Do you remember talking to a little boy when we were in Florida? He had to be around three at the time."

I shake my head. "No." My voice is barely above a whisper.

"You can't remember anything?" Jax starts to pace the room. "You need to try harder, Adalynn. Asher's life is at stake!"

"Don't you think I know that?" Again, I try to reach him but he takes another step back, putting the island between us. "Did she tell Stephen anything else?" I know the answer before I even ask, but I can't help but verbalize it anyway. "Did Mandy tell us who has him?"

"She was too afraid to give Stephen a name. She said if he ever found out, he'd kill her." When Jax pauses, looking anywhere but at me, I know he's hiding something. There's more.

"What else?"

"Mandy always thought Asher's mom was dead. She was told by her employer that his wife died the night Asher was born. That's why when he pointed you out, she didn't believe him at first."

"What changed?"

"I'm not sure."

"He kept his name though?" Jax keeps calling our son Asher. That must mean whoever took him didn't change it, right?

Jax nods. "His first and middle, yes."

"You know his last name?" For the first time in years, we have a solid lead!

"Yes."

None of this is making any sense. Why steal our child, keep everything but his last name, just to raise him as your own?

"Asher James Daniels," he spits.

It's too hot in here. Breathing becomes impossible. I'm almost too afraid to speak, but somehow I find the strength to ask, "Daniels? As in—"

"I can only think of one Daniels."

No, no, no. It can't be him. It's impossible. I would have known if Kohen had our son. I've been to his place, multiple times. There was nothing to indicate he had a child, *our* child. No, this is just a coincidence.

"Jax—" I don't even know what to say. What can I say? Did I really date my stalker, the man who apparently kidnapped our son when he was a baby? That seems impossible. Kohen has never been to California.

Jax doesn't say anything as he slides the manila folder towards me. I see the devastation written on his face before I notice the picture in his hand. Ignoring the fear racing through me, I stare at the two pairs of almost violet eyes.

Asher isn't alone. I'm in the photo too, right beside him. My hair is short, almost to my shoulders, which tells me this photo is a few years old. Asher's sporting a toothy grin as he seems to be chasing a bird. I recognize the place almost instantly. We all went to Florida for vacation. That morning, I left to walk the shoreline. Later that night, Jax found me in a ball, shaking, unable to speak or recall what happened and why I was missing for hours. We all thought it was because of the date. It was the anniversary of the crash, my birthday.

We were all wrong. We were so close. I was so close and I let him go. I can't even look at Jax right now. I can't even imagine how he feels. Knowing that the mother of his son, the same mother who forgot all about her child, allowed Asher to go back with Kohen. I wouldn't blame him if he hates me.

I hate me.

"When's the last time you saw our son, Adalynn?" Jax's voice is devoid of emotion. I've never heard him sound so detached.

Pinching my eyes closed, I shake my head. "I don't know," I whisper but I may as well have shouted.

"What do you mean you don't know? Why didn't you grab him? Why didn't you recognize him?" The desperation in his voice is hard to miss.

I look up. "Maybe because I didn't even know I was a mother! How could I possibly recognize a child I wasn't even aware I had?" It's a low blow but I keep going. Somewhere in the back of my mind, I know I'm doing this to push him away. I don't deserve him. "Maybe if you guys didn't hide him away like a dirty secret, I would have known it was him right away!"

I need Jax to hate me. All this time, he's done nothing but search for our son while I did the exact opposite. I forgot we even had a son. Finding out that I've met him and did the unthinkable... let him return to Kohen? It's... I don't even have the words. I'll never be able to forgive myself.

Picking up one of the barstools, Jax slams it into the ground until there's nothing left but the piece he's holding in his hand. I'm transfixed, staring at all the broken pieces of wood on the floor unable to be mended together, just like me.

"Jax..."

"You keep telling me that when you see him, you'll know. You have no motherly instincts! I spent years making excuse after excuse for you, while I waited for you to come back! I wanted us to be a family again, to be us again." Careful to avoid the carnage I left when I shattered the plate, Jax steps over it all and says, "I was wrong," before leaving the kitchen.

I panic, and start apologizing over and over again but no matter how many times I utter the words "I'm sorry," they won't fix what I've broken.

Jax doesn't care though, and I can't blame him. He talks over me, refusing to hear my pleas. "I need space. I thought I could be around you, but I was wrong."

Before I can look up, he's gone and I'm left alone in the kitchen. I watch the clock on the far wall, willing him to come back to me. Seconds turn to minutes. Eventually, my attention is pulled to behind me. Dawson is standing on the other side of the kitchen, broom in hand.

"How much did you hear?"

"Enough." He silently walks past me and starts to sweep up our mess. "You should go to bed, Adalynn."

Somehow, I manage to climb the stairs. I'm rooted in place as I stare at our closed bedroom door. I keep turning back to Asher's room. I've spent time with him, seen his smile.

And I took it all for granted. I don't belong here.

CHAPTER THIRTY-FIVE

Adalynn

"I'm here now, Ads. Please stop crying," he says at the same time he slides into bed behind me.

I scream at the unfairness, the pillow muffling the sound.

Wrapping his arms around me, he hugs me, making it impossible to escape. "I'm so sorry for everything. I shouldn't have ever left you. I love you."

I don't turn over to return his embrace. I lay here, immobile, paralyzed with fear. With the slightest misstep, this can all go horribly wrong. Reaching over me, he yanks the pillow from my grip, and suddenly we're face to face. It isn't until he crawls over me that I lose it.

"Tell me, how does it feel to be a mother, Adalynn? Is it everything you thought it would be?"

"FUCK YOU!" I scream at him.

His hit almost knocks me out. I'm dizzy, fighting to stay conscious. I bet he expects me to cry, to beg him not to hit me. I do neither. Instead, I laugh in his face. There's nothing more he can do to hurt me.

He's taken everything from me. I keep laughing. He's staring at me as if I belong in an institution. Maybe I do.

"Stop laughing," he orders, and I laugh more. He grips my chin, forcing my mouth closed. "Stop laughing, Ads. I'm not going to ask again."

"Where's my son, Kohen?" I demand once he releases my face. "Where's Asher?"

"You don't understand."

"Understand what?"

Kohen caresses my cheek. "You don't understand how much I love you. We're a family now." His blonde hair falls in his face. I used to love fixing it whenever it did that. Now, the only thing I want to do is hurt him. "You can meet our son when you're ready."

"HE WILL NEVER BE YOUR SON!"

The slap across my face is swift. I didn't even see him move. I welcome the sting. I touch my warm cheek. When I pull my hand away, there's a trace of blood. Is it from the slap or the punch?

It doesn't matter.

"I'm sorry I had to do that. Sometimes you make me so angry."

He looks exactly the same, with his crystal-blue eyes shining down on me. He's sporting a white shirt and jeans. Simple. Casual, as if he doesn't have a care in the world. I'm repulsed by him. How could I ever find the devil attractive? Kohen's mask has forever slipped away, revealing what lies beneath. Anyone passing him on the street would find him charming, attractive—blissfully unaware of what he's capable of.

I'm alone with a monster, with my son's kidnapper.

"I hate you.

He runs his nose against mine. "You love me." Nuzzling my neck, he whispers into my ear, "Our son is safe. Even after you forgot him, I've protected him all these years."

Where's Dawson? How did Kohen get in here and past both him and Reign? Should I fight or wait until they come rescue me? I need to keep this psycho talking until someone realizes he's in here with me.

"Why?"

Kohen ignores me. Instead he starts lifting my sweater. His ice-cold hand grazes my stomach. I do nothing to stop him, to fight him. He's won.

"How did you get in here?"

He licks my throat and whispers, "Oh, you mean past your body-guard?" He practically laughs. "She's taking a much-needed break, just like the other one."

My blood runs cold. "What did you do to them?"

He smirks. "Nobody is going to be bothering us tonight." After tugging on my earlobe with his teeth, he whispers, "Scream all you want."

I'm not going to scream. I'm not going to give him the satisfaction. "Take me to him."

Kohen pauses. His hand is right under my bra. His thumb traces the underwire. "Not yet."

"Please," I beg.

He kisses my collarbone. "Don't worry, Ads, we'll be a real family soon. I promise."

I can feel him start to harden on top of me. He yanks my legs open, settling between them. "Please, Kohen." I'm trying desperately not to cry, but when I feel his hands slip under my bra and trace my nipple, a tear escapes. "Don't do this."

"The harder you fight, the longer it will be until we're happy again." I flinch away from him when he attempts to caress my face. "Good thing I'm a patient man. I'll break you all over again and bend you to my will."

I glare at him in defiance. "I'm not afraid of you."

Kohen leans down and licks my trembling lips. "You only have to be afraid if you disobey me. Once you heel, you'll only find pleasure."

"I'll do anything you want. Please just take me to him."

Instead of listening, he starts pulling down my tights. I gulp, hating what's going to happen. "Soon, Ads. I promise."

I can't just lie here and take it. Nobody deserves this, not even me. "HELP!" I shout, as I desperately attempt to kick him off me. I gasp in horror as the blade—one I hadn't noticed until now—is pressed against my neck.

"Why do you fight this? I know you love me. Don't make me hurt you." He presses a little deeper, in warning. I should be terrified. Instead, I'm numb. He's so close to ending my life, and all I can think about is how much better the world would be without me.

"DO IT!" I scream as I arch my neck up. The blade bites into my skin. The pain barely registers as I arch higher, practically begging him to end my life. He thinks I'm bluffing and pushes a little deeper. It's not deep enough. I'm still breathing. Blood is running down my neck, pooling on my chest. "You don't have the power here. I do."

"You sure about that?" He licks a trail of blood off me. "You think you have nothing to live for. I'm here to remind you how wrong you are."

"Death doesn't scare me," I hiss at him as he slices into the next layer of my flesh.

He now has me in just my underwear; my leggings are bunched around my thighs. "No, but leaving Asher with me should." He thrusts against me. I gasp at the feel of him there. I think I'm going to be sick.

Kohen

I suck on her neck, loving the way she quivers underneath me. I do this to her, cause this reaction, not Jax. "I love you, Ads."

Before she has time to say anything, I kiss her. She tries to fight her attraction to me, no doubt because she still thinks someone is going to stop us. She doesn't realize I've been planning this for too long. We're safe. I bite her lip, urging her to open for me. I thrust into her, and her mouth parts on a cry, just like I knew it would. I savor the taste of her. It's been too long.

"I've missed you so much, Ads," I moan into her mouth. She tries to scoot up the bed. Grabbing her hip, I yank her back to me until her spine is flat against the mattress again. "Haven't you missed me?" I take my time, climbing up her body and caging her in. "Tell me nobody makes you feel the way I do." I emphasize my point by rolling my hips against her, hitting that spot that drives her wild.

She spits in my face. I use my thumb to wipe it up before sucking the digit clean. I missed how feisty she could be. Just another reason we're perfect for each other. I doubt she's this wild with her precious Jax. No, he'd never let her get away with spitting on him. He doesn't love her the way I do. There's nothing she could do that would disgust me. Her fire turns me on even more. Makes me crave her.

"Please, Kohen, let me see Asher."

As much as I want to give her what she wants, I can't. Not yet. I'm still working out the plan. Once I have our new documents, we'll leave. We'll go where nobody will be able to find us. That's when I'll take her to him.

"No, Ads, I can't."

"I HATE YOU!"

Why does she keep saying that? "Stop saying that! You love me!" I know she loves me. She has to.

"I HATE YOU! I HATE YOU! I HA—" Her violet eyes are wide and she gasps in shock when I pull the knife back and see the blood dripping from the blade's edge.

"FUCK, FUCK, FUCK!" I shout when I realize what she made me

do. Her head falls back against the pillow, her eyes close, and I'm frozen while I watch blood pour out of her.

Why did she make me do that?

I was so distracted by what she was screaming, I forgot about the knife in my hand. I work on autopilot, desperately trying to stop the bleeding. "You can't leave me. I won't let you!" Grabbing her torn shirt, I use it to apply pressure as I call 9-1-1. Fuck, how am I going to fix this? I smack her face a few times. "Keep your eyes on me, Ads. I can't lose you too."

I rattle off Jax's address, letting them know where we are and that a woman's been stabbed. Thankfully, I missed her artery. Once I sew her up, she'll be fine. I won't lose her like I lost Em. I can't... I just found her.

I kiss her lips over and over again, whispering, "It's okay. I'm going to save you."

What feels like a lifetime later, paramedics finally burst through the door. "Hurry, I'm her husband. I got here just in time." One of them tries to pull me away. I don't let him separate us. I can't. "I'm a surgeon! I can save her." I rattle off everything I need.

The one closest to me pauses, as if he doesn't believe me, then he relents. While I'm tending to her wound, they get her pulse, blood pressure, and prepare to move her. Once I know that she's okay, I feel like I can breathe again. Fuck, that was close. I almost lost her.

"Sir, if you can come with us, we have a few questions."

It isn't until I hear that, that I finally take my eyes off Adalynn and realize that more than the paramedics are here. "I'm not leaving my wife." I relay directions to the medical personnel before turning to the officers blocking the door.

One of the officers follows the paramedics and Adalynn. When I try to leave, the other one stops me. "I'm going to need your statement."

"I need to go with my wife." Before he has time to react, I inject him with the tranquilizer I was going to use on Addie if she became too difficult. By the time he hits the ground, I'm already fleeing.

Fuck, I can't believe I did this. It's not my fault though. She made me do it. Fuck, there's no way I can go back to being Dr. Kohen Daniels. Not after this. Too many witnesses. I never thought I'd leave without her, but I don't have a choice. I need to flee the city tonight. I just hope she'll be able to forgive me. She has to know that if there was any other way, I would have stayed.

Everything I do is for her.

Forgive me, Ads.

CHAPTER THIRTY-SIX

Adalynn

I wake with a start. I'm screaming, trying to push him off me, when I'm suddenly bathed in light. It's Jax, not Kohen. It takes me a moment to remember that I'm safe. It's been almost a week since that night.

He feels guilty. If he were there, none of this would have happened. He's repeated that so many times it's now engraved in my memory. I want to tell him he's wrong, but I can't. If he didn't leave me after our fight, maybe Kohen wouldn't have been able to sneak away. I was so close to finally putting this all behind us. If someone would have come back to check on me, maybe we'd have Asher home.

"I'm so sorry, Ads." Jax brushes the hair out of my face. "You're okay."

All I can do is nod. I've lost my voice. As much as I need to talk, I can't. I have no words. It's as if Kohen stole them all from me. My mouth won't work and I'm trapped in my body. I thought, after everything, he'd never be able to touch me again. Dawson promised he'd protect me. Logan promised. Jax promised too... They all broke their promises.

Kohen has Asher. Kohen broke me.

Turning away from Jax, I try to close my eyes and go back to sleep. I know it's no use. Sleep is hard to come by these days. Whenever I close my eyes, I'm haunted. I replay that night over and over again in my nightmares.

Jax left me... Kohen stole our son... I've... I've met our son...

The ring on my finger taunts me. Just a few nights ago, I was everything to Jax. He promised he was never going to leave me. He promised he loved me. That's all changed now.

He doesn't love me. Who could?

I'm the mother who not only forgot her child, but allowed him to go back to his kidnapper. No, worse than that... I dated his kidnapper. I shouldn't be here.

"Please don't cry," Jax whispers into my hair. He's in bed with me, his arms wrapped around me as if he can protect me.

Almost a year ago, I thought I was deserving of Kohen. That's why I stayed with him. With time, that feeling went away. And with therapy, I started to see that I'm worth so much more than what Kohen gave me.

Now, things have changed. I'm the mother who forgot her child... the mother who allowed him to go back to his kidnapper... I deserve everything life has thrown at me.

"You're okay, Ads." Jax's hand rubs up and down my arm. I barely feel it. "I'm not going anywhere."

He's only here because he feels guilty. He doesn't love me. Nobody can. I'm unlovable. I destroy everything. All I want to do is run away. I should have gone with Harper. It would be easier if I disappeared. Maybe then, Kohen would give Jax his son back. I don't deserve to call myself a mother.

"Let it out." Jax presses another kiss to my temple.

I stare at the sapphire on my finger and feel the band getting tighter. The longer it's on my hand, the more it hurts. I can't do this. Not anymore. Pulling away from Jax, I yank the ring off me. It isn't until I place it back in Jax's palm that I feel like I can breathe again.

For years, we've been playing this game. For years, I've built walls around my heart to protect myself from him. I should have known that I was never going to be able to keep him. I didn't deserve him then and I still don't now.

"Don't do this," he pleads. "I shouldn't have left you. I'm sorry." He grips my face in his hands and kisses me. I remain immobile against him. "Please don't do this to us," he says when he realizes I'm not going to kiss him back.

I can't. I'm done. *I'm the mother who forgot her child... the mother who allowed him to go back to his kidnapper...* The though repeats over and over in my head.

"We'll get him back. We'll save him," Jax promises. "I'm not letting you go."

I'm not giving him a choice. He deserves so much more than me.

"I think it's time to put you back on the medication," Liv says for the second time in the hour-long visit.

I'm already shaking my head. I'm done feeling groggy. It's been almost a month since I left Jax. It took another week to finally find my voice again. Logan has forced me back into therapy. Each evening, Jax comes by to sleep on my couch. He says it's because he can't let me go, but I think we both know it's because he thinks Kohen is going to come back and he'll be able to stop him.

During yesterday's session, I finally told Liv how I feel. She says that I need to talk to Jax. I can't keep assuming what someone can handle, how much is too much until they give up. She thinks talking to him will give me peace. I don't know if I'm deserving of peace.

"You were drugged, Adalynn. You can't blame yourself."

When Jax explained to Logan what we recently uncovered, Logan admitted that he knew something was off that night in Florida. And that he took a blood sample. When it came back that I had Rohypnol in my system all those years ago, he let it go. He didn't know what happened to me on the beach, and he was too afraid to ask. So, instead of telling anyone, he pretended it didn't happen. Until now.

He was trying to protect me. He thought I was raped. How could he possibly know that I spent the day with my son and Kohen? Rape was the easier guess. I can't help but blame everyone, including Logan. What would have happened if he told the truth? Would it have even mattered?

I didn't think it was possible to hate Kohen more than I already did, but I was wrong. I can't believe he gave me a moment with my son just to erase it. How many more moments have I had with Asher? What else has he done to me that I can't recall? I don't think I've ever hated anyone this much. It's at the very core of my being.

I never thought I'd have it in me to kill anyone. But this...? This is what drives someone to murder. If I ever find him again...

"Adalynn, did you hear me?"

Escaping my thoughts, I focus on my therapist. "I don't need them." How can I explain that I never want to take another drug in my life?

She sets her tablet on the table beside her. "You're unable to sleep for more than a few hours. Take the Ambien, Adalynn. You're only hurting your body when you refuse to address the issue. Your brain needs time to shut down. Think of it like a laptop. If you keep closing it without shutting it off, the hard drive will get viruses. It needs to be shut off to reboot. Just like your brain."

"So you're saying I have a virus?" Ugh, even to my own ears, this sounds bad. I knew I should have skipped today. There's nothing like paying someone to tell you just how crazy you are.

"I'm saying if you continue running on fumes, you're going to be in worse shape. You could develop high blood pressure, a weakened immune system, even diabetes. Your body needs sleep." She nods to the to-go mug in my hands. "How many cups have you had today?"

Five. "This is my second."

"I sincerely doubt that your hands are shaking from your second cup. You can't survive on coffee."

She doesn't understand. Nobody does.

"In your short life, you've had to deal with the loss of your parents, your sister, and your only child being kidnapped. You spent years going through the motions, and when you finally thought you could trust someone again, Kohen broke it. And Jax broke it when he left." She pauses to let her words sink in. "I can't imagine what you go through on a daily basis, Addie. Kohen stole your sense of safety."

"Kohen stole *everything* from me," I correct, and she looks away. Good. I'm glad I'm not the only one uncomfortable here.

"Adalynn—"

I sigh, long and slow. She doesn't deserve this. All Olivia has done is try to help me. It's not her fault I dated my son's kidnapper. I picture Asher. He's why I keep trying, why I continue to see Liv, when most days I feel as if all hope is lost. That's why I come here so often. I need to be better for Asher. One day, he'll be home.

"When we get Asher back, he's going to hate me." I can't even blame him if he does. Heck, I wouldn't even fight Jax if he wanted to take me to court for full custody.

"What are your favorite places in the city?"

I glare at her. "This concerns my son how?"

She shrugs as she remains silent, waiting for me to answer. Knowing that I won't get out of here until I do, I humor her and name a few.

"Do you notice a recurring theme?"

"Nope." The P makes a popping sound.

She doesn't waste any time making her point. "There's a park or an elementary school in every single spot you mentioned. Your mind might have forgotten him, but subconsciously, you have always remembered him. You've been searching for him without knowing it, Adalynn."

Minutes tick by as I mentally visit each and every one of the places I mentioned. It doesn't take long to realize she's right.

We spend the next half hour talking about Jax. At the end of the session, Liv hands me a prescription. "Promise me you won't throw this away."

I slip the note into my purse. "I promise."

"I'm going to check tomorrow to see if you fill it."

I sigh as I leave her office.

Sawyer unlocks my apartment for me. I'm not even surprised to find Jax in my kitchen cooking. My days are filled with routines. Someone escorts me to the bakery, where I picked up working again, then to therapy after work three times a week, then back home. Jax is always here, and the next day, we'll eat breakfast in silence before he goes to the office. It's almost as if we've gone back in time. Except now I'm the one pulling away, and he's the one begging me to stay.

"I'm not giving up on us, Ads," he says without turning around, focusing on whatever he's making.

I wish I could tell him to keep fighting for us, but I can't. I've done too much. He deserves so much more than me. I take a seat at the bar and grab the waiting glass of wine. It tastes bitter on my tongue. Ever since I found out the truth, nothing tastes right. Almost as if even my taste buds hate me as much as I hate myself.

"You can't keep blaming yourself," he says when he pivots to face me.

Watch me. "I've met our son, Jaxon. There's nobody to blame but me."

"Almost seven years ago, I chose to ignore the fact that I had a son. I chose to stay with you. I chose to not meet him."

"That wasn't your fault."

"You were fucking drugged, Adalynn! What excuse do I have?"

"Jax," I choke out. "I dated him. I let him into our lives and the whole time he had Asher. He still has him!"

I can see just how much my words affect him. He closes his eyes as if that will somehow drown out the truth. It won't. Nothing will. "You didn't know. This is not your fault."

Yes, it is. "Jax—"

"Wait. Just let me get this out, Ads."

My heart beats erratically as I wait for him to crush me even more. Everything he's been telling me for weeks is trying to penetrate my darken soul. Yet it physically sickens me, because I'm just not ready for us. Not yet. Not now.

"He had everyone fooled. There's no way you could have known who he truly was. I don't blame you."

"You—"

"I shouldn't have left that night. I took my anger out on you and I shouldn't have." He comes around the island until he's right beside me. "We're going to be a family again, Ads."

"How can you possibly forgive me?" I ask, desperate for the answer I've been seeking since I woke up in the hospital. How could he ever forgive me when I can't even stand to look at myself?

Everything that's happened to us is my fault.

Jax clasps my face in his hands. "You did nothing that warrants forgiveness." I close my eyes, wanting to block out his words. "When I did the unthinkable, somehow you were able to forgive me. I helped you forget him. I'm just as much to blame here. What if we never lied to you?"

Yes, what if they never lied to me? What if they didn't help me forget Asher? What if Jax refused to let me lock everything away? Would that have changed anything? Would Kohen have let me meet him? Would he have even come into my life if I knew the truth?

"There's an endless list of 'what ifs.' We can never know for sure. None of them matter, Jax."

"Tell me what matters then."

"The truth." I pull away from him. "I forgot him. I met him. I let him go back to Kohen. I dated that man."

"Okay, let's go over the truth. You didn't choose to forget him. That was your way of healing, of protecting yourself." I go to talk over him but he shushes me with a finger to my lips. "You were drugged when you met him. It was impossible for you to remember what really happened."

"I still let him go back to him."

He shakes his head. "I refuse to believe that. You don't know what happened, because he drugged you. There's no telling what actually happened."

"Jax—"

"No, Adalynn, I don't want to hear it. I remember when I found you. You seemed broken. There's no way you didn't know who he was when you met him. There's no way you wouldn't have fought to keep him with you."

"I—"

Jax looks away when he whispers, "When I found you that night on the beach, I saw the blood on your nails." When he finally faces me again, his eyes are filled with unshed tears. "I thought—"

"You thought I was raped." Just like Logan.

He nods.

"It doesn't matter, Jax." Nothing but finding Asher matters.

"I'm not giving up on us. When you're ready, I'm here. I'll always be here, waiting for you to come back to me." He crowds my space until his lips brush against mine while he vows, "I promised I was going to marry you one day, Ads."

I can't help the tear that falls. Absentmindedly, my finger plays with the ring that isn't there anymore.

"I'm done pretending you don't own me. When you're ready, I'm yours. Heart, body, soul, I'm yours. Forever and always."

Forever and always. That's what we used to say to each other every night under the stars when we were teenagers. My mouth moves to say them now but I can't. "I'm not ready."

He smiles down at me. "I know, but don't worry, Ads, we have all the time in the world. I'm not going anywhere."

The next morning, we eat our breakfast in silence. Not much has been said since he declared, yet again, that he's not giving up on us. As a little girl, I dreamed about having a life with him. There was never a time when he wasn't a part of my future. Then, everything changed. We changed. A future with him has become something that seems impossible. Yet here he is, putting his jacket on, kissing the side of my head, and telling me he loves me before he leaves.

Something happened between the time I closed my eyes last night and opened them again this morning. His love, our future, it's all in my grasps. We've always been able to find our way back to each other, no matter what the other has done. This time is no different. Jax forgives me, even when I can't forgive myself. He tells me I'm worthy of him, that there's not a world where our son could ever hate me. He promises that we're going to get through this. Connor told me Jax's still planning our wedding in a few months. He hasn't given up on me.

Jax is my soul mate. Love isn't easy. The heartbreak we've caused each other makes it seem as if we're fighting an uphill battle. We're worth it though. He's worth it. Together, we can overcome anything. No more hiding. No more fantasies. I want everything he's offering and more. When it comes to us, I want it all.

"Jax, wait," I say as I run after him.

Chapter Thirty-seven

Kohen

Standing in the shadows, I watch him twirl her around the dance floor. I have to hand it to Jax. With the lights strung all around them and the ocean crashing into the background, this is definitely Adalynn's dream wedding rehearsal. Too bad she's dancing with the wrong guy. Not for long though.

Her pathetic excuses for bodyguards are nearby, no doubt waiting for me to attack. As if I'd be dumb enough to do so *here*, with them around. Connor is talking with his parents while Logan finally puts me out of my misery and takes my girl into his arms for a dance.

I tried to stay away. I really did. But I couldn't wait until tomorrow to see her. I'd hate for her to feel as if I abandoned her. I don't want her to think she has to marry him because I'm gone. I contemplated drugging everyone, so that it could be me on this dance floor with her. I'm even dressed in a freshly tailored suit just for her, but I know that's not what she needs. She needs to make the decision to leave her life and come to me.

I'm the only person who truly loves her.

It's been almost three months since I accidently stabbed her. They all think I've been on the run. They're all very wrong. I've been out of the country building a life for us. Once Adalynn sees everything I've done for us, she's going to come back to me.

I know she doesn't love Jax. How could she? He's the reason she's so empty.

With me, she'll never have to worry about anything. I'm going to right all of Jax's wrongs. I couldn't save Em, but I will save her.

After dinner, she excuses herself to go to the bathroom. The first time, I stood by and watched as Reign escorted her inside. Then Adalynn said something to the woman that made her not accompany her the second time. Taking a quick glance around, I spot her far guard following her movements, and everyone else stays in their places. They're letting her go to the bathroom again by herself.

This is the perfect time to give her the ultimatum. Jax or me?

When she's done washing her hands, I make myself known. I close the small distance between us, my steps as certain as I am. Before she can utter a sound, my hand covers her mouth. I pull her against me, her back to my chest. Wishing I could take her now, I breathe her in.

Her hand goes to her necklace. I stop her before it's too late. "Don't."

I can't help but stare at her reflection in the mirror. For a second, I forget how to breathe. She's beautiful. Just like all the times before, her eyes captivate me. They've always drawn me to her.

"You're breathtaking," I whisper into her ear, my hand slinking around to trace the scar above her collarbone. "This healed nicely." Not my best work, but it's still better than what anyone else would have been able to do.

She tries to pull away from me.

"If you scream, or do anything to bring anyone else in here, you'll never see me again." If she ruins this for us, she'll never see her son again. I don't need to tell her this, because she knows. Still, I can't help but remind her that I'm the one with all the cards on the table. "Asher needs a mom. Don't make me have to find a stepmom for him."

I relish the fear in her eyes. I wish I had time to gather her dress around her hips and show her just how much her fear excites me. When she finally nods, I release her.

Chapter Thirty-eight

Adalynn

"Are you sure you're okay" Jax asks again as he closes the door to our room. We're all staying at the villa. Connor tried to remind us that we were breaking tradition by spending the night together. Nothing could tear me away from Jax, not tonight.

There're so many things I wish I could tell him; instead, I'm forced to lie to him and everyone else here. Nothing I say will ever make what I have to do okay. I just hope one day, when he finds out my secrets, he'll be able to understand and forgive me.

So, tonight, I'm going to pretend that I'm not keeping *everything* from him. Tonight, I'm going to pray that he somehow finds it in his heart to forgive me, to still love me when this is all over.

"Everything is perfect." The lie taste bitter on my tongue.

I'm already breaking. With each passing second, I'm that much closer to destroying what we have. I don't know how but I'm going to bring Asher back to him.

"You're shaking," Jax says as his fingers play with the straps on my shoulders.

Don't hate me.

"Are you okay?" Jax asks again, concern written on his face.

All I can do is nod. I'm terrified of what will come out of my mouth if I try to speak. I know this is our last night like this. After tomorrow, he's never going to be able to look at me the same way again. I'm doing the one thing I promised him I wouldn't.

I can't trust him. Not with this. I'm terrified that if I tell him the truth, he'll try to stop me. He'll try to find another way. He won't understand that this is our only chance, and I can't lose the *only chance* I have of saving our son.

"Kiss me as if we don't have tomorrow. Kiss me as if this is our last night."

"Ads—"

Then I kiss him before he's able to see through my lies. I don't want to talk anymore. I want to have one more moment with him that I can cherish. I need this night with him.

Wrapping his arms around me, he pulls me flush against him. Jax angles my head back so he can deepen our kiss. His groan sets my body on fire. Without breaking contact, I strip his jacket off him and make quick work of unfastening the buttons of his shirt.

"I need you," I whisper when he starts to trail kisses down my throat. His fingers follow the path of his lips. His touch is my undoing.

"You have me." He licks the scar near my collarbone.

I moan his name when I finally have his shirt undone. Unabashedly, my hands roam his hard chest. The well-defined muscles have my core pulsing with need. His lips continue their assault on my body, placing featherlight kisses until they make it to my wrist. There, he pauses at the sight of my new tattoo. Asher James is scrawled across my skin. Without taking his hunter-green eyes off mine, he places a kiss on the fresh ink. My heart skips a beat. Tears threaten to fall as I press my lips to the matching tattoo over his heart.

Forgive me. Forgive me. Forgive me, I say over and over again in my head.

"I love you," he whispers.

"I love you." *Remember that.*

Reaching behind me, he unzips my dress. I help him slide the dainty straps off my shoulders. It pools at my feet, leaving me in nothing but the beige Valentino heels. "Fuck, you've been naked this entire time?" His hands feel as if they're everywhere, lighting me on fire.

All I can do is nod.

"You're going to be the death of me," he vows before sealing his lips against mine. Grasping my butt, he lifts me and I wrap my legs around his waist. I shamelessly grind myself against him. I love feeling how hard he is for me. I do this to him. He walks us backwards, one of his hands holding me up, the other tangled in my curls.

"I need you," I all but moan when my back finally touches the mattress.

His tongue traces a path from my throat to my breast. He spends extra time on my nipples. I shiver in anticipation. I'm so wet, desperate to feel his mouth somewhere much more south.

"Please, Jax," I beg when he releases one nipple to offer just as much attention to the other. My hips come off the bed, seeking his cock when he bites down on me. "Argh."

"Tell me what you want."

"You." *Forever and always.* He is all I want, all I need..

His tongue leaves a blazing trail in its wake as he licks his way down my flat stomach. When he gets to where I need him most, he breathes me in. Holy hotness, if that's not the sexiest thing ever. "I love the way you smell," he says as he breathes deeply again.

"Jax." I arch into him, seeking.

His smile is wicked as he stares into my eyes. Jax grasps my thighs, spreading me wide and opening me to him. I grow impatient and try to bring myself closer to him. Refusing to let me move, he tightens his grip on me.

"Jax—" That's all I get out before I finally feel his tongue where I need him the most.

Clutching the sheets, I get lost in the feeling of him tasting me. His finger traces my lips, teasing me when they dip inside, just to go back to gliding along the outside again. Jax is driving me wild. "Please," I beg when he doesn't let up. I need more.

What feels like an eternity later, he finally inserts his finger in me. When he curls the digit, my toes curl with it. He nips my clit at the same time he adds another finger. I throw my head back and moan, shouting his name. As I come back from my high, I see him leaning over me. His smile is smug. At some stage, he lost the rest of his clothes. He brushes the hair away from my face, supporting himself with his forearm as he cages me in.

"You're magnificent." He peppers my cheek with kisses. "I can't wait to make you my wife tomorrow," he whispers into my ear the same moment he thrusts inside me.

I cry out in ecstasy... and in pain. I'm breaking and I don't know how I'll ever mend. I'm losing him and there's nothing I can do but destroy him along with me.

Wrapping my arms around his neck, I pull him closer until there's nothing separating him from me. His tongue tangles with mine. He kisses me the same way he makes love to me. He completely consumes me. I'm drowning in him and I never want to come up for air.

Jax grasps my hands in his. I swallow his moans and tighten around him, my walls milking him dry. We come together, moaning each other's names.

"What are you doing up?" Jax asks, taking a seat beside me on my towel.

I was so lost in watching the waves crash against the shoreline that I didn't hear him walk up behind me. "I couldn't sleep." I tell him the only truth I can. I don't tell him that I watched him sleep until I was afraid my crying was going to wake him.

He wraps a blanket around my shoulders. "I didn't like waking without you."

I lean into his embrace. "I'm sorry." *I'm sorry for everything. I'm sorry for what I'm about to do.*

"You can tell me anything, Ads."

I can't face him. I'm too much of a coward. I'm afraid of what I'll do. I can't risk our son. Not taking my eyes away from the ocean, I whisper, "I know."

We don't speak another word to each other, watching the waves ebb and flow in silence. It isn't until the sun starts to rise that I realize I'm crying.

Today was supposed to be my wedding day, the happiest day of my life. With each passing second, I feel as if I'm going to throw up. That organ in my chest, the one that beats only for him, is filling with lead with each breath I take. Today isn't what I've been envisioning since I was eight. No, today is the day that I shatter Jax's heart into a million pieces.

In my head, I tell him all the secrets I'm keeping from him. I tell him everything that I should have told him the moment Kohen slithered back into our lives. As much as I tell myself to say something—anything to make what I'm about to do easier—nothing comes out.

Please forgive me. I repeat it in my head over and over again until Jax helps me to my feet and guides me inside to get ready for our big day.

CHAPTER THIRTY-NINE

Adalynn

Three months ago, Kohen bypassed my security team and broke into my and Jax's apartment. He almost took something from me that I could never get back. Now, I bare the wounds of Kohen's ice-cold blade, the ones he inflicted on me when he pinned me down on our bed. Self-consciously, I trace over the ugly gash right below my collarbone. It's stylishly hidden under the white lace gown I'm wearing.

Last night, when I should have been celebrating with everyone else, I went to the bathroom. And just like a scene playing out in one of my nightmares, I realized I wasn't alone. Kohen was in the stall next to mine, patiently waiting for me to come out. I can still feel his hand wrapped around my mouth, preventing me from screaming for help.

Kohen told me his plan. If I didn't want him, if I truly wanted Jax, he'd let me go. He was done competing for my love. Instinct told me to keep quiet. I knew if I screamed, it wouldn't matter. He'd be gone before someone would break into the bathroom. What then? If Kohen was really willing to leave me alone, I knew we'd lose every chance of ever rescuing our son.

When he mentioned Asher having a stepmom, it was over. In that moment, we both knew I wasn't going to do anything. I was his prisoner all over again. This time willingly.

"I'll come for you tomorrow," he whispers into my ear as he holds me close.

The party rages on. I can hear Jax on the other side of the door talking with Logan. It would take less than a second for them to barge in here. Kohen wouldn't have time to escape. He'd finally be held responsible for all of the chaos he's caused.

"Go ahead, Ads, scream," Kohen dares me.

It's too risky. Even if he were to be caught, what would that mean for our son? As much as I want this to be over, he's won. We both know I'm not going to do anything to risk Asher. Jax's and Logan's voices fade as they walk away, unknowingly leaving me with a monster.

When this is over, Kohen's going to take any light I have left inside me. I know once he's done with me, I won't ever be able to recover. I don't matter though, only our son does.

For him, I will endure anything Kohen throws my way.

Spinning me around, he smirks down at me as he fingers my now-permanent necklace. My heart threatens to beat out of my chest. My mouth moves but no sound escapes. His expression smug, he moves towards the open window, never once looking anywhere else but at me. "Lose the trackers," Kohen says as he sneaks off into the night.

Jaxon was the first to find me. I could tell the second he noticed a shift in my mood. However, when he pulled me to the side of the room, he didn't ask me anything. Never once did he question what was wrong. Instead, he pulled me into his arms and held me while I fought back tears. I silently begged him to make it better, to fix the impossible. But he never asked and I never told him. With each second that passed in his arms, I died a little more. This time tomorrow, I wouldn't be the only one broken.

No, tomorrow I was going to break his heart and there was nothing I could do. He wouldn't know that breaking him meant saving us both. I just wish there was a way for him to understand that I was doing this for us.

I vowed to make this right, while he squeezed me tighter, almost as if he knew our time was fleeting.

Earlier this morning, Dawson knew something was off. I kept telling him I was nervous but he wouldn't drop it. When he mentioned beefing up security so I felt safer, I knew I had to tell him something. I couldn't have him ruining everything Jax and I've worked so hard for. So I told him the only truth I could live with.

Connor stepped out to make sure everyone was in their places, leaving Dawson and me alone. I know Reign is standing just outside the door, ready for anything. Lucas, my far guard, is somewhere on the property with eyes on me. Reign and Dawson will be easy to get rid of. Lucas is another story. I have to get to him before he can radio anyone else.

"You'll keep your promise?" I ask Dawson, needing to triple-check.

"Of course. Nothing is going to happen."

I sigh. "I know. I just need to hear you say it." I'm stalling, buying time as I try to think of a way to get Lucas here without notifying everyone else. I can't try to run. Too risky. I have to get to Kohen before Jax finds out. He'll try to stop me.

In less than five minutes, Jax is going to hate me. He won't understand that it's the only way.

"Is everything okay?" Dawson's voice has changed from the casual one to that deadly calm, killer tone. Not good.

"Just prewedding jitters."

He hands me the bouquet of peonies, two roses, and the single Stargazer lily. The two roses are for my parents, the lily for Hadley. "If the worst happens, you're not the priority," he says at last.

For the first time all day, it feels like I can finally breathe. Everything is going to be okay. Dawson won't betray me. "Thank you."

Logan pops his head in. "Waiting on you."

"Don't forget to smile, Addie. I promise nothing is going to ruin your wedding," Dawson whispers the last part so only I hear.

I can't speak. Afraid if I do, I'll tell everyone the truth. As much as I want to have faith in him and everyone else, I can't. They're hired to protect the wrong person. No, I can't put my trust in him or anyone else. It has to be me.

With one more final glance in my direction, Dawson leaves. I only have a few more minutes before I have to go. Everything is going according to plan. My phone buzzes on the table. My heart rate skyrockets as Logan picks it up. Thankfully, he hands it to me without glancing down.

"Thanks," I say, without checking the screen.

He kisses my cheek. "If you promise you won't cry, I have something for you." Reaching into his jacket, he pulls out an envelope with the familiar cursive of my mother's writing. My hands shake as I take it. "I'll give you a moment to read it."

My heart is pounding. In my left hand, I have a letter from my mother that states: *on her wedding day*. And in the other, my phone. I'm standing here, on the day of my wedding, and I can't will myself to read her words. I don't want to hear them. Today isn't my wedding day.

I unlock my phone.

Unknown: Ten minutes.

Another text comes through. This time with a picture that seals my fate. Kohen's won.

Unknown: Don't do anything stupid!

With tears in my eyes, I open the letter and set it face down on the vanity, along with the bracelet I'm wearing. It's Hadley's. I can't risk Kohen thinking it's a tracker and throwing it out. Then, running as fast as one can in a wedding dress, I head for the back door. Sawyer scans me, ready to whisk me away from any threat.

The lie I practiced all morning falls easily from my lips as I jog past him to the parking lot. "I dropped Hadley's bracelet in the car."

I hear him mutter, "Lucas, stand down," into his mic and he quickly tells them what's happening. "I'll get it for you."

I shake my head. "It's okay. It will be faster if I do it." I point to the door. "Can you make sure Jax is still waiting for me?"

Sawyer glances my way, then at the car that's a few feet away. After what feels like an eternity, he says, "Okay. Be careful."

I rush the short distance to the car, my heart pounding and my hands shaking. When the guys were getting ready, I reached into Henry's jacket and grabbed the keys. Without any thoughts other than getting to Kohen as fast as I can, I turn on the ignition and drive away.

Today was supposed to be my wedding day. The day I've been waiting for since I was eight. Instead, Kohen gets what he's been after all along.

Me.

Chapter Forty

Jax

Connor is standing beside me on the beach as we wait for Logan and Adalynn to come down the aisle. We went back and forth on whether or not we were going to have empty chairs for the people we'd wanted to share this moment with, those we lost before their time and those we hope to be reunited with soon. Ultimately, Ads decided it would be too depressing. So, instead, I thought it would be best to have her family represented in her bouquet. Then we each tattooed Asher's name on our skin. My hand traces over the spot on my chest.

Glancing around, I make sure that everything is just right. Flameless candles light her path to me while the ocean is our backdrop, and the small band is currently singing a Vance Joy cover of "I'm With You." She's going to walk down the aisle to Dermot Kennedy's "Kiss Me." I can't wait until she sees the surprise I have in store for her.

Chris Martin, and the rest of the band, is waiting for us at the reception. She's always wanted to dance to them for real. I can't wait to make all of her dreams come true.

Marrying her today is the dream I've held on to since I was a kid.

Eleven years ago

Staring at her like the creep that I am, I can't help but watch her in her sleep. She looks so peaceful. My eyes trace every inch of her face, committing it to memory before I transfer it to paper. After everyone went to sleep, I sneaked into her room. She wasn't even surprised to see me climb through her window. I've been doing it frequently, even on the nights when my dad doesn't hurt me.

I just need to see her, to be with her.

I know I should probably stay away. Each time I come over here, I'm putting her at risk, chancing that my dad will see what she means to me, but I can't stay away from her... I've never been able to.

After cuddling in bed, whispering our secrets to each other, I held her hand while she went to sleep. I promised I wasn't going anywhere, that I'd be here in the morning, but we both know I'm going to break my promises.

One day, I won't leave. One day, I'll stay.

I spend the next hour listening to her soft snores as I draw her image. I capture the way her hair spreads around her on the pillow, her hand clutching the blanket closer to her chest. My fingers help shade her lips with the charcoal. The shirt she stole from me slips over her shoulder a little.

It takes another ten minutes to finish the last few details of her face. With a deep breath, I turn it over so I can write on the back: one day, I'm going to marry you. I tuck the sketch under her pillow so she can find it tomorrow when I'm gone.

Pressing a soft kiss to the tip of her nose, I whisper, "I love you," before turning off the bedside light and slipping out the way I came.

"Relax, man," Connor says, snapping me back to reality.

"What's taking so long?" I check my watch. The band should have started playing her song a few minutes ago. I see Reign talking into her mouthpiece, her eyes locked on mine. Usually, she's impossible to read. She's always sporting that bored expression, but now she's staring at me with pity.

Something's wrong.

I don't realize that I'm running, until I hear Connor say, "Slow down, man. I'm sure everything is fine."

I don't slow down. I run past Reign, back into the villa, and head towards the room Adalynn was using to get ready. I gave her the master since it had the best view. I wanted her to see me standing there waiting for her. I know you're not supposed to see your bride or groom until the ceremony, but fuck tradition. If she wants to watch me, I'll let her. We've been through enough. Nothing is going to break us.

"Jax... I... fuck..."

"Move, Logan." I push him out of my way to open the door.

"She's not in there," he says when I walk into an empty room. He keeps talking, trying to tell me everything he knows, but I can't listen to him tell me that she left me. No, she wouldn't do that to me. I search the room, my movements frantic, as if she's magically going to appear and tell me that I'm worrying for nothing.

"She left," he says again.

Spotting the letter on the vanity, I pick it up. My hands shake as I take in Quinn's writing. Logan handed me a similar envelope this morning after we came back from a run on the beach.

"She took one of the cars. Dawson is trying to track her," Logan tells me, but I'm too focused on the words in front of me.

My dearest Adalynn,

If you're reading this, that means I'm not here to celebrate today with you and Jaxon. There's not a doubt in my mind that he's going to be the man waiting for you at the end of the altar. You've been in love with him for as long as I can remember, and I assure you he's loved you even longer.

I'm going to share a little secret with you that you might not remember. After he and his family moved to town, he'd come over every single day after school, asking if you could come out and play. And each time, your brother would tell him you were at practice. He would play with Logan and Connor while waiting for you to come home. He thought he was so clever, but your dad and I knew right away that he had a crush on you.

As much as you two try to pretend that you're just friends, I know the truth. Whenever I see the way he looks at you, when he thinks nobody's watching, I'm reminded of your father. I'm glad he's finally stepped up to the plate and he's marrying you.

Your dad begged me to write something about someone else, in case I'm wrong, but I know that I'm not. What you and Jax have is rare. Cherish it.

With all my love,

Mom

"She didn't leave me." There's no way she'd leave me, not voluntarily. Kohen did this. I know it.

Logan and Connor both look at each other before facing me. Connor is the one who breaks the silence. "I know you don't want to hear this but—"

He's right. I don't. "She didn't leave me," I repeat. I refuse to believe what they're telling me. Logan explains that she said she went to look for Hadley's bracelet before getting in the car and driving away. He says that she seemed off when he checked on her right before he was meant to walk her down the aisle.

I pinch the bridge of my nose. No, we just talked last night. She told me that she loved me. I can still practically feel her hand on my cheek as she whispered, "*Kiss me as if we don't have tomorrow. Kiss me as if this is our last night.*" Before I could ask her what she meant, she kissed me and I got lost in her embrace.

Connor keeps trying to call her, but her phone is off.

"Why weren't you with her?" I yell at Sawyer. He was supposed to be with her.

"Jax, you need to calm down." That's the last thing I need to do. I need to find my bride.

"I know where she is," Dawson says, entering the room, phone in hand. "The car stopped at a cemetery. I sent Lucas ahead of us."

"Let's go," I say as I follow Dawson outside to a waiting car.

Before I can get in the passenger seat, Logan stops me. "She might not be ready for this."

This, as in our wedding. "You don't know what you're talking about," I growl before slamming the door on his face. I refuse to believe what they think. She wanted this. She didn't leave me. She just needed to talk to them one more time. I bet she's on her way back to me right now. We're all worrying over nothing.

Since Dawson was the one to accompany us the last time we went to the cemetery, he already knows where to go. Before long, we're headed south on the 101. It's southern California right before sunset. Our car barely moves as we follow the sea of red brake lights. It's going to take close to an hour to reach her. By then, she'll be heading back to me.

Maybe I should have waited for her.

I laugh, imagining her reaction when she finds out that I went out of my mind looking for her. Dawson takes his eyes off the road to give me a glare that clearly states he thinks I'm losing it. I'm not. I'm fine.

She didn't leave me. Maybe if I say it enough times, it will be true. She just needed a moment. It's not like anyone can blame her. She's been through a lot recently. *I love you.* The sound of her voice plays over and over again in my head. My knee bounces, my nerves getting the best of me.

"Yes," Dawson answers his phone through the Bluetooth.

Lucas is frantic as he says, "She's on the move again."

"How long until she's here?" I ask, shaking my head. I knew it. She's coming back to me. "Get off at the next exit to turn around," I instruct Dawson. It isn't until I notice that he didn't put his blinker on or follow my directions that I realize Lucas never answered me. "Where is she going?" I ask him, dread filling my gut. Before he utters the three words that are going to destroy me, I already know.

She's not coming back to me. She's leaving me. Our love wasn't enough to save us.

"To the airport," Lucas says at last.

The End.

Stay Tuned for the third
installment of the Beautifully Series.
Beautifully Forever.

About the Author

Courtney Kristel graduated from The Fashion Institute of Design and Merchandising, but she couldn't shake her true passion for writing. In 2014, she started the process of drafting her debut novel, *Beautifully Shattered*. Courtney hopes to release the third book, *Beautifully Forever*, soon. Followed by books for each of the other main characters in the Beautifully Series.

When she isn't thinking up new stories and creating new worlds, Courtney usually has a book in her hands or is hanging out with her husband and their dog Astrid as well as their three cats: Mildred, Zulu, and Maverick.